LOVE WILL COME AGAIN

MARGUERITE SHAW

Old Bakehouse Publications

© Marguerite Shaw

First published in Great Britain 1996
by Old Bakehouse Publications

ISBN 1 874538 90 5

Published in the U.K. by
Old Bakehouse Publications
Church Street
Abertillery, Gwent NP3 1EA
Telephone: 01495 212600   Fax: 01495 216222

Made and printed in the U.K.
by J.R. Davies (Printers) Ltd.

Cover: From a painting by
Phil Davies, artist,
48 Fountain Road, Pontymoile, Pontypool.

To family and friends who have given me encouragement and have asked for another novel about the Watkins; to the warm-hearted people of the Afon Lwyd and Pend Oreille Valleys of which and for whom I write; to my mother who taught me how.

STR		ALC	
SHI		ALM	
SHM		SDL	
KTN		HEN	
WEI			

The words and music of the song, 'The Exile' are by Gordon C. Shaw (Copyright MCMLXXXV) from whom they may be obtained.

Whilst the setting and historical background for this novel are based on researched facts, the characters and families therein are entirely the product of the author's imagination and bear no relation to actual persons alive or dead.

3

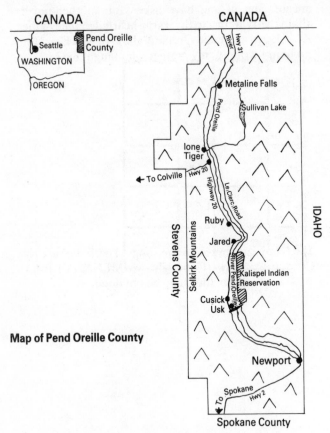

Map of Pend Oreille County

⋀ = Mountains

Map Scale: 2cm - 24km (15 miles) approx

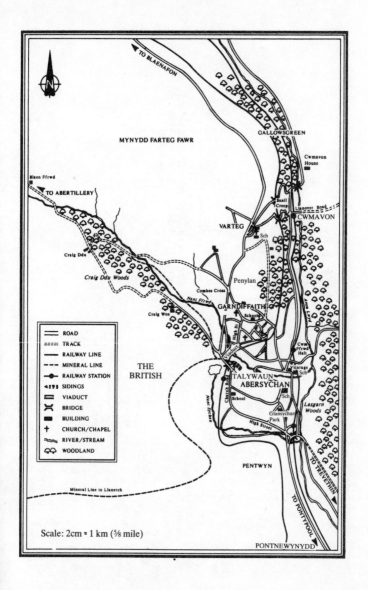

Scale: 2cm = 1 km (⅝ mile)

The Watkins Family

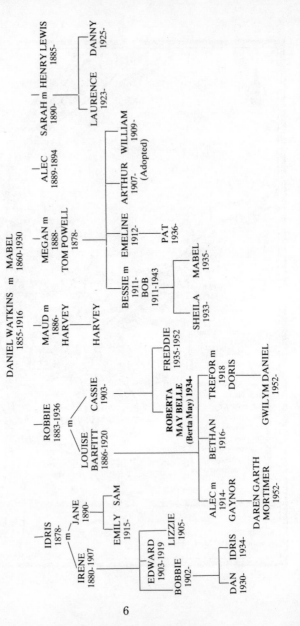

Chapter 1

Momma picked up Freddie and made for the door saying, 'Be a good girl now, Berta May and be sure to help Auntie Sarah all you can. See you supper time.'

They were gone; I was visiting, all on my own and wearing my best blue velvet frock and my patent leather shoes that I'd had for cousin Laurence's birthday party. But Laurence was in school and I was in his house with Auntie Sarah and I had the whole long day ahead of me, for playing with the toys he had outgrown.

'Now don't you fret, honey,' said my auntie, 'your mom will not be long away. Do you see the toy box by the porch door there? Just you have a lovely time playing, while I get a few clothes washed out and cut up the vegetables for our dinner.'

'All right. I'm fixing on making a castle first off, but just you call me if you need any help, Auntie Sarah. And I'll be real careful not to leave anything for you to fall over.'

At four years old, I was far from fretting at my mother's having left me for the day. True, I would have liked to ride on the train with her and Freddie but, all things considered, I felt much more important for having been allowed to stay in town. I did not often get to visiting on my own. Much as I loved our homestead on the mountain, I thought it high time I dressed up and met company.

'And after dinner, why, we'll go down Washington Street and you shall choose yourself some candy and cookies. Then if we have the time.....' Auntie Sarah's voice drifted companionably from the kitchen while I played.

'May I go out in the yard a while, Auntie Sarah?' I asked at length. 'It's perfectly dry and warm and I want to play skittles and you wouldn't want me throwing balls in here, now would you?'

'All right, my lovely, but make sure and come in if you feel chilly. Uncle Henry said there was a touch of frost last night.'

'There was a real white frost in the meadow this morning when we woke,' I told her, 'But now it is hot.' I ran outside, counting 'one, two three' as I went down the steps from the porch.

Within an hour, I was tiring of my own company. I was too hot in my velvet dress, for the chill of the autumn morning had given place to a still, warm day.

'What can I do now?' I asked. 'Is it nearly dinner time?' I trailed around the house on the heels of my aunt, getting in the way while she tidied the beds. Stealthily, I opened a drawer of the dressing table and took a peek inside, knowing she could not see what I was doing. But there was nothing wrong with her ears.

'Come out of there, Berta May,' she said surprisingly sharply, 'you know better than to pry. Now could you be a big girl and pour a glass of milk for yourself while I make a cup of tea? And if you look in the jar on the left hand side of the range, you'll find a few cookies. Bring one for me and one for yourself and we'll sit on the porch for a spell. Only one mind, or you'll spoil your dinner.'

After that, she told me a story while I sat on her knee and next I helped her lay the table for dinner, then suddenly the house was full of people and I sat at the table tongue-tied. They all had so much to say, Uncle Henry looking strangely important in his business suit and cousins Laurence and Danny so grown up and all. It took some minutes of coaxing before they got me to say a word, but I did full justice to my dinner and I played peekaboo around my uncle's chair while he was smoking his pipe after the boys had gone back to school.

'Now curl up in Uncle Henry's chair,' said Auntie Sarah when he left us, 'and cuddle your dolly and look at your picture books while I wash the dishes. Then I will let you have look in my box of treasures.' She put a cushion behind my head and a rug over my knees.

An hour must have passed while I slept. I went to the bathroom then. Washing my hands under the tap, I wondered at the running water and the porcelain basin with shiny faucets in which I could see my own reflection.

'May I see your secrets now?' I demanded and followed Auntie Sarah up to her bedroom. Out from the closet she took a wooden box, set it in the middle of her bed and lifted me up to sit high on the feather pillows. Kicking off her

8

shoes, she settled herself alongside me.

'Now, what shall we look at first, Berta May?' she asked, opening the clasp and raising the lid. 'Who can you see on this photograph?'

'I can see a lot of people standing in front of a big house and that one is my Poppa when he was a little boy and there is his brother and his big sister and they've all got their best clothes on. And that one is you, with the big bow of ribbon on your hair. Didn't you-all just wear the funniest clothes?'

'Chapel Anniversary 1911,' said Auntie Sarah. 'Tell me now about this next one, cariad.' It was a small framed photograph showing two rows of children and a few adults. 'That was when you all got prizes at school,' I told her proudly, pointing out each member of the Watkins family in turn.

'There's you in your frilly pinny and Poppa in the front row with his books and there is Auntie Maud with a silver watch and Auntie Megan with a medal there at the back. Wasn't your momma just too proud of you-all that day?'

I knew very well how to get Auntie Sarah talking about her childhood in far away Wales. With every picture and yellowing newspaper cutting there was a story; with every tissue-wrapped souvenir a memory for her to share with me.

'Feel the smooth silk ribbon. Look at the bright green prize purse and see what you can find inside. Half a crown! That was a fortune to me, the day I won at the Eisteddfod.'

There were postcards, with views of seaside places, streets and old stone buildings. Dainty embroidered handkerchiefs with messages worked in coloured silk were unfolded for inspection and then replaced with care, but the greatest treasures of all lay at the very bottom of the box. Grandpa and Grandma Watkins' silver watches rested side by side on a bed of cotton wool.

Then I listened again to the story of my family's leaving their homeland and my infant brain received and understood the love and the longing that came through the words of Auntie Sarah, whose voice regained its native lilt the while she spoke.

One more item remained in the box.

'Here's Poppa's song,' I said, pulling out the sheet of

music. 'Let's go down and sing it.' I was tired of sitting and the novelty of the box had worn off. I wanted action and began to shuffle towards the edge of the bed.

'And who is going to pack these things away? Would you like to do me a favour and help me put them in tidily, before we go to sing?' And I must perforce hand her the treasures one by one and watch her neatly pack them into place, though she could hardly see a thing.

Then down stairs I ran, to open the lid of the piano, put the music in place and pull the padded stool into position. By the time my aunt arrived, I was fingering the treble keys.

We sang it through twice over and had no need of the sheet of music, for Auntie Sarah could not see and I could not read, but this was our favourite song. From my birth, I had been soothed by it, while my father had sat on our deck overlooking the meadow, holding me on his knee if I were fretful and singing, singing, singing.

'How I wish I were back in the valley,
The valley I left long ago.
How fair was my valley in summer
In winter how warm the fire's glow.
How friendly the sheep on the mountain,
So lively the town down below,
Yet nothing could match the deep feeling
In the fam'ly I left long ago.'

'In a land far away from the valley
Surrounded by friends new yet dear,
And with my own family around me
The voice from the past sounds so clear.
We built here a home for our children
To grow, holding everything dear
We learned from the far away fam'ly
In the valley that ever is near.'

After that, we sang other songs like Hickory, Dickory Dock and Ring a Ring o' Roses and I got down from the stool and danced around, until suddenly the door was opened.

'Momma!' I cried in dismay. 'You can't come back yet awhile. We haven't been to buy my candy.'

'Shame on you, Berta May,' laughed Auntie Sarah, 'that's no sort of welcome to give your Mammy. Now you play with Freddie while I make a cup of tea and then you and I will take him along with us to the store while Mammy has a rest.'

So I got my candy and cookies after all and was proud of myself as I guided Auntie and helped Freddie slowly along the side walk. Poor Freddie had a twisted foot, which was why he had been taken to the big hospital in Spokane for a specialist to examine him.

'He'll have to have an operation,' Momma was saying later as we put on our coats to go home, 'but he can have it done here in Newport. He'll still have to wear the calliper. That old leg may never be truly straight but he'll surely be able to walk and ride in time. Thank you for having Berta May, Sarah, I can see she's had a lovely day. What do you say now, Berta May?'

'Thank you Auntie Sarah,' I recited obediently, 'and please may I come again soon?'

2

It was dark before we finished our uphill route through the forest, but a welcoming light gleamed across the meadow to guide us home. Home was Greyroofs, a farmstead built by my mother's parents thirty years before, when they made their claim as homesteaders after travelling for months over the mountains in a horse-drawn wagon. High above the Pend Oreille Valley in Washington State, they found the acres of their choice and set about felling trees to make a shelter for themselves before the onset of winter. Here in the remoteness of the backwoods I was reared, with the sound of the wind in the forest above and the Greystone Water in the ravine below.

We found Alec, my oldest half-brother, feeding the stock in the barn.

'Hi.' he greeted us cheerfully. 'How y'doing? Everything ok? I've nearly finished in here and the stew pot's in the oven, Mom.'

'Can I help Alec?' I asked.

'Yes you may, but mind you don't soil your best frock,' said Momma. 'I'll go right on in and give Freddie his supper and by the time you're through, I'll have everything ready. I sure am hungry myself after nothing but sandwiches for dinner.'

Alec and I soon finished the chores while I kept up a constant flow of chatter about my day with Auntie Sarah. Then we secured the barns and shacks for the night and rinsed our hands under the water pump over by the drinking trough. We were totally in tune, Alec and I, for he had taken me under his wing as soon as my baby brother was born. I had trotted round the farm at his heels and shared his saddle out riding the trails. My play was in imitation of his work and he rarely lost patience with me or excluded me from his activities.

'Can I go with you?' I pleaded early the next morning when I saw him saddling his big grey horse. I fastened my workaday trousers, dragged my pullover on and reached for my leather jacket which hung behind the door. He was obviously preparing for a day's journey.

'Not this time. I'm going to the other side of the mountain and will be too long away.'

'But I can ride that far and it's high time Dusty had some exercise for we haven't been out since Sunday. Please, Alec?'

I knew I could more often than not twist him round my little finger and I put on my most persuasive voice and smile, but on this occasion he was adamant.

'No use, Berta May. I have to go a long way in a short time. But you can ride as far as Elk Rock with me if you like, so long as you promise to come straight home from there.'

I ran after him across the yard and helped saddle my beautiful chestnut pony.

'Now listen carefully, Berta May. I want you to let all the horses into the meadow when you come back, but make sure of the gates being shut fast before you do. They might as well have a run around, once the sun lifts the frost off the grass, for it won't be long before they are shut in for the winter. Ready?' and Alec led the way through the first gate.

There was nothing more surely guaranteed to make me obey his orders that the feeling that he was relying on me, so I took careful note of his instructions as we crossed the meadow and set off up the forest trail. It was cold between the dark conifers and the horses' hooves struck sharply on the frozen dirt. For a mile, we followed the meandering track until a high red rock appeared on our left.

'Bye now, Berta May. Mind how you go - let Dusty feel her way at her own pace on this hard ground and remember what I said about the gates.'

He watched me turn, then set his horse at the higher track and kicked her into action, while Dusty and I retraced our route. For a while, I was content to go slowly because I wanted to prolong the ride, but after some minutes, the silence and gloom of the dark forest began to undermine my confidence. I remembered stories of lost children; I thought of the bears which even now might be approaching in search of food; I wondered whether there really were wolves in the woods. I urged Dusty into a trot, which became a steady canter as soon as the ground levelled off a little.

It was with some relief that I dismounted and tied her up while I dealt with the gate into the meadow. Then I enjoyed a canter all the way round before approaching the homestead, where I carried out Alec's orders and took saddle and harness into the barn. The saddle was too heavy for me to lift onto its rightful rail, so I rested it on the chopping block.

'Something smells good,' I said on entering the kitchen. 'Is it for me?'

'Sure is,' laughed Momma. 'You went without your breakfast, but I put some hashbrowns and bacon to keep hot in the side oven. Just a minute while I lift them out. You want an egg?'

I was hungry enough to eat anything offered, but at last was satisfied. It was time for us to get out to the barn and attend to the hens and geese. Momma put Freddie's coat on and helped him down the steps, saying, 'Bring the basket for vegetables, Berta May as well as the one for eggs.'

The yard behind the house was brown and lifeless, all

13

crops having been harvested weeks ago, but our larder was full of preserved fruit and our store shack held potatoes, carrots, turnips and other vegetables, carefully packed against the winter's cold.

In a corner of the big barn, the poultry was fenced in. Freddie's job was to slide up a little hatch through which they could run out to scratch around the farm yard. Mine was to collect their eggs from the straw and count them.

'How many have you got today?' asked Momma, busy scooping up a measure of grain from the barrel.

'...nine, ten. One. I got ten and one,' I told her.

'That's eleven all together, so two of them hens is still laying away. Go and see if you can find where, will you?' Freddie and I hunted in all the likely places and a few unlikely ones, for you never knew what those old hens would do next. It was Freddie who found the hiding place behind the water trough.

'Eggs!' he cried. 'I got eggs.' But he could not reach far enough to get them out and he almost got stuck in there behind the trough, lying down on his tummy to try.

'We need a pole,' I said and rushed back to the barn. We soon had the two eggs out and nestling in the basket with the others.

Then we amused ourselves for a spell, while Mom was busy cleaning out and laying fresh straw and by that time Freddie was tired and it was time to go indoors to make his dinner.

Life had not been easy on my mother, left an orphan at fifteen and twice widowed before her fortieth birthday, but there was not a trace of sadness about the life she created for Freddie and me. She was easy-going and the sun shone from her eyes. Her physical strength was almost as great as that of the menfolk who helped her with the farm work and she was rarely silent, her singing and whistling and shouting being audible from one end of the meadow to the other. In marrying my father she had taken on not only an invalid husband but his three grown children and then got two babies of her own.

'The best day's work I ever did,' she was used to saying to any who wondered at her courage. 'Got myself a ready-made family at one fell swoop and the darlingest pair of babies that ever drew breath' and she would hug me and Freddie and break into a song.

And it was true enough that Alec and Trefor, my big brothers from Wales, were as much at home on the ranch as I was and worked as hard as Mom, though Trefor had a job in town which kept him there all week. They had a house in town, too, left to them by Poppa, and when sister Bethan came visiting she usually stayed there. Thus, with Auntie Sarah's family and a cousin called Zeb who did odd jobs here and there and every which where, Momma had plenty of family folk on whom to call for help after Pop died.

He was buried above the ravine in the birch grove, within sight of the house and within sound of the creek. There were wild flowers growing round him and sometimes we put a posy of forget-me-nots in a pot of water there. It was a restful place.

The animals and plants of the forest gave us our livelihood and horseback was our usual means of travelling, though Mom could drive the old motor car, Trefor had a motor cycle and the men had made a little horse-drawn wagon in which we all could go visiting while Freddie was small. Dirt roads and rough tracks linked us to our neighbours and to the lakes in which we caught fresh fish. There was never an idle minute in our days, though we did take time out for church or for picnics or other celebrations, for Mom was as partial to dancing and singing as any of the Watkins.

'Roberta Maybelle Watkins' they had christened me, on the porch of the homestead in the spring of 1935 when I was nine months old. My father being too frail to take a journey to the nearest church, our minister and relatives had come up the mountain as soon as the snows of a severe winter had cleared from the road. By the next winter, I was at Alec's side wherever he was working, woollen leggings and layers of tiny hand made jackets to keep me warm while Momma nursed Freddie.

Alec was twenty years older than I, so by the time I was four, he was a real grown man. An engineer by training, he had turned his hand to inventing what he called 'Labour Saving Gadgets', though some of these made more work than they saved. His water-wheel, however, was by and large a god-send, said Momma. By some means not understood by anyone but him, he had harnessed the power of the Greystone Water to make electric lighting for the homestead. So, while most folk in the outback were using candles or kerosene lamps, we were enjoying the luxury of bright, clean, modern lights. We were very proud of Alec.

I heard him ride in while supper was being cooked, so there was no peace for Momma until she allowed me to run out to greet him.

'I did everything you said,' I told him, 'and we got the horses in again before dark.'

'Good girl,' he smiled. 'Here, catch this fish and put it in the store until morning, then you can help me clean it.'

'Oo, good. Me and Freddie like fish and we got in plenty of vegetables this morning and we found all the eggs so there'll be lots to sell. And Momma said she clean forgot to tell you she brought the new blade you wanted from town yesterday.'

'Where did she put it?'

'Right there on the bench.' I stood on tip toe, trying to see over the edge of the work bench at the end of the barn. I stretched out my hand but could not reach far.

'Never mind that now. Hop up into the loft and toss some hay down for me, just enough for the horses.' I scuttled up the ladder, while he took a pitch fork in hand and waited for the fodder to fall. Together, we fed all our stock and secured the doors against wind and storm. Then we went indoors.

'You aiming to spend time in town this weekend?' Momma asked Alec. 'I see there's a Gene Autrey movie at the Rex.'

'No. I'm just as happy here and want to fix the rail fence down the meadow, before we have snow. I could do with Trefor's help, though, so I hope he comes.'

'I'll help, too,' I piped up.

'Come and get your hands washed before you have your supper,' said Momma. 'You look like a lumberjack.'

'Me lumberjack,' shouted Freddie, pushing his toy truck across the hearth rug. It was loaded with twigs.

'Lumberjacks don't drive trucks,' I told him. 'Alec,

16

lumberjacks don't drive trucks, do they?'

'Nothing to stop them,' he replied. 'Up you come, Freddie. If you're going to be a lumberjack, you need to eat a good supper.' He swung my brother above his chair as steaming dishes were taken off the stove.

'Hands together,' said Momma and we bowed our heads. 'Make us thankful, Oh Lord, for this food and for all Thy blessings.'

'Amen,' we all said before our plates were heaped with the good stew.

I had a little idea how lucky I was to be well fed and warmly clothed at a time when children in all parts of the world were starving. In our corner of the States, a severe depression had robbed hundreds of their jobs, the mining and timber industries had declined and prices for furs had fallen until trappers could not make a living. Farming was precarious, but at least it provided us with food and home, while many had lost everything.

3

When Trefor arrived the next afternoon, he brought letters with him.

'From Wales?' I asked, knowing how much Alec and he loved letters from their cousins overseas. Who they all were, I could not say for sure, but I knew they were Watkins and therefore Family.

'Yes,' he laughed. 'You'd better get your scrap book out, Berta May, because cousin Emmie has sent some pictures for you and there's a packet of scraps from Doctor Liz.'

'Things are going from bad to worse over there,' he was saying to Alec while Mom settled me at the table with glue and scrap book. 'Here, have a look yourself and then we'll go and get on with that fence.'

The envelope was bulky. They usually sent several letters at once, to save on postage, and addressed them to the whole family. This time, three of them had written.

'Dear Cousins,' wrote Emmie, 'I got up to chapel last Sunday and saw everyone up Penylan, who send their love and will write soon. They said to tell you not to worry about us, whatever you read in the papers. We are all managing, though times are hard.

Bobbie is running the farm because of Uncle's lumbago. It's a squash for them all now the children are growing, but our Emily says if it comes to a war, she'll be on her way and make a bit more room for the rest. What a way to talk, but she's never had a really good job and I think she fancies the chance to get away. Not my cup of tea at all, wild horses wouldn't drag me from home, but then I have my husband and baby to look after,

I am glad to say both are well and as yet no sign of Jack's shop closing like so many have done because there isn't the money about. The co-op seems secure enough. Our Bessie has had a bad spell with her two getting mumps and her hubby out of work so she has to turn her hand to anything. Mam and Dad are well and she is writing to you as well.

I got the post card from Maud and the cuttings from the paper, so after you've all seen them, Roberta can have them for her scrap book. I wish I could see her and Freddie. How is his leg? They say they can do wonders to straighten the kiddies legs nowadays, but poor little thing, I wish he didn't have to suffer.....'

Then there was a letter from Emmie's mother, Auntie Megan, who told us how their farm was doing and how she looked after Bessie's children for two weeks.

Good as gold they were, but so poorly and their necks so swollen they looked like big red footballs,' she wrote. 'Still, they might as well have it while they're young and save complications later. I brought them down to our house as soon as they were well enough, so they had plenty of fresh air around the farm and I got on with my jamming. Plenty of blackberries for the picking and tons of apples in our orchard, so we shalln't starve.

There's a terrible mess we are in with Hitler. No end to his mischief, to judge from all reports, though they don't tell us the half of it. I can't believe what they say about another war though. Surely not after the last time. Our boys lost their dad through that one and I dread to think they would have to be fighting the next time.

Tom sends his love and I'll write again before Christmas. Your loving Auntie Megan.'

I was too absorbed with my pot of paste, brush and scrap

book to pay much attention to what the grown-ups were saying about the state of the world. Of far greater interest were their plans for our own entertainment during the weeks to come.

'If Momma is to take Freddie down to the hospital, I shall have to visit with Auntie Sarah again. May I come and see your office, Trefor? Please? You said I might, when I had growed some.'

'Why so I did, though I had in mind to wait a year or two. Little girls like you wouldn't be interested in seeing a stuffy old newspaper office.'

'I would so. Please, Tref - you promised,' I wheedled.

'There she goes again,' laughed Alec. 'You might as well give in now, Tref. You'll not hold out against her persuasion.'

'Nonsense,' said Momma. 'If you mean No, say No and stick to it. You'll spoil the child between you if you give in every time.'

'Tell you what, Berta May,' said Trefor, 'we'll save it as a birthday treat for when you are five. I promise to show you my office as near as possible to your fifth birthday and I'll get you a reporter's notepad just like mine as well.'

With that I had to be content. I helped my big brothers fix the old zig-zag fence, between sessions with my paste brush and scraps. We all went down to church Sunday morning and heard about the plans for Thanksgiving, which gave me new hopes of excitement. There was to be a whole day of festivities, with competitions and races and pumpkin pies for supper.

Chapter 2

By the end of October each year, our winter had begun in earnest, with frost almost every night and the threat of snow before long. Our store cupboards and barns must be well filled before travelling became too difficult and I loved to see the neat rows of canned fruit, jams and preserves along the storeroom shelf. Some of these Momma had made, some had been gotten from neighbours in exchange for eggs or wood or farm meat, but there were in addition cans and sacks and stoneware pots filled with boughten goods. Everything we could not grow or make ourselves had to be carted up from Newport or from the store at Cusick.

It was a wonderland to me, the general store with its groceries on display, butter and cheese and sacks of potatoes as well as jars of candy. There was a section for dry goods and another for hardware, where we got replacements for broken crockery or leaking saucepans. Then there was a small selection of clothing and bolts of material, with a catalogue to study if you should want to order by mail.

Momma did not favour mail order shopping. She liked us to be able to try on our shoes and such clothes as she could not make for us, so what the local store could not provide, she got on our visits to town. Knowing that it might be the last time we could get there before Spring, she was armed with a long list of necessities on the day of Freddie's next appointment at the hospital in Newport.

'We better get through with the shopping first,' she said as the Ford picked up speed along the highway after we were safely down the hill. 'Auntie Sarah is expecting us for dinner at one and then you can stay there, Berta May, while I take Freddie over the road. You warm enough now, Freddie?'

'Sure am, Momma,' he smiled from under his fur-lined cap. 'Look, Berta. Boats.'

'And logs,' I said. 'Just look how many logs is coming down to the mill.'

'How many? Kin you count them?'

'No I can't. Near a hundred, I reckon. You reckon there's a hundred, Momma?'

'More than a hundred, honey. We'd be all week, counting that lot.'

We were travelling south from Dalkena, the road and river close together and although snow lay thinly and ice was covering ponds, traffic on the Pend Oreille was flowing normally.

A laden motor truck caught up with us and overtook.

'Lumber truck. Is it going to the mill, Momma?' asked Freddie. 'Is that Joe's truck, Momma?'

'Course not,' I told him. 'Joe gotta brand new rig, Alec said only the other day. Besides, Joe would have surely waved to us and he generally works the mill. They got paid truckers now they own the mill.'

Joe was a friend of Alec's, living down river and running a business with his father.

We came into Newport and began our errands on Washington. At first, it was exciting to be amongst the bustle of people and to see the passing traffic. I held tight to Freddie's hand to prevent him straying while Momma talked to friends and we said Thank You very politely when they gave us a stick of candy. Not an hour later, after I had tried on about seven pairs of boots in Penny's and none of them had been found to fit, I was weary and Freddie was tiresome.

'I just never seen anyone with such troublesome feet as yours' Berta May,' sighed Momma. 'There's nothing to be done but to have your feet measured and get the boots made special. Just pray the snow don't come to stay before they are finished.'

'I don't want no new leather boots,' I declared. 'Why can't I have some of those red rubber ones? I like them far better.'

'Because rubber galoshes ain't no use in snow, let alone keeping your toes warm against twenty below, for all they look so nice and shiny,' said Momma. 'Hurry now, we've not done the half of what we set out to do and time's flying.'

We crossed the road to the drug store to get things for the bathroom, then went into Kimmel's Hardware, where

Momma wanted to leave a long list of items for delivery. Freddie and I gazed at the rows of goods, the things hanging from the rafters and stored on shelves, as if we were in Aladdin's cave, while the list was carefully checked. Tiring of standing still, I wandered over to look at fishing tackle.

'Freddie!' I heard Momma's voice half a second before the building echoed to the clatter of a dozen falling zinc wash tubs. I waited, concealed, to hear whether she would laugh or scold.

'I'm real sorry, Mr Hunt. They're having a dreary day but I have nearly finished.' With the help of other customers, she was beginning to rebuild the stack of tubs. 'Berta May, come here at once and hold his hand while I pay for all this stuff we need.'

After that, there was one final errand to do. Mom ordered some lengths of fabric - shirting and tweed and calico in which I had not the slightest interest. I would far rather she had paid attention to the pretty spotted pyjamas displayed on a model my own size, but her head simply would not turn that way.

At last, she was through. We were out on the sidewalk and nothing between us and Auntie Sarah but the hotel and two blocks of houses. I skipped ahead to tell her we were coming.

She had on a dress of striped red and green material with a contrasting waistcoat and looked very pretty even while wearing her pinafore. Her fair hair made a curly halo round her face, a sharp contrast to my mother's practical thick braid. Our woollen shirts and pants and jumpers looked a mite homespun against her town clothes and I wished I had worn my best frock.

'But you couldn't run a farm with your best dress on, my lovely,' she comforted me after dinner when I told her what I had been thinking, 'and think how silly I would look if I wore these clothes to feed your horses.'

She sat beside the stove for warmth, for even in town it was a cold day. She pulled me onto her lap, saying, 'Now guess what I had in the mail on Tuesday.'

'Letters from Wales?' I said. I could not imagine the mail serving any other purpose than to link the Watkins with their family overseas.

'Why yes, I did have letters, but something else too.'

'A new frock?' Perhaps Auntie Sarah had been shopping from Shears catalogue.

'No. One more guess and then I shall have to tell you.'

I looked around the room, wondering what the mail could possibly have brought. Something for decoration, perhaps?

'A new story book?'

'Very good, but not quite right. It is a book, but it has songs in it, not stories. See, I hid it behind the cushion here. Bethan sent it for us, all the way from California and she says there are some beautiful songs for us to sing.'

'Is that in Wales?'

'No. California is part of this country where we live, but a very long way beyond the mountains it is, and quite different from Pend Oreille. Shall we try this song to start with?'

We settled at the piano for our favourite pastime and it seemed a very short while before Momma and Freddie were back, though four o'clock was striking as they took off their coats.

'There we are then. He has to come back in April for the operation and by this time next year he will have legs nearly as good as Berta May's,' said Momma with her happiest smile. 'Yes please, Sarah, just one cup and a gossip and we must be on our way. Have you-all had letters from home this week?'

'Yes. Not very good news, is it?'

'Not from what your Megan said in her last letter. You think it's really as bad as that or does she exaggerate some?'

'I doubt it. Calls a spade a spade, does Megan. Oh, Cassie, what a shame and a waste - Rob and all those other young men fought for our freedom in fourteen-eighteen and now the governments can't keep peace amongst them. I thought last Spring they had defused the situation and things would settle down peacefully.'

'Get up to the table you two,' said Momma to me and Freddie, 'and tuck into Auntie Sarah's buttered fruit cake to keep the cold out until we get home. Aw, maybe they'll sort it out without coming to blows.'

'Meg says she'll send a bundle of newspapers next, so we can read for ourselves. It seems the authorities are making preparations in case of war, so there must be something in it.'

'Well come to that, I did hear tell our own senator was predicting all-out war. He wants the Government to start a general draft in case the worst comes to the worst.'

2

That was our last visit to Newport before winter shut us in. Before Thanksgiving, snow had fallen to a depth of two feet or so, but we managed with difficulty to get to the party down at Church. After that, it really did its best to cut us off from the rest of the world.

The snow plows did their daily sweep up and down the highway, keeping the trucks and cars, horse wagons and buses moving. They plowed up the Creek road too for the first two miles where six or seven families lived on the lower farms, but at the point where the Greystone's valley narrowed and the ungraded road began to climb, they did a turnabout and went back to the Calispel Road. It was left to us to clear our own road.

Alec had a light plow-blade that he could tow behind Misty and it was always his first job after a snow fall, to scrape his way down the hill and back again. Then we could travel on horseback or on foot or by sled. Only after many storms with wind, when the snow would drift into high curving spurs too deep for the little plow, did the task become impossible.

In one respect, we were pleased to have snow, for once it froze and the surface hardened, we could haul logs from our timber stand on the mountain, sliding them out of the places where Alec had felled them and towing them home by sled.

'After Christmas, I shall get Joe's team in. Those decks up there are ready to go to the mill,' he said. 'There's some good white pine and tamarack and I'm looking for a better price this year.'

He kept the track open until Christmas, when Trefor came with packages and added to the excitement of

Freddie and me. Mom had been baking and sewing, we each had a little corner where we had hidden small gifts she had helped us to make and I don't know just how many times I had put on my coat and boots to run as far as the meadow gate and look to see could I spot Santa's sleigh passing by. We had deer all round us and I was certain sure ⅞ should catch him harnessing a few whitetails if I kept watch.

Trefor tramped in, just as darkness fell on Christmas Eve. Our festivities could begin. He told us he never would have got here, had he not carried a shovel over his shoulder in readiness for clearing the worst of the drifts.

'Pile up my plate please, Mom,' he laughed. 'I could eat the whole goddurned rooster, bones and all.'

'You'll get not one feather, boy, if I hear you using that language,' said Mom, but her face was smiling all the same. 'You may be a real tough guy, but I'm still your Mom and I'll have none of your cussing in here.'

'And you sure won't get no gifts from no-one,' I lectured him. 'Freddie and me shall get them all. We been real good for days and days, ain't we, Momma?'

'Santa's going to bring me a b-i-g new sled,' said Freddie, stretching his arms as wide as he could reach. Trefor leaned down to tickle him under the arms and we all ended up in a rolling, laughing heap on the floor. Mom got around us some way, to put the food on the table.

For three days, we feasted and played, fitting the chores in night and morning but even Alec and Mom took a break from their usual work. I was glad to find that Trefor had brought my new leather boots as well as some gifts from Auntie Sarah, for my old ones had pinched my toes most painfully and there was no end to the cold, snowy weather. Nice though it was to have new jigsaws and books for playing indoors, we could not stay in the house for ever.

January through March, the cold intensified and the snow deepened. Watering the stock became an hour's hard labour daily, for the pump froze and we had to fill a tank down at the creek, pulling it up to the yard on a sled. In the house, our hand-pump was still working, but heating the water for washing seemed to take an age and we all hated the days when clothes must be laundered.

'Before next Fall,' promised Alec, 'I shall get piped water to this house if it's the last thing I do, and a hot water system with a bath and all.'

'Then you better get some prices on bathroom fittings when you get out to town and tell Zeb we'll be needing his help,' Mom said. 'We been talking about this long enough and I reckon this old place could do with modernising some.'

Not that I was concerned at not being able to wash too often. I was out in the yard come hail, come snow, tending horses, bringing in dry kindling, carrying cord-wood to the porch or helping Alec in the shop. That was where he sawed and planed, sanded and polished the things for farm and house when he could not work outdoors. Slowly, we built a store of new fence posts, repaired Mom's chairs and made wooden toy trucks out of pale ponderosa pine.

3

It was March before the promised newspapers arrived at our place, Trefor finally getting through from town although he had walked the last two miles where the snow lay too deep for his motor bike. We were all delighted to see him, for the sake of a change of company as well as for the mail and news he brought. To my joy, he readily agreed to take me and Freddie tobogganing while Mom and Alec settled down for an afternoon's reading. There were the Newport papers, the National papers and those from Wales to enjoy, as well as letters from Auntie Megan and the others. It was so long since our last visit that even Auntie Sarah had written bits of news to bring us up to date with what was going on in the valley.

'My, to think people have been sick and dying from Flu and we never knew there was an epidemic down there,' Mom was exclaiming as we buttoned our coats. 'Sarah says it has hit real hard and some businesses were barely able to carry on in January.'

'True enough,' said Trefor over his shoulder. 'I bumped into Joe Walker in the store Thursday and he said the boys in the mill had gone down like flies.'

'I guess I'd better get on down to see can he come soon

and haul our logs, before the ground softens...' Alec was saying as we closed the door and went towards the barn.

For two hours or more, the three of us played outdoors. The thaw which had reduced the snow covering in the valley had barely changed conditions around the homestead, though the surface was no longer frozen everywhere.

'Pull us up the trail to Elk Rock,' I begged, as we took the large sleigh out of the yard. 'Then we can all ride down together.'

'That's nearly a mile!' Trefor said. 'I can't pull your great weight all that way.'

'Well then, pull us across the meadow and then after that I'll walk with you and we'll both pull Freddie.'

'OK. Jump on and hold tight. Ready?'

When we got to the far end of the meadow, the gate was too deeply buried in a drift for us to open it, but from where we stood on top of the snow, it was no great chore to lift the toboggan over the rail. We put Freddie safely in place again and I took hold the rope to help Trefor as the incline grew steeper.

'That's far enough,' he said at last when our breath was quite gone and his arms could pull no more. 'Turn it round, Berta May and then we'll all get on. All aboard for Greyroofs!'

What a tremendous ride we had then, speeding down the snow trail between the tall pines. Freddie squealed in delight and sometimes in fright, for now and again we swerved off course and found ourselves careering towards the trees.

'Phew, that was a narrow escape,' whistled Trefor as we picked ourselves up from a deep drift ten feet to the left of the track.

'It's a good thing snow is nice and soft,' I said.

'And a good thing there were no low branches. You all right, Freddie?' he asked, brushing off snow and straightening my brother's cap. 'Not hurt your legs, have we?'

'No. I wanna do it again,' laughed Freddie. 'I did head over heals. Did you see, Berta May?'

'No. I was thinking would we land safe or not. Guess we

better not say too much to Momma about that spill, had we, Trefor? You hear, Freddie? Not a word else she won't let you out with us again.'

We repeated that run and then sought other routes, riding three-up or turn and turn about. Freddie's new sled then had to be tested and by the time we went indoors, we had taken so many more tumbles and were so wet and cold that the first exciting ride was almost forgotten. In any case, Momma had other things pressing on her mind and was not inclined to worry about our safety.

'By all accounts, they've had as bad a winter over there as we've had,' she was saying as she hung up our coats on the airing rack. 'These towns they write about - Garndiffaith and Varteg and Blaenavon - are they as far apart as Newport and Ione?'

'No,' said Alec, 'There's only a couple of miles between them.'

'How come they get so cut off then? Don't they have no snow clearance programme over there?' She was setting about making tea, I was glad to see, for I was famished.

'Well I only know what I read, the same as you,' he answered. 'I was only nine when we got to leave there, but one thing I do know, there are villages all up the valley sides, not just along the river like we have here. Blaenavon is quite a big town, built right above the altitude where trees grow. Imagine a town up here at Greyroofs - it would be cut off like we are. And another thing: they never know what to expect, for one year there may be little snow and another there will be a lot. Out here, winter is more predictable; we know for certain how to prepare and for what length of time, so we don't get taken by surprise.'

'Have they been tobogganing then?' I wanted to know.

'Sure to have,' Trefor said. 'Mom, you are the darlingest, best maker of gingerbread I ever did hear of. Could I beg another slice? Or could I have Berta May's, since all she wants to do is chatter?'

'Cupboard love,' laughed Momma. 'You know well it's your own dear Grandmother's recipe I use and as likely as not I have a spare cake in the tin ready for you to take away with you, but I can tell you we shall be running low on stores unless we get out of here pretty soon.'

'I'll ride on down mid-week,' said Alec. 'Just to stock up on essentials for you and get a call through to Joe. And maybe when it clears better, I'll go over and visit with them. We missed their company at Thanksgiving and I'm real sorry to know the flu struck the mill so badly.'

'But it's all this preparation for war that is the worst worry.' Momma was back with the newspapers, reading out from the Free Press: 'Local Authorities are to make a house to house survey by the end of February in areas considered to be safe from the danger of bombing.'

'It's past February now,' I said.

'Don't interrupt, Berta May. Go and play quietly if you have eaten enough. We are discussing serious things.'

'They seem to be planning to send all the children out of the cities into the country for safety. What's this? Ten stroke six per week for the first child to be paid and eight stroke six for others. Do you understand that, Alec?'

'It means ten shillings and six pence, Mom. At the present rate of exchange that would be possibly four dollars.'

'Same price as a gent's overcoat in the Sales,' said Trefor, pointing to the front page of another paper.

'So your Garndiffaith and those other places are on the safe list. Will Megan and the others be taking in lodgers, then?'

'Sure to be offering. She took in Arthur and William last time, didn't she? Finished up adopting them, too.'

'What's adopting?' I asked.

It seemed to me the whole weekend revolved around talk of war and work and winter and I could not find a single picture of interest to me, when I got my hands on the papers at last. My scrapbook got not one new thing from the whole of that bulky mail bag.

When Trefor left, he had a long letter from Mom and one from Alec in his pocket, for despatch to Wales. Each of them told of family affairs and of the general situation in Pend Oreille. From what I heard, those letters must have made real dull reading, telling of programmes to educate adults and get them set up for finding jobs and so on.

'Guess them kids over there won't be wanting to hear that old stuff,' I thought to myself when Mom read bits aloud. 'Why don't you send some pictures, so's they can make a scrap-book like mine?' I asked.

'...and I wonder what the situation in Europe will be by the time you receive this letter.' wrote Alec to Uncle Idris. 'If Eden had stayed in and hadn't been bluffed by the dictators, I wonder if they would have gone so far? The other morning on the radio I heard that Italy has called all men of 38 in to train....'

'Man's inhumanity to man is one thing we women cannot understand,' finished Momma to Auntie Megan.

As for Trefor, he was, unknown to any of us, in the throes of mental torment, for his love of the country of his birth was so strong that he knew he could not stand by and see it under attack. Beneath his normal calm and happy manner he was secretly harbouring a desperate plan.

4

Mid April saw me sleeping on a little folding cot in Auntie Sarah's back room, while Mom was living temporarily with Trefor and Zeb on Third Street. It was time for Freddie to have his operation, so we left Greyroofs in Alec's care, dusted down our sturdy old motor car and chugged away from the still white hills to take up residence in town. I was swelled with pride as Mom dropped me off at my aunt's door and handed me my very own luggage. I had packed the bulging bag myself while she had folded clean underwear, shirts and dresses into a flat leather suitcase. I'd insisted on locking it and the key was safe in my new pocket book which I was clutching in my left hand.

'I do declare you have grown five inches through the winter, Berta May,' exclaimed cousin Laurence when he saw me. 'Carry on that way and your feet will stick over the end of your bed before you go back home.'

'Momma had to let down my best frock and my skirt and my cord trousers,' I agreed. 'She says I get to be more like my poppa every day.'

'I don't remember your poppa being such a chatterbox as you,' laughed Auntie Sarah. 'Now there's room for all your clothes in the corner closet, Berta May, and you can put your books and so on in the toy box to be handy when you want them.'

'Can we go down Washington for some candy?' I asked.

'Just this once,' she said. 'Laurence can take you today, but we don't get candy every day you know. People who live in town just get it for special occasions.'

'Like birthdays,' I nodded. 'Did you know it will soon be my birthday, Laurence? I shall be five and Trefor promised to take me to visit his office. He might take you, too if you care to come.'

It was my first time of staying away from home without Momma but there was never any doubt about my settling. No matter that town life and manners were different or that I must needs wear frocks most days, I made myself at home at once. The days passed quickly and pleasantly and in the evenings when Uncle Henry and the boys were home, we all played Chinese Checkers.

Meanwhile, the clever surgeon was at work on Freddie's leg. I heard talk of X-ray pictures and bones and incisions and they said the operation would be next Monday. I think it was tea time Tuesday when Momma called to tell us that all was well.

'He came out of the anaesthetic asking for his dinner,' she said, hugging me and grinning. 'They've had a tough job keeping him in bed and tomorrow he can have visitors. Would you bring Berta May at three o'clock, Sarah?'

I was none too keen on going. Memories of what I had heard about doctors and surgeons and Matron and some of the accidents which had resulted in patients being admitted here were overpowering. The wooden hospital building did not look inviting to me and I was tongue-tied as we crossed the reception hall, afraid of what I might see.

It was a total surprise, to find Freddie seated in a low chair beside his bed in a room full of children. I looked hard at his legs, not knowing what to expect as evidence of the surgeon's work, but all I could see was a fat white bandage from his hip to his toes. He was cheerful and talkative, playing with a box of metal animals on a low table beside him while Momma talked to his nurse.

'Come here, Berta May,' he commanded. 'I wanna fence round my farm. Get the bricks from the box there. Hurry now.'

So the hour passed easily, but I was glad to be going home with my auntie instead of staying in the hospital ward.

'He'll be out within the week,' said Momma, 'but we shall have to stay in town a while because he will need to see the doctor every day. Did you show Berta May the plaque, Sarah?'

'No, we came straight in, and I thought you would find it better than I would.'

Momma lifted me up.

'See here, Berta May. This is the plaque they put up to remember your daddy. Do you know what that says?'

'No, Momma. I never seen that before.'

It was a shiny brass plate attached to the wall. 'To the memory of Robert Watkins, MD.' she read aloud. 'Physician of this town 1923-1934. He served the community well.' As she lowered me to the floor, I fancied a tear was in Momma's eye and she took out her handkerchief to blow her nose.

Chapter 3

A fine spell of Spring weather enabled Auntie Sarah to take me out and about a good deal and we had a walk most afternoons. Sometimes we went towards the river and I told her all I could see. In the distance, the mountains were still snow-covered, the green conifers dark against the background and here and there a patch of grey-brown trees without foliage. Riverside meadows were beginning to show new green growth.

The highway in Oldtown, however, was not the place in which little girls were encouraged to linger, I gathered. My questions as to what the various buildings were and who lived in which house did not meet with satisfactory answers. I was urged to walk quickly. On the other hand, our strolls along Second past the schools were leisurely and we often went as far as the airport, where I was thrilled to see light aircraft landing now and then. Once, a big white ambulance rushed past us, to take a patient towards a waiting aeroplane.

'I expect someone needs urgent treatment in Spokane,' said Auntie Sarah.

'You don't suppose they've taken Freddie away, do you?'

'I'm sure they have not,' she said, taking my hand and turning towards home, 'but we'll call at the hospital and make certain if you wish.'

On Sunday the whole family went to church and I was introduced to some little girls about my own age. I was invited to go round to their house and play sometime. Elderly ladies patted me on the head and said how well they remembered my father and grandmother and what a good little girl I had been to sit still through the service.

'The pity is, so many children are growing up without a spiritual upbringing,' said the Minister's wife to Uncle Henry. 'Is it the same back home do you know? Are the churches and chapels in danger of closing for want of support?'

We children were given fruit juice in the school room and

allowed to play while our elders talked. The two Misses Beeching were introduced to me.

'We were your daddy's neighbours at one time,' said one, 'and watched his first family grow into American citizens so you wouldn't know they had not been born under the Stars and Stripes.'

'Ah me, how time does fly,' said the other. Then they turned their backs and I heard them whispering.

'A well-mannered child, all things considered.'

'Such a shame, him taking up with that outback horsey woman. The way she dresses, even when in town.'

'Can't expect to make a silk purse out of a sow's ear, as Mother would have said.'

Walking home between my Aunt and Uncle, I was happy to hear that I might go to play with other children during the coming week, but less pleased to know that the Misses Beeching had invited us to visit.

'I really do not care to visit with ladies who whisper things about people,' I announced. 'Momma says it is rude to whisper. The Misses Beeching were being rude. I heard them.'

After a short silence in which Auntie and Uncle probably exchanged glances above my head, he said, 'Quite so, Berta May.'

'Perhaps we will decline then,' said Auntie Sarah. 'We cannot fit too many engagements into a couple of weeks, can we?'

Once Freddie was out of hospital, we went round to see him each afternoon. Momma was planning to take him out for a short daily drive and said she would pick me up next day, so we had a spin to Diamond Lake which gave us all a lot of pleasure.

'Only a few more days and we shall be able to go home,' she said at the end of that week. 'I shall be real glad to get back. Alec has had the responsibility of the farm for too long.'

'But he has Zeb with him now for company,' said Auntie Sarah.

'Oh, sure. And Zeb's a great worker so things will be in hand. Probably putting in a bathroom at this very moment, but well...I suppose I've gotten home sick, being so long away.'

To tell the truth, I was beginning to long for the homestead myself, for my pony and the fowls and for Alec. I would not have hurt Auntie Sarah for the world, but I was ready to pack my bag and head for the hills.

Then came a day when I could not eat my breakfast.

'What ails you, my lovely?'

'Are you sick?'

'Her cheeks are flushed. Has she got a fever?'

All four members of the family were concerned but all I could answer was, 'I want Momma.' Then I burst into tears and was carried back to bed.

I had rarely had even a chill in my short life, so the affliction of a raging sore throat and a throbbing head was a new and nasty experience. The doctor diagnosed Tonsillitis, said I must stay in bed and on no account go near my little brother.

'We cannot risk his catching it as this stage,' he said, 'and I must ask you not to let their mother near the patient either, lest she carry the infection.' So no matter how I might need her, Momma could not come. Dear Auntie Sarah lavished her tender care on me, bringing me soothing syrup and sitting beside my bed to sing me to sleep until at last the pain receded and I felt a little better.

'See here, Berta May,' she said. 'Momma has sent a package for you. Open it now and see what is inside.'

Propped up on pillows, I untied the string to find a pretty rag doll, just the right size to hold in my arms in bed. I had never taken greatly to dolls and their frilly dresses, but this one arrived just when I needed her and I snuggled down to cuddle her beneath the warm quilt.

The third day after that, I was demanding that stories be read to me. Out came books which Laurence and Danny had outgrown and Auntie Sarah told stories until she was hoarse. Uncle Henry came home with a new little book for me and read 'Our Button Book' over and over again. I liked best the one about marketing;

'We buttons go to market
On Kate's new flowered dress;
Her pocketbook is open-
She's buying food, I guess.'

The picture showed a girl with her hair braided just like mine and two boys playing a shop clerks behind a low counter.

Next day, I said it over and over to myself while Auntie Sarah was keeping house, then she allowed me to sit by the stove for a while after lunch. We browsed through her treasure box on the following afternoon and I tried to fix in my head who was whom of all the Watkins. At last, I was feeling better.

'Can I go home tomorrow?' I asked.

'Not until the doctor is certain you will not give Freddie your bad throat,' she told me. 'Maybe Saturday. Momma is just waiting until you're ready, but first you are going to have a surprise.'

None of them would tell me what it would be, no matter how I tried to persuade them, but three days later I was up and dressed for breakfast and they let me into the secret.

'What day is it today?' asked Uncle Henry.

'Friday, I guess,' I said.

'And what day comes next?'

'Saturday. Why?'

'What else is Saturday?' asked Laurence. They were all grinning at my puzzled face.

'I don't know. Tell me, please'.

'Stop teasing her. It is May 31st,' said Auntie Sarah. 'Your birthday, Berta May.'

'Well, fancy you forgetting,' teased Laurence. 'Who cares about an old birthday, anyways? C'mon, Danny, time for school.'

'I care!' I cried. 'I shall be five and I'm going to see Trefor's office. I can go see it can't I, Auntie Sarah?'

'Yes you can, cariad. Trefor is coming for you right after dinner and then when you come back we shall have a birthday tea.'

What a relief, to know I had got better just in time. At one o'clock I was ready, wearing my warm blue pleated skirt and jacket, kneeling up on a chair to watch for Trefor coming. Hand in hand, we went along Third and Union and I tried to match my stride to his.

'Hi,' said a tall smiling lady who stood behind a polished counter inside the door of the Miner. 'You must be Berta May. I am Sadie Beeching. How are you?' She stretched out her hand and I reached up to shake it, feeling very grown-up.

'Much better, thank you,' I replied.

'And today is your birthday? Happy Birthday, honey.'

'Thank you. I'm five,' I said.

'I know you are and boy, are you just cute? My aunts told me they had met you in church, before you got your sore throat. I hope you will enjoy looking round our office here.'

She seemed a lot nicer than her two old aunts, I thought as Trefor unlocked the door to the inner room.

'Now whatever you do, don't touch anything,' he warned me. 'It may look a mite untidy, but we reporters and typists know exactly where to find things and I'd be mighty unpopular come Monday morning if papers had been moved around.'

'Of course I won't touch things,' I declared, indignant that he should think a five-year-old needed to be told. 'Which desk is yours?'

'Over in the corner there, with the brown box files and big pile of photographs on top.'

'Is that your typewriter?'

'Yes it is, but I have to share it with another reporter. Now first I'll explain how we collect the news and arrange the pages for the paper and then I will let you try typing.'

So we did the round of the desks and I saw some letters and pictures of baseball games awaiting attention. I heard a telephone shrilly ring more than once in the outer office.

'Sadie's having a busy day,' said Tref. 'Sometimes, Saturday afternoon is just dead. Now, come and sit on top of these books and see can you reach the typewriter.'

It was about level with my chin, so he got another thick book from somewhere and then showed me how to press the keys. With a lot of rattling and determined effort, I got two lines of letters printed on the page. I thought it was magic, the way a black shape appeared out of the end of one lever after I had pressed hard on another.

'Now we'll type your name,' he said, guiding my fingers to the correct letters so that BERTA MAY WATKINS was printed large and clear in the centre of the page.

'Show me how to do it real good,' I demanded, slipping down from the chair.

'What do you want me to type then?'

'Put about my birthday and that I came to see your office today.'

'OK, I'll write a report about you.'

I watched in fascination as his fingers tapped one key after another at rapid speed, while the lines of clear letters spread over the paper.

'What does it say?' I asked when he stopped.

'It says Berta May Watkins of Greyroofs, Greystone Water Road near Cusick, was a visitor at the Miner today. This being Berta May's fifth birthday, she was privileged to be given a tour of the office, by her brother Trefor. She was wearing a stylish blue jacket with white trim at the wrists, a matching pleated skirt and a white knitted jumper. Miss Watkins was recently suffering from Tonsillitis but has made a full recovery. Happy Birthday, Berta May.'

'Read it again, I want to remember it,' I said.

Then he bought a brand new reporter's notebook just like the one he used, for me to take home along with six sharp lead pencils and Miss Beeching put them all in a brown paper bag. I showed her what Trefor had typed and pretended to read it.

'You're cute,' she said again. 'Have a nice party now.'

Home for tea then, and we went in through the door to hear a chorus of 'Happy Birthday Berta May' from more voices than I had expected. There was Momma, large as life in the middle of the room, her arms spread wide to hug me, as well as Freddie and our two big cousins, a friend I had played with before being sick and of course, Auntie Sarah and Uncle Henry. On the table was a feast of goodies, a cake with candles in the middle and a pile of wrapped gifts at one end.

What a party we had. The food was delicious and although my appetite was still small, I sampled everything before starting to open my parcels.

'How did you know I just wanted a pencil box for the pencils Trefor gave me?' I asked Laurence.

'A little bird told me and I made it myself,' he said. 'You like the picture on the lid?'

Of course I liked it, liked everything and everybody and became so excited that they thought I might become ill again.

'I figure an early night is what the doctor would order,' said Momma at last. 'Off to bed with you quickly now, Berta May and I will read you a story before I take Freddie home.'

'...and speaking of home,' she added as she kissed me goodnight, 'we are all going back to Greyroofs tomorrow.'

2

We twisted and turned on our seat in the car, Freddie and I as we trundled up the highway. A hundred times, Momma told us to be still, for fear of our being thrown down at a sudden swerve, but both of us wanted to be first at seeing round every bend, first to find the well-known landmarks that led us homeward. We sang and we laughed as if we had known no happiness for weeks, forgetting the kindness and love of those who had cared for us in town.

Slowly, we crept up the steep pull through the forest, our cries echoing under the canopy of green until at last we had first sight and sound of our own Greystone Water as it rushed through the gorge below us.

'We're home, we're home,' we cried when the brow of the hill was passed and the homestead came in sight. 'Alec! Alec! We're coming!' and we wound down the windows to lean out and wave.

Gone was the last snow from the high land and the forest and it felt like a big new country to me after the closed horizon of town streets. I leapt down to open the yard gate, dancing for joy and shouting, 'Alec!'

'He's away over Tacoma Creek,' said Zeb, coming out of the house, 'but I should think he'll have heard you, the racket you are making.' He swung me high in the air to sit me atop the gate while he pulled it shut.

'So how's our little man then? Doctor get you a new leg,

39

did he?'

'As good as Berta May's,' declared Freddie, 'when I get my plaster off. I got crutches for now see, Zeb. Look how I can walk and my foot don't twist no more.'

We had hardly got our bags unloaded when Alec trotted into the yard and I was first to rush out and hug him. With a thousand questions, I followed him round the barn and yard and tried to help with the chores. The skirt I was wearing was soon speckled with straw and bran mash, my shoes and white socks dusty, but I would not leave him for a minute to change my clothes.

'Tell you one thing, Mom,' he said when we were having supper. 'It's been mighty quiet up here without this chatterbox. I don't know whether we can stand it, me and the stock, listening to her night and day from now on,' but I knew from his smile that he was teasing me.

It was nearly bed time when he looked at Zeb and said, 'I guess we'd better go and get a bit more wood from the barn,' and they both went out so quickly that I had no chance to tag on. Five minutes later they were back, carrying between them something covered with a piece of sacking.

'There you are then. Happy Birthday, Berta May, from both of us. Zeb made the desk and I made the chair and Momma brought the painting set from town for you.'

My happiness was complete. I arranged and re-arranged my papers and pencils and paint box inside my polished wooden desk and asked for it to be placed beside my bed. What more could a five-year-old want?

As for Mom, she was kicking up her heels for joy over the new bathroom that the men had fixed up while we'd been gone. There was running water to the tub and the basin, with faucets every bit as bright as Auntie Sarah's and the furnace had been made to heat all the water we could want.

'And come summer and you don't want to light the furnace all you have to do is switch on the power for an hour,' they told her.

'Now ain't that just neat?' she exclaimed.

'And when we finished that bit of tiling in the corner, all it needs is a lick of paint to finish off the room,' said Zeb. 'I'll do that before I leave.'

He had some trouble, for Freddie and I were so intrigued with the new fittings that we were in and out all day long on supposedly urgent business and he just got no peace for more than twenty minutes at a time.

'You better give these kids some kinda medication to settle their stomachs, Cass,' he said at last. She banned us after that, saying we must use the old place until all work on the bathroom was finished.

I took it for granted that I would resume my daily chores and that Alec would tolerate my company about the farm. As summer advanced we rode further afield, first bringing our stock up from the lower pastures to graze on Sutton's meadow. That lay about a mile beyond Elk rock, some two hundred feet higher than the homestead. It was a two-day operation to drive the cattle up from the valley and this was the first time I had been allowed to join in fully. The Stork and Davies farms which lay below us two miles down the creek moved their animals at the same time, so it was a great time for me to meet their families. We rested the stock overnight in our home meadow, then finished the ride by the following midday, after which all hands stopped off at our place for cool drinks and giant doughnuts.

There was work to be done on our timber lots high above, taking out a small amount of mature timber and removing trees infected with rot. Zeb stayed long enough to help with the heaviest work and sometimes all five of us were out there from dawn to dusk, but we children were strictly forbidden to approach the felling area. Looking after Freddie was a chore I did not like.

When Momma took him back to the hospital for treatment, I stayed home with Alec. We planted the vegetable seeds and cleaned out the stables, brought home wood for burning, sawed it and stowed it under the eaves. I was not pleased to be told that he would be leaving us for a week or two in July.

'But I can't do everything myself,' I protested.

'No, but you can help me all you can,' said Momma, 'and Zeb will come back to do the forest work. Alec deserves a holiday and you must not let him think he should not have it.'

Meanwhile, several more letters had come from Wales

41

and the adults were always talking of the tense situation that existed in Europe. Much as I loved to have pictures for my scrapbook from Auntie Megan and the others, I hated the evenings when dreary items were read aloud and discussed over supper.

'There's only one bit of good news in the whole paper,' said Zeb on the first day he was with us in July. 'There's a new factory opened down the valley, making valves and taking on two hundred workers. But the rest is all gloom. Measuring folks for gas masks and getting teams of volunteers to learn about dealing with emergencies. All this talk of dugouts and A.R.P....'

'But they're still writing of holiday trips and going to the theatre,' said Momma. 'Life seems to be pretty much as usual and here's a page of advertisements for cars and all about new radio programmes. Do they have radios most everywhere there, I wonder?'

'Sure to have by this time. Probably all electric now, same as ours, though would you believe it the valley still has no main sewer? Still pouring the filth into the river they are, same as fifty years ago. Just look at this bit - the councils are thinking about the cost.'

So it went on. Alec had his holiday, back-packing in the forest above Sullivan Lake with his friend Joe and returned saying he was well rested and glad to be home. August through September, we had a glorious time with fruit and vegetables in abundance, our stock all in good heart and our family likewise. There were picnics with our church and visits to friends over Ione way and once Alec took me to the very top of Timber Mountain, where we climbed the fire tower and talked to the Ranger on duty there. If only there had not lurked the unvoiced fear that some disaster was about to overtake the nation.

Mostly, I was living outdoors in meadow and forest, a thriving, growing girl secure in a stable family. Even Freddie got to leaving the homestead now, for with his leg improved he could learn to ride horseback and Momma took him out for an hour or so each day when I was not needing Dusty.

'By next summer, you will have outgrown her,' I was told, 'and we'll get you a bigger pony so's Freddie can have her.'

'But I don't want another pony.'

'You cannot stop yourself growing, child. By next year, your feet will be trailing on the ground and think how silly you'd look, riding to school like that.'

She persuaded me thus, for I was eagerly awaiting the time when I might start to school, once I turned six. Not for the world would I look silly in the eyes of my fellow students.

I began to look intently at our horses and those of our neighbours, wondering which one to choose as my new mount.

One Friday evening when Trefor came, he told us that Auntie Sarah had received a parcel from cousin Bobbie.

'It was so heavy,' he said, 'it cost nearly a pound to mail it and it took her ages to untie all the string. And when she got through, she found our Grandma's Welsh Bible all wrapped round with layers of cloth.'

'Land sakes, why did he send that then? Do they think we are such heathen we have no Bibles over here?'

Trefor laughed. 'This one would do us no good, Mom, in that case. It's all in Welsh.'

'Then why....?'

'Bobbie sent a letter with it, to say he wants it kept safe. Gran gave it to him when we left, see. She used to write all our dates of births, marriages and so on in front and she charged him to carry on with the record. Quite a family heirloom it is, see?' Trefor shook his head. 'I take it as a bad sign, him thinking things so bad he has to send the Bible here for safe keeping.'

Then he asked me if I wanted to ride out with him.

'If we take a can with us, we may get some huckleberries and then we can have pancakes for supper. I won't take her too far, Mom.'

Of all the adults in my life, he was the least inclined to talk about the national or international news. As soon as war and unrest were mentioned or the radio was switched on, he would find a job needing his attention or would ask me and Freddie did we want to play in the yard. That suited me, for the daily dose of air-borne gloom through which I was bidden to be quiet was as unwelcome as a spoonful of

43

bitter medicine.

He was not with us on the day when the solemn voice invaded our sunlit porch where trickling water made background music as we ate our supper.

'Britain and France have declared war on Germany.'

3

'Dear Sarah, Henry, Cassie and all you dear people,' began the next letter from Auntie Megan.

'This will not be a long letter. I will send all details later but we want you to know we are perfectly safe as of now. You will know of course that the worst has happened and the preparations that have gone on for months were necessary after all. I thought some of it was a waste of time and money but now I am glad I took notice of what they said in the Women's column in the paper. I got in as much tinned food and stuff as I could manage like it said to make an 'ARP Store cupboard.' Jane and Bessie likewise, so far as our money went. One way or another, most of us got involved - can't say No that's our trouble so our Will and Arthur and the young lot been taking Gas Masks round and by all accounts even the Scouts and Guides are useful carrying messages. Evacuees arriving now.

What a shame, though maybe I should not write such things. Last month was perfect and a good harvest. We all went to the opening of Glansychan Park where they have made a playing ground in the middle of Abersychan. Used to be a big house there, where our Jane had a job as maid. Sarah will remember. I think she sang there in the old days. And the Garn Gleemen was on the radio on the 25th, our Idris, Bobbie and Will amongst them, but now here we are at war and dreading them all being called up. No room for more. Sending this by the Air Mail. More soon. Megan.'

It was six weeks before papers and letters arrived by sea and the initial shock had worn off, there being no dramatic developments which we could understand at this distance. Mid October was time for Freddie to have his check up at the hospital and Momma declared we might as well make a shopping day out of it and stock up a bit for winter. So Alec

44

got out the car, tinkered with the engine and brushed straw off the bonnet. We put our overnight things in a bag, for Auntie Sarah's church was holding a concert and we fancied some entertainment.

'I'll come down myself Saturday morning,' Alec said, 'after I've done the chores. Hope this rain eases up.'

It was still pouring down when we arrived and put our things in the spare room up top of Trefor's house. Zeb came from his basement to welcome us and gave us a hot drink.

'How about you staying with Auntie Sarah, Freddie, while Berta May and I get the supplies?' asked Momma, thinking how difficult it would be to drag him around in the rain.

'Why not leave him with me?' said Zeb. 'He can help me in my workshop. Like that, wouldn't you boyo?' and Freddie nodded.

So Momma and I scurried from store to store, umbrellas in hand and glad of our long pants and boots no matter that we were not too tidy. It took some time but at last we were through and our arms were full of packages. Even my awkward feet had been obliging, so my new winter boots had been purchased.

After dinner, I went to Auntie Sarah's while Mom took Freddie to the hospital and I got to look at the family Bible which Bobbie had sent.

'Read it to me, please,' I begged, but poor auntie could not see to do so, though she pointed out the names written in the front.

'In any case,' she told me, 'I never could read Welsh. I'm real sorry about that. Your daddy could read some, when he was a boy, but it had virtually gone from the valley by the time we were born and the only bit we had was a few songs we learned for Saint David's day. And for Eisteddfods.'

'Sing one to me then. Please.'

'Oh dear. Now let me think.' She hummed a few bars of a tune, then changed her mind and began another. When finally she started to sing, it was a haunting lullaby and we swayed to and fro together in her fireside chair. The strange words meant nothing to me but I loved the music.

'Another. Sing another,' I begged. After that we sang

The Exile together and then some nursery rhymes, but I got her to repeat her first haunting lullaby before the end of the afternoon.

'Trefor must read all the names to you,' she said as we closed the old Bible and put it away in her bookcase. 'And by this time next year, you'll be able to read a bit yourself.'

'Alec says he will start teaching me my letters this winter,' I told her. 'He says they start school at five in Wales and I ought to be doing sums and reading before I get to be six, like Poppa and you-all did.'

From my bedroom that evening, I could hear the grown-ups talking, Momma and Zeb, Trefor, Uncle Henry and Laurence who had come round to visit. Freddie was asleep and the drone of voices made a comforting music to my sleepy childish thoughts as I lay in the strange bedroom.

Suddenly, I was startled to hear angry words. I raised my head in alarm and there was no doubt about it, Trefor was shouting.

'I know, but I can't help it. This is something I have to do.'

Astonished, I picked up my ears. I had never known Trefor shout so. In fact, none of us shouted much, unless on a windy day we needed to be heard across the yard. Mom had the loudest voice of all, but she sang rather than shouted and was rarely angry.

'You God-dammed stupid boy,' she bellowed now and my mouth fell open to hear her language. 'I never in my whole life seen any boy less like a soldier. You never raised your fists to a soul your whole life long, how can you talk of fighting?'

'Calm down now, Cass,' came Zeb's deeper voice, which then continued quietly so I could not hear. At length, I must have fallen asleep and heard no more of the argument, but the morning soon brought a renewal of discord. Alec trotted into the yard before mid day.

'Now you tell your brother what you told us last night,' ordered Momma to Trefor and then I heard the awful truth.

'I shall go home to fight for my country,' he said.

'Your country? But this is your country. And mine and

Berta May's and Freddie's.'

'Theirs, yes, for they have known no other, but I am Welsh and I am British and my homeland is in danger of invasion. I am going to go there and fight. No God-dammed German army is going to march into my valley and crush my people while I have breath to fight.'

His dark eyes flashed fire, he stood tall and wiry and determined and I imagined him armed and ready to quell the foe.

'You sure are brave,' I said, 'as brave as knights of old. Auntie Megan will be pleased to see you because she wouldn't want the Germans to burn her homestead and get her horses, would she? But have you got a gas mask? They all got to have gas masks there, you know.'

For some reason, they began to laugh. Alec gave me a playful punch and said, 'Saved by Berta May. No use getting our tempers up now. I have to go order some harness and take my saw blades for sharpening. Coming with me, Tref? You can buy me a drink in Kelly's and try to convince me I'm wrong.'

'Can I come?' I begged, but was refused and had perforce to stay in and eat my dinner. There were no more angry words, but an intermittent discussion went on throughout the day and the adults mostly wore frowns. In the early evening, we all got well wrapped up to go to the concert, even Freddie being allowed to come because it was posted a whole family programme. We got to stand on stage when they called for children to sing a chorus for the wedding of the Princess and her noble rescuer, who was none other than cousin Laurence.

'Your pop would have been so very proud of you,' whispered Momma as she kissed us good night. I know that he would also have been proud of Trefor for holding to his determination to serve his country, though at that time I was heartbroken at his leaving us.

'Take this packet and keep it safe in your desk until I come back,' he whispered to me next morning after church. 'I want you to have my diaries and poems. You can read them when you are big enough, but for now just you keep them safe. Be a good girl now, Berta May and help Momma all you can, for she may be lonesome on times.'

Little did he guess, as he hugged me close to him, that we too were to be invaded. An invasion of another kind was imminent, one that would fill our houses, our hours and eventually our hearts.

Chapter 4

Papers, papers, papers. Momma and Alec had them spread all over the kitchen table and were reading bits aloud. Fall was slipping into winter with the shortening of days and increasing cold at night; our long evenings were spent around the warm furnace, so there was no escape from the latest news.

'Please Alec, will you show me some more letters?' I asked. 'I copied all yesterday's and know their names real well, see.'

Seated at my wooden desk, I was busy with paper and pencil. A card with the whole alphabet lay to my left, but Alec was teaching me bit by bit and we had got as far as 'p'. I thought it was time he gave me some attention.

'I knew it,' exclaimed Momma. 'Listen to this: Passenger steamer torpedoed. 'I saw shells hit the water,' said Mrs Doreen Ford of Toronto, Canada, who had been recently staying with friends in Abersychan. Ships being sunk and our Trefor on his way across the Atlantic and who's to know, has his ship gone down already? Oh wow! Fancy a Sir and a Lady having to take to the lifeboat, too.' She buried her head in the Free Press again and we heard no more for a while.

There were photographs of children arriving by train and I gathered they were Evacuees, come to Wales for safety from the cities which might be raided by German bombs.

'Aw, listen to this,' said Momma. 'Abersychan's little guests saw their first blackberries in Lasgarn Woods when they all went out for a walk. But they were surprised to see no snow on the mountains in September.'

'Silly things,' I snorted. 'Anybody knows snow don't come before October.'

'Not kiddies who probably never seen a blade of grass, let alone a whole green mountain. Snow doesn't fall in Abersychan until at least mid-December as a rule and sometimes not before January.'

After that they got onto reading letters from Auntie Megan and cousin Bessie.

'There's one from Lizzie as well. She doesn't often find time to write, let's see what she has to say first,' Alec said.

'Dear Folks,   22nd Sept. 1939

'Before we all get swept up in this awful turmoil and mail has to be censored, I thought I should write. Your last letters arrived safely in September but with ships now being torpedoed who can say whether we can expect more, or when?

I am still in my post at Pontypool, where we opened a new Out-patients department recently. It was built at a cost of £17,000 and contains consulting rooms, waiting rooms and all modern facilities even to two iron lungs, X-ray and Electro-therapy units. Can you beat that in Newport? Yet even while we make progress in medical treatment, the evils of Man's actions make it likely that we shall have unforeseen situations to deal with. Only last week, we had a cyclist killed, probably as a result of carrying his gas mask on his handlebars, our first war casualty.

Megan, Bessie and I have managed to fit six children into our houses and strange little creatures they seem to us, these waifs from Birmingham. The two I have taken are under four years old and so have their mother with them, a necessity as I am out at work. We hear some sorry tales and some very funny ones. Some families that arrived had the mother with five or six children refusing to be split up, so you can imagine the difficulty of finding homes for them. Our people have been tremendously hospitable, though some say it is costing too much and they cannot carry on for long. There have as yet been no Air Raids.

Petrol (gasoline) is to be rationed, 200 miles per month being allowed though as a doctor I will have more for essential travel. The price is one shilling and six pence a gallon. No doubt you can convert that into dollars. Our houses all have to be blacked out at night. Megan got a bargain lot of black satin from Fowlers' Sale at 1/6¾d a yard, enough for her and Jane and Bessie but as I don't have time to sew, I got shutters made.

Do write with your news and especially about Freddie's leg which of course is of professional interest to me. Tell Berta May I shall look for a letter from her as soon as she can write. I counted how many of the family are of an age for military service and it could be as many as twelve, though some of us would be exempt, I think, being farmers or in the coal industry. My conscience tells me I ought to volunteer my services, so who knows where we shall all be this time next year.

With my fondest love and best wishes,
Yours, Lizzie.'

'Another one with a conscience. I suppose they'll be crying out for doctors and nurses as well as service men.' He passed the letter across to Mom and picked up another.

'Is Lizzie a doctor?' I asked.

'Yes she is, just like Pop.'

'Is there a Mister Lizzie?'

'Not yet. Lizzie is still Miss Watkins.'

'Is she as old as you?'

'Older. About thirty five, is Lizzie.'

'I shall write her just as soon as ever I get the hang of these letters. And Trefor. I shall write him first and Lizzie next. Look, how'm I doing, Alec? Am I shaping up all right?'

I held my book for him to see and he said I was doing fine and just to write another line of p to z.

'Tomorrow, I shall show you how to write a little word,' he said.

Now and then through the winter, Momma told him he was filling my head with too much learning.

'I never heard of no little girls writing and reading before they got to school,' I heard her say one day round about New Year. 'Sue and Jack Barker down Two Mile, they got a boy in school already and he barely started reading last time I saw them, though he's rising seven.'

'But Sue and Jack Barker don't have to amuse Berta May like I do. She needs something to do beyond colouring pictures and building bricks and if she didn't want to read, I would not have started her on it.'

'You sure she ain't straining her eyes none?'

'Absolutely certain sure.' He came over to my desk where I was slowly copying a line of lettering. 'That is good, Berta May. Read it to me.'

'My name is Berta May and I am five years old,' I read. 'Can I start my letter to Trefor now?'

'Tomorrow,' he said. 'You've done enough for today and Freddie wants you to play with him. Be a good girl now and keep him out of Mom's way while she bakes pies for supper.'

We all missed Trefor's weekend visits. News from town was rare at this time of year, but he had always struggled out to us if the roads were passable, whereas now we had barely any visitors from November through March. Only old Lon Withers, who lived in a cabin high up the trail above Sutton's Meadow, had banged on the kitchen door after supper one dark night.

His beard was snow-flecked and his breath sent white clouds along our porch while a strong north wind threatened to tear the door from my hand.

'You got a corner where an old-timer can rest till morning, Missis?' he asked. 'I been to Cusick for a few supplies but me and my Bess is clean wore out and there's a storm brewing.'

'Come right on in,' said Momma, getting up to welcome him, 'but you'll want to settle Bess in the stable first.'

'I'll show Lon where to put the mule,' said Alec, 'while you make coffee. How long did it take you coming up from Cusick?' I heard him ask as they went down the steps.

I did not do any writing that evening. Once he had thawed out and disposed of two bowls of Mom's thick broth, old Lon entertained all four of us. He told us local gossip that he had picked up that day and pulled a tattered newspaper from his pocket, but before they could launch into a wearisome session of talk about War and Want, I sidled up to him and said, 'Please will you tell me some stories about the old days, Mr Withers?'

'Why bless my heart, I ain't had no-one call me Mr Withers in a month of Sundays, so I ain't,' he laughed. 'Come up here on old Lon's lap, my little Princess, and I'll tell you how me and my folks came over the mountains in search of a fortune long before you was a twinkle in your daddy's eye.'

'It was in the year of 1883, see, that my folks packed into Calispel valley by way of Rocky Gorge, my Ma and Pa and his old Uncle Wes as was the last of the Withers that came over from England in the fifties. A real good woodsman, was Uncle Wes and thanks to him, me and my baby sister got a roof over our heads before winter come.

That was a fine cosy cabin he built us, down near the lake where the camas grew thick and the cows we brung with us did thrive so's we had a-plenty and to spare. But my Pa and Uncle Wes, they had the wander thirst in them. They was restless to be finding a place higher up the mountains and my Ma, why, she figured it was bad for our chests to be living by the lake. So do you know what we did?'

'Guess you upped and came right on up the trail,' I said.

'Yup. Only there weren't no trail before we come, not even an Indian trail. It was Withers made your trail for you, cutting a way through the forest for mile after mile. A month or more I guess it was, before Pa got where he wanted to be, and all that time we was camping out nights and living off whatever we could shoot and the bit of food Ma had packed in the ox-cart.'

'And did you like it, when you got to the mountain top?'

'Sure did. Clear on up to the pass we went and they cleared a patch of ground to put up our log cabin. I been living there ever since and do you know how long that is? Seventy three years and I'm not kidding. And I'll tell you sump'n else. I found Gold in the creek. Why, there was a time when I was all set to make my fortune. It was like this......'

I got to stay up real late that evening, for after the stories came songs and Momma did not have the heart to put a stop to the old man's pleasure, though she whisked me off to bed sharp enough when he pulled a flask of whisky from his hip pocket.

'Now just you come right on up to visit with me come summer, little missy,' he said, 'and I'll teach you the lore of this land. Not many can survive on top the mountain like I do and I got no family to pass things on to.'

'Thank you, Mr Withers, I sure will. Good night.'

He was up and gone before I was dressed in the morning, in spite of a new fall of snow which had obliterated the track again. Standing on the second rail of our fence, I studied the line of footprints heading across the meadow.

'Why is he walking, Alec?' I wanted to know. We were beginning the daily round of feeding the stock.

'Because Bess had a good weight to carry without him on her back. How he has survived so many years alone up there I cannot think, for he seems to run out of the essentials most winters. Once it was flour he needed and the way down to Cusick was blocked. Mom gave him half a sack to tide him over. And sometimes it's potatoes and sometimes beans.'

'Poor old man. I shouldn't like to have no-one at all to talk to all winter.'

He laughed. 'Berta May, I should think you would talk to the birds and the bears rather than be silent. Did you see old Lumberfoot was here this morning? Go and look behind the wagon shed.'

Timidly, lest I should have an unwanted encounter with the black bear which sometimes came looking for food, I peeped around the corner. There was nothing behind the shed but clean white snow, but a clear trail of footprints led out from the forest fence to the shed. I followed it from there to the orchard, where Lumberfoot had been scratching big holes in the snow in his search for fruit. Poor thing, I thought, he must have been really hungry to have woken up and come looking for fallen apples. I hoped he had found something to make his walk worthwhile.

Alec never hunted bear. He hunted deer and elk, shot duck and geese and wild turkey, all to help feed us, but got no pleasure from killing wild animals. Varmints like coyotes had to be controlled; it was a continual battle to protect our vegetable patch from deer and our poultry from mink; sometimes we set traps to get gophers, for they dug just about everywhere we planted, but he taught us not to kill for fun.

By April, we were mobile. Alec went down to collect our mail from the box at the Post Office and there was a letter from Trefor telling us he had arrived safely in England in November.

'I went home to Wales first,' he wrote, 'and got to know everyone. I found I could just remember Uncle Idris, Auntie Jane, Auntie Megan and Uncle Tom, but none of their families. I went all round the Garn and Varteg and they showed me the house where we used to live. Then I got to work on signing up.

As I don't have any particular skills, I thought I'd not aim too high, but put my name down for the army. The Monmouthshire Regiment is what most men here go for, but our William is going into the Royal Engineers and suggested I went for that in the communications line, so that is what I did. I am presently in Training Camp but am not allowed to tell you where. The recruitment officer showed some interest in the fact I had been a journalist and I have a faint hope of becoming an official Correspondent.'

So for the time being, Momma could stop worrying about him and as the countryside came to life we got out and about. Neighbours could visit with ease and contact with our relatives in Newport resumed. Our Sundays once more included going to church in Cusick and it was not long before we were all riding horseback, for Momma had bought me a new pony and Freddie could have Dusty.

'This ought really to be for your birthday,' she told me when we went over to the Barkers' place to look at him, 'but if this chestnut is as sturdy as Jack makes out, I would be a fool to pass up the chance. All depends on size in the end though.' She kicked her horse into a canter along the trail and I urged Dusty to keep alongside. I was feeling at that moment that I should never love another pony as I loved her, but when they saddled up the chestnut and told me to mount, I could have burst with pride and pleasure. He was a dream. With no trouble at all, I walked him round the Barker meadows and then out some way up the mountain with Jack and his son. Chuckie was riding a chestnut, too, the older brother of mine.

'You coming down to Stoney School, come September?' he asked as we trotted homewards.

'Sure am. That where you and Sue go?'

'Not Sue. She starts September, like you. I'll be going up to second grade then.'

'Doesn't Sue want to ride Storm, then?'

'No. Sue ain't so big as you and when she has growed some, Pa's got another ready for her. Look, there she is with Mom on the fence. Race you back.'

He won easily. I made pretence of racing, but was not fixing to take a toss in front of an audience and Storm seemed big and strong to me. We took him home on a halter behind Mom and I wasted no time in getting used to him.

2

We all went to town at the end of the month. There was by now a host of things we needed for the house and farm and quite a bit of trading for Alec to do. It was good to see Auntie Sarah and the rest of them but there had been a sickness which had made her quite poorly. She was pale and tired, so Mom said we would call back later and did not leave me or Freddie there. When all the errands were done, we picked up a bunch of flowers for Auntie Sarah and took things for our dinner with us so she did not have to cook.

'There are three letters for you to read, from Megan,' she told Mom, 'though no doubt you have heard from her yourself.'

'There was nothing in the mail last week and we only picked this week's up today, so I haven't read it yet,' answered Mom. 'One from Trefor though - I must open it first and find out what he's doing.'

'You won't learn much. His letters are censored, but at least you will be glad to know he's well. I had a really long one after Christmas, telling about the old place on the Garn and all the people he had met, but it wouldn't be of much interest to you. Zeb and I had an evening of reminiscence over it.'

Momma ripped open Trefor's letter. It was short but made her happy. 'Anything important from Megan?' she asked then.

'They seem to be making out all right. You'll see all the war news in the paper. Lizzie has gone into the Medical Corps, Emily's in the Land Army and William in the Royal Engineers. But what do you think about the children, Cass? Is it time we were offering to have the little ones?'

'What, here? You mean, have them come over and live with us? But I thought they were supposed to be safe in Wales - that's why they have taken the city children there.'

'Yes, safer than in the big cities, but Britain is a very small country, Cass. Once the Germans got across the channel, there would be no stopping them rolling right on

56

through England and into Wales. Oh, it makes me shudder to think of it. They've done it to Belgium and there seems to be no force to equal theirs.'

I pricked up my ears but decided that this was not the moment to ask questions.

'How many children are there?' asked Mom.

'Well there are seven or eight under fourteen I think - I keep having to ask Henry to read the list of birthdays to see how old they all are. But I haven't said a word to them yet, so I don't know whether they would even think of it. Give the idea time to sink in, Cass, then let me know how you feel.'

'Ok. Now can we do anything for you before we go, Sarah? I'm real sorry to see you not well.'

'So'm I,' I said. 'Would you like to have me sing you a song, Auntie Sarah? I learned it from Mr Lon Withers back in February when he dropped by.'

'It would do me good to hear it,' she smiled, so I gave her a cheery rendering of 'Lil'l liza Jane' and they all clapped my performance.

'Time you went to school and got took down a peg or two,' said Momma, but I knew she was just kidding by the way she hugged me.

'Come on, kids. Pack up that toy box and get your jackets. We'll be back to see Auntie Sarah in two weeks when Freddie has to have his leg checked and let's hope she feels better by then.'

'Will I have my birthday at Auntie Sarah's again?' I asked as we drove home.

'I was thinking about that,' said Momma. 'There's a whole month to go before then, so anything could happen to spoil our plans, but what say we ask Uncle Henry to bring them all up to our place and have a family picnic? It's a year or two since they visited with us and time we did something for them.'

'Good idea,' said Alec. 'It would do Auntie Sarah good and if you want them to stop over, me and the boys could sleep in the hay loft for the night.'

'Me too,' chirped Freddie. 'Let me sleep out with the boys, Momma. Please.'

'And we could ask Barbara and Chuckie and their Mom

and Pop. I'd like the children to get more friendly,' said Momma.

Then Alec said he would ask Joe Walker and I said what about old Mr Withers and the Davieses and by the time we were home, just about the whole county was included.

We were sworn to secrecy on our next trip to town, just until Momma found out for certain was Auntie Sarah quite better, for we wanted it to be a surprise for her. I hardly knew how to contain the secret for the two hours that I stayed with her. Luckily, she was intent on going through a new lot of songs which Bethan had sent her and on teaching me one of her Welsh lullabies, so I managed to hang on to my tongue.

As she seemed more like her old self, Momma gave me the nod after tea and I got out my pocket book in which I had been hiding the invitation.

'For you all,' I said. 'Would you like me to read it to you? I wrote it all by myself.'

'Thank you, I should like to know what it says, otherwise I must wait until Laurence comes home.'

'Mr and Mrs Henry Watkins and family are invited to a picnic party at Greyroofs on Saturday, 30th May at 3 o'clock.'

'Oh, how lovely,' she exclaimed. 'Now that is something to look forward to.'

'It's a birthday party,' I told her, 'though my birthday is the Sunday, but Mom said Saturday was best for a party and you can stay overnight and the boys are going to sleep in the loft and all our best friends is coming.'

'Are coming. I hope you can make it, Sarah. I'm trying to restrain Berta May from inviting every last soul she meets, but we'll be quite a party, I guess. And about that other business - I think you should start asking Megan now. I'm ready to do all I can.'

My head was full of plans, most of which made work for Mom or Alec, but it was not long before I had to do my share of the preparations.

'Now we are going to clean this barn from one end to the other,' announced Alec about a week before the party date.

'Why?'

'Because it will be needed for your visitors if we get a rainy day. I've put the horses out early and shifted things around to make a bit of space, so you can help me sweep and shovel until the floor is shining.'

He meant it, too. He took the chance to tidy accumulated odds and ends of harness that had lain around for years and to arrange everything in order.

'This floor's gonna be clean enough to put the white linen on,' I commented, stretching my arms and groaning after three days of toil.

'I aim to have it so,' he laughed. 'Now let's have some fun. See these buckets of water?'

'Yes.'

'I'm going to pour the water over the floor, starting at yon end. I want you to swoosh it along with your broom like we did in the stables. Don't let it run back towards the pens, aim for the door, will you?'

'Ok. All set.' As the first bucketful came my way, I frantically pushed my broom to drive water down along the barn. He picked up a bigger broom and came to help and for half an hour we had a wet hilarious time.

'That looks good enough to me,' I said as we stood by the door looking back at our achievement, but he said there would be more to do tomorrow.

'I'm none too sure I want a party after all,' I told Momma. 'Alec makes me work so hard, it's hardly worth it.'

'Then perhaps he'd better have Freddie help him instead,' she teased.

With Freddie's leg so much more like normal, he was getting around and taking part in farm life along with me, but the last thing I wanted was for him to take my place as Alec's chief assistant.

'I guess I'll carry on,' I sighed.

3

I could count up to ten, but how many there were on our picnic for my sixth birthday, I was never quite sure, for just when I thought I had got it right, some more would arrive and throw me out. More than two tens, a lot more, anyway.

The weather held and we took our hampers and boxes up Sicley Creek Road and clear to the top of Calispel Peak. We twisted and turned through the forest, past clear-cut lots where ancient lone cedars marked where their comrades had fallen, across crude log bridges and under gloomy bluffs. There were some of us on horseback and some in wagons, some came up in motor cars and Joe Walker brought his father and mother along in their lumber truck. When the cars could go no further because of the stones and the wash-outs, he picked up their passengers and that is how Auntie Sarah arrived before I did at the very end of the road.

'What a ride!' she said. 'Are we at the top now?'

'Just a mile or so to walk,' I told her, 'but you can have a ride on Storm if you like.'

'No thank you. I leave that to you, Berta May. Uncle Henry and I will come on foot while you go on to get the kettles boiling.'

Through the final twisting mile of dark pines then, where only a narrow footpath led steeply upwards, we climbed until at last we came into bright sunlight and there were no more trees. The view from the summit was magnificent and groups of people were standing to admire it from all angles while Alec and Zeb and Momma got down to work. Rocky outcrops made seats for all and we tackled the food with good appetites. Tea was nearly over before we noticed two stragglers walking up the trail.

'Why look, Berta May,' said Momma. 'Someone else is coming. Can you see who it is?' She stood up. Then the next minute Alec leapt to his feet and ran away from us, waving his arms and shouting. A voice replied.

'I know that voice,' said Auntie Sarah. 'It's Bethan.'

And so it was. My half-sister had arrived all the way from California to find none of us in town or at the homestead. Luckily, Mom had pinned a note to the door in case anyone came late, so Bethan and her friend had followed us.

'Mom, meet James,' she said. 'James, this is Mom, this is Alec and these two are Berta May and Freddie.'

'Why ever didn't you send word you were coming?' asked Mom.

'We only made up our minds a few days ago. We are

resting at present and found time to spare for a vacation, and having got as far as Seattle, made up our minds to come on over.'

She was a very smart young lady, dressed more for a fashionable event in town than for a mountain-top picnic and her friend wore a striped blazer and grey slacks. While they chatted and ate tea, we children scattered, to run, to hide or to play jumping over low bushes. After, I heard music and ran back to see what was happening and there was James strumming a ukulele while everybody sang.

It went on for quite some time, that concert on the mountain top, and it made my birthday joy complete, yet there was more to come when we got home. It was just the family by then, plus old Lon Withers, but that was still more than I could count. Into the barn we trooped and out came the old man's fiddle for a few dance tunes before bed time. We did our dosey dos and ladies chains; we dipped and dived and turned the star till it seemed to me the clock would crow at any minute and the animals must have wondered at the merriment. Then Freddie got his dream come true and slept in the loft with the boys, for Bethan must have his bed and I wished I had been born a boy. However, there was some compensation in having a cup of cocoa in the kitchen while Bethan told the ladies about her life on the stage. She was getting to be quite famous, by all accounts.

'Berta May, you better not be six every day,' groaned Momma next morning, nursing a sore head. 'Now get on out and bang the tin tray outside the barn to wake the menfolk, for there's work to be done, Sunday or no Sunday.'

4

I remember there being much adult talk during the next few weeks and I knew that Bethan's visit had in some way made Momma sad. She had enjoyed the company of the theatrical couple, I knew, but must have learned some unwelcome news. I supposed it was the war again.

Then she and Auntie Sarah had their heads together more than once about some plan they were making and a

61

letter of great importance was sent to Auntie Megan in Wales.

'Dear Megan, We are perhaps reading too much into the reports we hear of the war. If so, you must tell us, but it seems to us that the time has come when we must offer what help we can.

As we understand it, many families are making arrangements for their relatives in Britain to send children to the States where they will be cared for. We would like you to know that there will be a welcome here for your youngsters. We can offer them homes along with our own and all the care we can give them. The journey across the ocean is of course at present dangerous and then there are five days by train to Seattle, the nearest point where we could collect them, but travel can be arranged and we believe Matrons are provided to escort them.

We hope you will discuss this with the children's mothers if you think fit and let us know of your decision. We are thinking of you all the time.

Sarah and Cass.'

We had made the most of summer and had been to fairs and picnics as well as having an outing to Sullivan Lake before a reply came to this letter. My schooldays were about to begin and I could think of little else, never mind that way out east in the White House a man called Roosevelt had authorised that guns should be supplied to Britain. Unknown to me, our national and regional economy was about to stage a recovery because of the need for weapons to defend those islands that Trefor called Home.

Momma drove me down to the school on the first day and I took my place with two other new girls. Barbara Barker was one and the other was called Mary Jane Pike. We brought the numbers on the register to twenty one and there were no new boys that year.

School was a plain frame building faced with clap-board set at the lower end of our creek where most of the houses were, two miles or so before the junction with Calispel Road. The people of Greystone Water had built it around 1920, when ten families had settled there and wanted their children to have an education. When I entered its doors in 1940, it had one teacher, who taught Grades 1 through 8, but the older students went to Cusick High.

After two weeks, Momma allowed me to ride to school on Storm, mostly alone though some days she or Alec came part way down with me for company. I unsaddled and tethered him alongside a handful of other children's ponies and at recess I made sure he had water in his bucket. A big boy called Randy Wesley was detailed to assist with saddling-up at the end of the day before he cleaned up the droppings, which his father took for manure.

After three weeks, I arrived home for tea saying: 'Mom, I have to tell you it ain't no use my going any more to school before I reach Third Grade.'

I threw my bag on the table, hung up my jacket and made for my room ready to change my clothes like I had been told, for school dresses were too good for wearing in the farm yard.

'Well now,' said Momma, 'and how you fixing to get through Third Grade without you attend First and Second?'

I raised my voice so's she could hear me. 'I got no use for them. All them kids do is play the whole day long, counting buttons and threading beads and putting bits of puzzle in place. I've done enough of that now, so I won't go back until I can get to use a pencil and write letters. Reckon they'll take a year or so to catch up with me, so can you use a farm hand for a while longer?'

I came back to find her shaking her head and Alec shaking with laughter.

'I told you!' she said to him. 'All that reading and writing and now she thinks the school can teach her nothing.'

'Well surely they ought to do something more than play? I'm sure I was counting in the infants' class, though I didn't take to reading as readily as she has done.'

I was tucking into my tea. Through a mouth full of muffin, I said, 'Oh sure, we do count some. Like I said, buttons, one, two, three little buttons. But we don't get to write it down and we done no reading as yet.'

'Berta May,' he said, 'you are trying to run before you can walk. Remember two things. One: the other little girls may need a little time to settle in before they get down to serious work, so the teacher has to move slowly at first. Two: there just might be one or two small things I've failed to teach you, me being first and foremost a farmer. So you must pay attention and look out for those things and then come home and tell me.'

By this time we were out in the barn, cleaning harness.

'Now how about you give it another three weeks,' he suggested, 'and see if you learn something new?'

'Aw, I suppose I will if you want it. And I sure do like playing with the girls and boys at recess.'

'Of course you do. You'd miss them if you stayed home.'

So I went back to school on Monday and watched like a hawk all that went on, not only in my grade but in the others. My ears were also tuned in to everything, so I soon had a list of things I had learned, though few of them related to the first grade syllabus. Alec and Momma were glad to have no more complaints from me, but they were not to know that my greatest advance in learning was in the field of disruption.

Boredom led me to seek diversion. I set my wits and my hands to making life more interesting.

'Barbara,' teacher would say gently, coming back to our group after half an hour teaching Second or Third Grade students. 'Is this all you have done this morning?'

'Yes ma'm,' whispered my neighbour who had but three coloured beads on her yard-long lace, but I swung my string of beads arrogantly beside my table, looking intently at my nearly-empty tin and knowing that I had twice snatched her string and whipped all her beads away.

Then when it came to counting out loud, I often missed out number four while teacher was elsewhere, so that the other two girls learned to count their buttons all wrong. I could get them into trouble in all sorts of ways. Older children, too, were blamed and punished for sins they had not committed. All in all, I was enjoying myself, while Alec was happy that I made no more complaints.

A meeting was slated, for parents to go hear the teacher speak about school policy, future plans and how best students could be helped to make the most of their opportunities. Mom left us with Alec for the afternoon and drove down, doing some marketing at the store in Cusick first. After an address by the District Superintendent, our teacher Miss Lucas spoke about her methods and hopes, then there was time for questions to be asked and for private talk with the teacher while tea was in hand.

Mom came home in a seething rage and dragged me in from the yard, slamming the door before Freddie could follow.

'Berta May,' she stormed. 'I never thought I would be tempted to lift a hand in chastisement to my own daughter but at this moment I am very near to tanning your hide as hard as I can. Stand there, you wicked girl. Listen to me and listen real good and take heed of all I say, for I am in no mood to tolerate one more jot of your naughtiness. I am ashamed of you.'

Chapter 5

Out of the many stern words my mother said to me that day, it was probably the threat of missing out on a trip to town that had the most effect on me.

She meant it. I knew that sure enough. Like she meant she would take a slipper to me if I should get one more bad report from Miss Lucas and she would escort me into school next morning to hear me say 'Sorry' like she hoped I truly was.

I was, too. Sorry to have been found out, at least, and sorry that I could be staying home if I played one single trick more, while Freddie got to stand on the train station meeting visitors. Our cousins were coming to stay.

All things considered, it would pay me to toe the line, so I made my apology and tried to contain my boredom. I behaved so well that after a week or two, I got given a thick black pencil and was told I might write my name. I asked not how this had come about, but joyously filled the paper with my best printing.

Then off we went to Newport on Saturday, after a certain amount of pushing around of beds and cabinets, to welcome the Watkins from Wales. We asked a thousand questions that Mom could not begin to answer and hopped about like mad marmots between her and Auntie Sarah until the train came in.

How in the world were we to find them in all that crowd? It seemed as if the whole world was arriving on the one train, and we clung to Momma's hands in alarm at the crowds and the smoke and the clatter of passing freight wagons.

'That must be her.' Zeb, the only one amongst us to have seen any of the expected party before, was pointing to a lady who had just left the carriage furthest away. She was helping some small children to alight and looking around as if needing assistance.

'Yes, that will be our Bessie.' He led the way forward and she smiled with relief at the sight of him.

'Uncle Zeb, was I ever glad to see you? Get the cases

from the luggage van, will you, while I d'count these kiddies. Now stand still a minute, do you hear, while I make sure no one is left on the train.'

'Sarah,' whispered Momma. 'I make it eight children with Bessie. We weren't expecting eight, were we?'

'All present and correct,' said Bessie. 'Now shall I tell you who is who? I recognise you, Auntie Sarah, for all I was no more than twelve when you left. As beautiful as ever, you are. So you must be Cassie.' She held out her hand to Mom.

'Yes indeed, but first we have to find the people meeting these three.' Bessie pointed out two boys and a girl. 'Two of them are to go to a Mr and Mrs Wilson who live near a place called Caspel or something and the other to a Mrs Clark of Newport. I wonder, do you know them?'

'Gee Mom, that's Wilson's Calispel Road,' I said. 'They are standing back there by the engine. Shall I run and tell them the kids are here?'

'Yes, you do that,' agreed Mom, so I scooted back along the train and soon the extra girl and one boy were gone.

'That makes two more for our school, I guess,' I said, but nobody was interested at that moment. We still had a boy to dispose of.

'There is more than one Mrs Clark in town, you see,' Auntie Sarah was telling Bessie. 'I think we'd better take him to the Sheriff's office,' but at that minute, as the train pulled out of the station with a cloud of steam and a piercing whistle, a woman arrived at a run.

'Sorry, lady, you missed it,' shouted the guard, but she was not interested in him.

'Your name Clark, by any chance?' Momma was saying and the woman nodded, trying to catch her breath.

'Then this one must be yours. Which is his baggage, Bessie?'

One way or another, we all got safely along Washington to Zeb's house, while he piled the luggage into our car and drove round.

'We thought it best to bring you here while we get to know each other and tell you who's to go where,' Auntie Sarah explained. Momma and I poured coffee and coke and offered cookies.

'I cannot tell you how glad I am to have stopped travelling,' sighed Bessie. 'Three whole weeks on the move with a cart load of monkeys would be heaven against what I have suffered, it would. Never again! But there, it will all look better after a night's sleep in a proper bed, isn't it?'

She had a lovely way of speaking, her voice rising and falling as if she were almost singing, but none of the children had as yet said more than a word or two.

'Berta May, show the little girls where to find the bathroom, while Zeb takes the boys down to the basement, then we'll all line up and say our names.' I did as Momma said, helping the two smallest with their panties.

We stood in a rough circle round the room and Auntie Sarah said, 'I am Auntie Sarah and I live along the street here in Newport.'

Then Momma said, 'I am Auntie Cassie and I live out at Greyroofs with my family.'

I was next. 'I'm Berta May and I am six and a half. That's my Momma and this is Freddie my brother.' I gave him a nudge.

'I'm Freddie Watkins and I live at Greyroofs,' he said clearly.

Next, 'I am cousin Bessie and I will tell you who's who amongst us. Now these two are mine and Bob's and their names are Sheila and Mabel. Seven and five they are. Pat is four and she's my sister Emmie's. Then the boys are our Bobbie's - Dan's ten and Idris is six.'

'After Uncle Idris, see?' said that one.

'I'm Sheila,' 'I'm Mabel,' said two of the girls, but little Pat hid her face and looked as if she would cry.

'I'm Dan,' said the big boy, 'and he's my brother Idris.'

'I can do it myself, see,' protested Idris. Then Auntie Sarah told them all that they were very welcome and we wanted them to feel at home.

'So as this is the biggest house and most of the time only Zeb lives here, we thought you and the three little girls could make this your home, Bessie. There will still be a corner for Alec or Bethan if they need it for a night or two, since it belongs to them, but they'll be glad for you to use it. Cassie has really room only for one and we thought young Idris would be best, as her own two are near enough of an age with him. And Dan can come to me, for my own are getting so grown up I am missing having a boy about the place. Do you think you'll be happy with me and Laurence and Danny?' she smiled.

'I'll do my best,' he said quietly and he grinned.

'There's funny it will be, to have two with the same name under the one roof,' said Bessie.

Auntie Sarah said she thought they would get along just fine and she'd know which was which by their voices. Dan grinned again.

'Momma, he looks just like Trefor, did you notice?' I said.

'Sure did, honey.'

'Trefor came to our house,' said Idris. 'Had dinner he did, and my dad took him up the mountain.'

'And I went with them,' chipped in Dan. 'Right over to Craig Ddu we went and would have gone further but a thunderstorm came on.'

'You can tell me all about it tonight,' said Auntie Sarah. 'Right now, we have to see Auntie Cassie off, as she has a long way to drive, so let's put Idris's bags in the car.'

I saw Dan whisper something in her ear and she nodded and said, 'Yes, I will.' Then she had a word with Momma while the boys and I were scrambling into the back seat.

'What did she say?' I asked.

'I know,' declared Idris, kneeling up on the seat to wave at the folks seeing us off. 'Told you our Dan was worried in case I was not happy and please to keep an eye on me. Does it all the time, he does, cos Mammy said I might be pining to go back home.'

'And are you?' I asked.

'Not much. Look, where does that road go to?'

He soon pushed me out of my window seat so's he could have a better view and asked hundreds of questions along the way. There was no sign of pining about him.

'Who lives there? Will we see any bears? Do you have reindeers? Why haven't we seen any Red Indians yet?' It went on all the way home, the three of us barely able to keep pace with him.

He was fun as a playmate, full of energy and enterprise. I got into more scrapes in the first week he was with us than I had for a whole year, but Mom and Alec tried to be patient because they thought he needed time to settle down.

'We could do with another pair of hands about the place,' said Alec, 'to help with the chores morning and evening. Watch carefully while I mix the mash and that can be one of your jobs.'

'I d'know all about that,' said Idris. 'My dad's a farmer isn't he? and my grancher. Give me that old bucket and I'll do it, then I'm going up the woods to look around.'

'You most certainly are not,' he was told. 'Nobody goes into the forest alone, particularly at this time of year when the bears are hungry. And children NEVER. You have a lot to learn, young Idris and we'll start with the mash, for our stock is different from your dad's and bad feeding makes sick animals.'

Proudly, I did my share of the chores and made no mistakes, then Freddie and I collected eggs while Idris was taken to see the horses.

'Does your dad have any horses?'

'No. He got a tractor though.'

'Then keep out of the stables until I have taught you how to handle them and when they are in the yard, your place is behind the gate. Understand?'

'Course I do. Are they for riding?'

'Some of them. When Mom thinks you are ready, she will teach you to ride.'

'Why do you call her Mom?' Idris asked Alec.

'Because she is Mom to me and Freddie and Berta May.'

'But you're grown up. Grown-ups don't have mams.' Then he found something else to question, so no-one need answer that.

He was a handful all right. We had fights as well as fun when his strong will clashed with mine, but his arrival did me a real favour as regards school.

Momma took us down in the car on Monday early so as to introduce him to the teacher and we all went into the schoolroom.

'This is Idris from Wales, come to live with us until the war is over,' she said. 'He is six years five months old and here is some information about his schooling up to date.'

Miss Lucas opened the envelope and pulled out a folded paper. As she read it, her eyebrows rose in surprise and she looked in disbelief at Idris.

'Can this be correct? You are adding tens and units? And learning the three times table?'

'Yes Miss, and I can do take aways and I'm on Beacon Book Three.'

She shook her head slowly. 'Five threes?' she snapped.

'Fifteen, Miss,' he said.

'Seven threes?' she said.

'Twenty one.'

'Twelve threes?'

'Twelve threes are thirty six. And if I hadn't left I would have started the fours by now.'

Then there was a knock at the door and in came Mr and Mrs Wilson with their two guests.

'Good morning, Miss Lucas. We have brought our grand children who have come from England to stay with us. We hope you can enrol them into school?'

Their ages were seven and nine and they too had brought reports from their previous schools. I watched teacher's eyebrows rise again.

'Well children, you are all welcome and I hope you will be happy in our community. I foresee a few problems as regards grades, but we shall overcome them. Berta May, will you kindly pull the bell rope now?'

Then our parents left her to work out how to accommodate a six year old who was equal in performance to third grade, a seven year old ready for third grade too, a nine year old doing fifth year work and me, already a thorn in her flesh.

Idris soon got a seat beside me, with a sum book, box of counters and pencil. By recess, the others were writing and reading and my baby-play days were over. As long as I was quiet and causing no disturbance, teacher no longer worried that I was not doing first grade activities, so I kept my eyes on my books and pushed ahead.

To Idris's credit, I have to say that he was generous with his help. Through him, I got to adding and taking with the aid of the box of counters. Through him, I learned new words and wrote out my tables in my note book at home. So as the weeks passed, we both got to sitting near the third grade row and listening to their lessons. School had become a treasure chest of knowledge.

It was an exceptional winter as far as the weather went, for the early snow did not lie. Rain was heavier than usual and warm winds kept the ice away.

'Be thankful for small mercies,' said Momma, in conversation with Jack and Mrs Barker after church one Sunday. 'How I would have coped with the three of them home from school December through March, I fail to think. I only wish I had made haste to teach Idris to ride a horse, for I am still having to drive him to and fro. Had I but known the roads would be open, I would have started soon as he arrived.'

'You got a mount for him then, Cass?'

'Well no, that's another thing. He could manage on Dusty for a while, but come next Spring, Freddie will need her. I guess I'll have to buy another. But then again, we'll have a riding mare of our own within the year.'

'No sense in wasting cash, Cass. How about I ask around, see if a neighbour could lend or rent you one to tide you over?'

'Why thank you kindly, Jack, I am much obliged to you.'

We talked of visiting town for a Christmas treat and planned an early start so as to get back in the one day, for there was no longer room for us to sleep down there. Idris was on his best behaviour lest he be left out and we worked in the evening making little gifts to take our cousins.

I was saddling Storm in the yard on the Saturday before that, for Alec had said I might ride out with him to see if he could shoot a couple of Canada geese down the valley. It was barely ten o'clock when I heard an engine growling its way uphill. I looked across the meadow to the far gate and saw a large black motor car.

'Alec, I see visitors,' I told him.

'I am sorry to do this to you, Cass, but he's such a loveable boy and not one bit of trouble and he's breaking his heart in town.'

I hovered near Auntie Sarah and Momma while Alec and Uncle Henry were walking into the yard with Dan.

'Then you done the right thing bringing him here,' said Mom. 'If it's farm life he's missing, why, we can but do our best to make him happy.'

'But how will you manage?' was the last I heard, for I had set off in pursuit of the men. If Dan was to come and live at Greyroofs, I wanted to be first to help him get acquainted with things.

'You want I should show you round?' I asked, and Alec gave me a nod which I took to mean OK. 'We better put Storm back in the stock yard first off, since I doubt we'll be going hunting now.' I unwound the reins from the hitching post and led him away, Dan at my side asking questions about all he could see.

Unlike Idris, he was quiet and receptive, interested in our animals and way of life without making out he knew all there was to know. I asked him about his father's farm and discovered they had bought a tractor for ploughing and haulage.

'We had horses when I was little, so I got to ride a bit with Grancher, but now we got mostly sheep and a few beef cattle. I like this place. Reckon your Mam would let me stay here, do you? Work for my keep, I would, and sleep in the barn if needs be.'

'Sure, Momma will love to have you stay. If we got a tractor too, you and me could get around the chores in half the time.'

Then Freddie and Idris came running up from the creek where they'd been playing and shouted for joy at seeing visitors.

'Come to see am I pining, have you?' shouted Idris. 'Well I en't, so you can go away.'

He took to running round the yard like a wild bronco, kicking out at fence posts and leaping over the chopping black, but his brother paid him no heed. We went into the barn and found Alec at the work bench.

'Can you use a plane and chisel?' he asked Dan.

Lunch time, we had to eat in two sittings, the adults standing round the furnace drinking coffee while we four got first turn at the table.

'Just for now,' Mom was saying, 'we'll put the ladder up to the roof loft above this room and Dan can have that for sleeping, but come Spring we shall have to extend some.'

'What do you have in mind?' asked Uncle.

'We been talking on and off about making more living space, so now's the time to get on with it. Either box in the deck out back of the house or build in between house and barn.'

'Twenty five feet or so there is, between the two,' explained Alec, 'and only the store shed need be taken down to clear the ground. We thought of maybe putting up a sort of separate bunk house.'

'I see,' said Uncle Henry, 'with its own door into the yard? You'd have to put in a bath of sorts.'

'Yes, but if we put it in the corner next to the house, it would feed into our drains, so no problem there. Make either one big room with six bunks and a furnace to heat it, or two smaller rooms.'

They spent a good deal of time after that, measuring and drawing plans on paper and Mom said she would order the lumber from Walker's saw mill.

'To be delivered beginning of April,' she said, 'so we can get on with it soon as Spring sets in.'

'Then you'll all be able to stay over when you visit, next time we have a picnic,' I told Auntie Sarah as I hugged her Good bye. 'See you next week in town.'

Dan settled in like he had always been part of the family and Alec was pleased at the way he helped out with the winter woodwork. We took him into school on Monday and Miss Lucas raised her eyebrows higher than ever.

'Another one two grades up on where he's supposed to be at?'

'I'm sorry, I don't understand, miss,' said Dan with a puzzled frown.

'Your brother and the two from England, they were so far ahead of my other students, I had to push them into the higher grades, no matter what my superiors thought about it.'

'Oh no.' He grinned and shook his head. 'No fear of that with me, miss. Not the brainy type at all, I'm not. I been working with fourth grade down Newport and just about keeping up, with a bit of help from my cousins after school.'

'Good boy.' I could see she had fallen for his smile. 'You take that desk by the wall then and I'm more pleased to see you than you imagine.'

The fact was that Dan's enrolment brought our numbers over twenty five, which gave her the chance to apply for an assistant. When Mom heard that, she groaned.

'Heaven help us if they send a raw girl fresh out of college to teach our Idris and Berta May. They'll run rings round her.' But Miss Lucas had got the measure of us now and had her many problems well in hand, so she was not fixing to make life more difficult for herself. When the new teacher came after Christmas, it was the top grades that went into a partitioned corner for their lessons while we remained under strict supervision and continued in tandem to learn at a great pace.

By then, our trip to town had been accomplished just in the nick of time. With all the folks down there, we took up two rows of seats in the theatre and I got to sit beside one of the little girl cousins, Sheila. We giggled at the clowns act and clutched each other's hands when the wicked sisters were being perfectly horrid to Cinders and we were firm friends by the end of the show.

'Come summer, I shall visit with you and be your friend,' I told her.

'My best friend, is it?' she asked. 'I got one best friend back home, but she's a very long way away. I guess you can be best friend with me, too.'

The little ones were already beginning to talk the same as we did and their voices no longer reminded us that they were foreigners, but to hear Auntie Sarah change her way of speaking when she and Bessie were together was funny.

'Next time you come,' she told me, tucking a rug round my knees as we got into the car to go home, 'you must stay long enough to let Bessie hear you sing. She has a lovely voice herself and we could nearly make a choir now so many of us are here.'

'We could sing in the pantomime next Christmas,' I said to Momma and all the way home, the boys and I had quite a chorus going with the songs we'd heard that day.

There was snow right after Christmas and it hung around as usual through March, but our trail was open most days and we did not miss much schooling. An occasional blizzard left drifts up the front of the house and over sections of the trail, so a few days here and there we stayed home, but it made a difference Dan being with us. Mom had to give up all idea of getting horses for Idris and him and settle for taking us to school daily, but a ten year old boy with a shovel was a good help when it came to clearing the odd blockage. She was no mean wielder of shovels herself and I'd had a bit of practice myself, so that old snow took a beating and we made it.

Thaws came now and then, with unseasonal rain and a patch of green showing through here and there after a few days. Alec and I got to riding out for shooting game for the pot a couple of times before winter closed in again. He did some preparation of the site for the new bunkhouse with our help on fine days, so that as soon as Spring should come, all would be ready for building to start.

Dan's coming had eased things for Mom too, for he knew how to handle Idris better than all of us put together. Quiet, hard-working and amiable Dan could quell his rebellious brother in a trice, without shouting or fisticuffs. I could never quite figure out how he did it, for his manner was so pleasant and smiling. But then, I could not always figure out just what the two of them were saying together in moments of crisis when they rattled off their words at top speed.

Idris had been a thorn in Mom's flesh all the way home one day and set about disobeying every order when we arrived. He left Freddie to do all the eggs and refused to shut the yard gate, got into the stable and disturbed Mom's grey stallion and as near came to grief with Alec's hunting knife as ever was. The barn looked all set to be destroyed by his wild caperings, while Freddie and I looked on in alarmed amusement.

In came Dan. He stood for a moment by the door, then

said, 'Idris.'

That was it. One word and the madness was gone. Idris stood still and hung his head, while a string of quiet sentences only he could understand drifted musically from Dan's mouth and found their mark. There was a lot of 'is it' and 'Our Mam' and 'you d'know well enough' and 'Grancher' but whatever I missed in hearing, there was no doubt of its meaning.

On other occasions, a single word from Dan was enough. In any case, his presence was having a calming influence on Idris and we were all glad he had come.

4

The new teacher was called Miss Petersen. She was young; blond and tall and slim, she soon had the older boys vowing they were in love with her, but she knew how to control them in class no matter that this was her first school since college.

'I know your face,' she said to Dan soon after arriving. 'Do tell me your name so I can recollect how that can be.'

'Dan Watkins, ma'm.'

'Which family of Watkins is that, Dan?'

'Watkins Penylan, Miss Petersen, but my brother and I come to stay with Auntie Cassie for the duration of the war, see.'

'Cassie Watkins of Greyroofs? Then of course I know your face. You are the image of my old friend Trefor. Have you any news of him? My mother told me he had gone home to enlist in the army and I pray he will be safe.'

Momma chuckled to hear that Leonie Petersen was our new teacher.

'She sure will have some old memories stirred, looking at you every day,' she told Dan. 'She and Trefor were best friends from first grade through graduation, but they grew apart when he went to work. I doubt he'd not have gone away fighting, had she but married him when he asked her. Give her my regards, Berta May and say she's welcome to come visit if she has a mind to.'

We had a real wet week in February, when there was no play outdoors either in school hours or at the weekend and Idris became tiresome again through boredom. Particularly on Saturday, when Alec had taken the car to town for the day and Mom was trying to get some baking done, he got up to every kind of mischief until we were all sick and tired of him. Finally, he threw a tantrum because he was told to clean up a trail of wood dust he had made in bringing fresh logs in for drying.

'And I won't make my bed, nor dry the dishes nor collect the eggs nor brush the yard,' he screamed, bouncing up and down on Mom's best sofa and throwing cushions about. 'I hate it here and I hate you all and I want to go home.'

I truly thought that time that at last Momma was going to raise a hand to discipline him, but in came Dan from the barn in the nick of time.

'Stop it, our Idris,' he ordered. 'What did Grancher tell you?' and the tirade ceased at once. Idris folded up in a heap on the sofa and looked as if he might be going to cry. Momma stepped over to scoop him up in her arms and sat quietly for a long time, just cuddling that naughty boy. Then I got my best story book so's she could read to us a while and soon he was smiling and happy again.

When Alec came in, he brought letters from Wales and the boys had one each from their mother.

'I shall sit right down and write back,' declared Idris after tea, 'and tell them what a good boy I'm being and what a lovely time I'm having.'

'You do that,' said Mom and hurried to give him paper and pencil.

'I wish I had a letter all my own,' I said. 'I think I'll write Trefor and Lizzie.' I settled down at my desk and got to work. Then Dan decided to do the same and we had a quiet hour while Mom sat knitting by the furnace and Alec read the papers. The only sounds were the ticking of the clock and an occasional sigh or rustle of paper and when I looked up I saw Momma had fallen quite asleep. So I wrote on a spare sheet, 'Mom asleep don't wake her' and passed it to the boys.

Freddie had climbed up onto a chair with paper and crayons by now, so Dan shushed him up when he made a sound and he was real good. He got to stay up late, too, since she didn't wake until nearly nine.

'My goodness me,' she yawned, 'what happened to the time?'

Well, she was mighty pleased with our letters and drawings and when Monday came, gave us the stamps to put them in the post, so we all looked forward to having replies. I daresay they would have quite a good time over there, reading that lot. It would take their minds off the worrying news about the war.

5

I found Alec sitting in the barn after tea one evening when I went to take my turn mixing feed. He was reading a newspaper and looking very solemn.

'How come you're sitting out here?' I asked. 'I can manage the chores and Mom's got a plate of food warming for you.'

'Thanks, I'll go in directly. Just doing a bit of thinking and trying to sort something out.'

'That pesky war again, I suppose?' Since the boys had come from Wales, our radio had not been tuned in so much to bad news, but I knew Alec and Momma listened to it and read the papers after we had gone to bed. I'd heard them talk of naval bases and armament factories and things that meant nothing to me.

'Indirectly, yes,' he answered.

'You wanna tell me?' I measured meal and grain from the bins as I talked.

'Yes I do. Glad to share it with you, old buddy, if you really want to listen.'

So I curled up on the straw beside him and he confided in me.

'They have started drafting men into the armed forces since October. They are asking for volunteers.'

'What's volunteers?'

'Men who wish to enlist, to be soldiers or sailors without being forced to do it.'

'Like they want to go to war?'

'Perhaps not to war. America is not at war, but they're making the forces stronger, just in case.'

'You won't go, will you, Alec? I don't want you to go.'

'No way am I off to fight, so don't worry your pretty head about that. If they don't get enough volunteers, I expect they'll call up the young men first. I'm not so young and farmers won't be drafted and I don't intend to volunteer.'

'Good.'

'But I'm an engineer by training and now is the time I could get work. See this column? It says they're going to harness the power of our rivers more and more and the Corps of Engineers is starting a survey. I knew they would get on with it one day and I want to be there at the start.'

'You mean to get a job and leave us?'

'Get the job if I can, but I'd not be far away. Back home for weekends, like Trefor used to do. You see, Berta May, there are three things to consider.'

I kept quiet, not understanding all he said, but glad he wanted me there.

'First, my own ambition to be a successful engineer. Second, the homestead here belongs to Mom. It was hers before she met Dad and it will be yours and Freddie's when you grow up, not mine. So I ought to start making something of my life although I love to be helping you all I can. And thirdly, the money.'

'Time was, this farm supported only Mom. Then she married Dad and the family grew until now there are six of us. Never mind how clever we are, keeping so many costs more than we can easily make. So if I had a salary coming in, things would be easier for all. Does that make sense?'

'No, I don't know what's a sal'ry'

'A salary is money. I could earn a lot of money.'

'OK, that makes sense, sure enough. I'm with you all the way, Alec.'

That's just what Uncle Henry said. He thinks I should apply for the job at once, but what Mom will say, I dread to think.'

'You put it to her straight,' I told him, getting up to go feed the stock. 'Three things to consider, just like you told me,' and I took the first of the buckets over the yard.

With the building of the bunkhouse starting after that, which meant labouring jobs for me and the boys, I thought little more about Alec's problem. Loads of sawn lumber arrived on Joe Walker's truck and Alec worked all hours putting in corner posts. Weekends, Joe and a mate came to give a hand and then Zeb moved up for a spell. Foot by foot, the walls went up and we marvelled at the speed they grew when all four men were at work.

Momma never complained, but must have cooked tons of food for her hungry workers and she herself had to clean the stock yard after the animals were turned out.

'My larder is clean empty,' she said to Babs and Chuckie's mom one afternoon in the store after school, 'but I reckon it will be worth it in the end.'

'You fixing on having a house-warming? asked Mrs Barker. 'Make it Pot Luck and save yourself some baking.'

'How about having it on my birthday?' I asked.

Chapter 6

The roof went on rather later than we had hoped, because the Spring work on the farm could not be entirely neglected. We had increased our herd of cattle in the rented riverside meadow and got a timber stand approaching maturity. Mom and Alec were needed every which where. There were days when we came from school and found the walls grown a full three feet, but this progress could not be maintained on a daily basis. We began to look at Fourth of July as a likely day for finishing the roof.

Our mail box was near bursting one afternoon when Dan and I took the key into the Post Office and we had a great time sorting what was for whom as Mom drove home. Even Freddie had a letter of his own and mine was fatter than anybody else's. It seemed most everybody in Wales had put a message in, for all the envelopes contained sheets of different sizes and colours as well as a few pictures for us kids.

'Now I call that real nice of them, to take time out for writing us all when they have so much worry of their own,' said Momma, settling down in her chair to read a long letter from Auntie Megan while we all spread ours out over the table and the floor.

With a bit of help, I got through my pages from Lizzie and Emmie, who said she had written at length to Bessie and please to ask for all the news when next I saw her. Uncle Idris and Auntie Jane had put a picture of their house in winter and said Dan was to show me his letter. They all liked the ones we had sent a few months back and said we had cheered them up.

From what Mom said to Alec, they could do with some cheer over there, for Britain was still in danger of invasion by the Germans. It was a year since the fall of France and she stood alone to face the enemy. Intensive bombing of her cities had failed as yet to crack her, but she was blockaded by sea and attacked from the air.

'I don't see how she can hold out much longer,' said Mom. 'See what Megan writes: 'Food, petrol and clothes are rationed and we farmers are called upon to do the impossible in the way of growing more food. Tom ploughed up our home meadow for potatoes, which is laughable when you think no-one wanted them eighteen months ago. And we had bombs in Abersychan last November but no one hurt, just the chapel and fire station damaged.' 'I wonder, are the evacuees still there?'

'Dad and Grancher have joined the Defence Volunteers. What do you suppose those are, Alec? Not going off to war are they?' asked Dan. 'Said he was too old for that, did Grancher.'

'He said Thank God for being over sixty, he did,' chipped in Idris. 'Here, let me have look at that, Berta May,' and he snatched my picture from me.

'Mom, make Idris give it me back,' I wailed.

'I d'want to have a look,' he said. 'My house it is, not yours. See, there's our bedroom and that there's the kitchen and the bosh is just inside the door.'

'The what?'

'The bosh. Like the sink where Mam d'wash up, see?'

'My, my, I never heard such a funny ol'language in all my born days,' I said. 'Kin I have my picture back now, please?'

We all knew by this time that Alec would be leaving for an Engineer's job, come end of July, so there was pressure on him to complete our bunkhouse before then. The final week in June, Zeb came up to be on hand and over the weekend we had Joe Walker and his mate, so with four workers full time, the walls were completed and timber sawn for the whole roof. Word went around, that Watkins would be house-warming come July Fourth.

A holiday for all, it started while the sun was still low over South Baldy, when Alec and I made sure all stock was well fenced away from the building and the gates were open to let traffic through. By seven, eight men were drinking tea on the porch and work was about to begin.

Throughout the morning, more and more food appeared on the trestle table we had erected in the barn, till I do declare the boards were groaning and me and the boys had tongues fairly hanging out with hunger. Not that we were inclined to stand around, for there were people arriving all the time and shouts from Alec when he wanted us to fetch and carry. It sure was a busy morning. I tried to count the crowd when it seemed our yard and house would hold no more, but then I saw Chuckie and Babs coming and we all ran off to play a while.

'You take good care don't no-one fall in the ravine now, Dan,' shouted Momma as we ran towards the creek, 'and Berta May, you take real good care of Freddie.'

Our curiosity would not allow us to stay away for long, though we had a good time leaping around the rocks at our usual playing place and one of Dan's friends whose Pa had come to help got both feet good and wet.

Dinner time came and the men stopped to eat. I had never seen Uncle Henry and Laurence looking like labouring men, but there they sat on the straw as sweaty and dusty as the Walkers and all. We put away a mighty pile of food between us. Mom and the ladies were running to and fro to fill jugs with lemonade and pots of tea, while the sun rose higher and the day got hotter.

'All hands on deck then,' said Alec at last, 'before the heat gets the better of us,' and the final section of rafters was hoisted into place. Nothing now but to secure it and start putting shingles in place, which progressed real quick with so many hands at work.

Meanwhile, a couple more motor cars crawled uphill, laden with friends and family including Bessie and the little girls, Miss Petersen and the Wilsons with their grandchildren from England. They all brought more food to replenish the table.

What a feast we had at the end of the day, the men now slaking their thirst with beer that we had cooled in the creek. Then they washed under the pump, shook dust from their shirts and were ready for celebrating.

'What are we waiting for?' shouted Lon Withers, taking his fiddle from its case and scraping up a tune for dancing. Toes began to tap and I seized Idris by both hands to skitter round and round in the centre of the yard.

'Take your partners,' called Jack Barker 'and circle left.' So we pranced and we danced, Mom with Zeb and Alec with Bessie, showing her how to make a star and dosey do. We did the Virginia Reel and Redwing, until we were all quite breathless and Mr Withers needed a drink. Then by and by, someone started singing.

'Get your accordion, Danny,' said Auntie Sarah.

The night midges were begining to bite, so we retreated to the barn and all found places to rest, then Danny began to play 'Li'l Liza Jane.' Well, we sang that in school regular, so we let rip in chorus, me and Idris, before most had got their tongues in action. We got a round of applause for that and then we went through just about everything Danny could play.

'Give us a song from Wales,' said Momma after a while.

'All right,' said Auntie Sarah. And beckoned Bessie and the girls to come and stand over by her in front of the work bench. 'You too, Dan and Idris, Laurence and Danny and Berta May.' But then she spotted Zeb and Uncle Henry lurking by the door, so with them we made a choir of twelve to sing Calon Lan and Sospan Bach. I barely knew the words and nor did the little girls and Idris, but we helped out with the tune and after that we sang the Bells of Aberdovey, which Danny was able to play.

'Please could we sing Poppa's song?' I whispered to Auntie Sarah and we started it off, very quietly.

'I wish I were back in my valley.....'

It was magic. There was a tingle down my back as the music echoed round the barn and drifted out the door to travel over farm and field, where the horses were invisibly asleep in front the acres of dark pines. You could have heard a pin drop when we finished and I saw Bessie wiping a tear from her eye, while Mom had gone out to stand looking at the sky alone.

'To absent friends and dear ones far away,' said Uncle Henry, raising his glass.

That brought us back to the present, with Lon Withers striking up another dance tune and the fun began again.

It seemed to me the night must be nearly gone and I should hear the rooster crow any minute, before folks began to look for their empty plates and basins.

'Let's all sing a couple of songs in the bunkhouse, test will the roof fly off before you go,' said Mom, so we trooped over to the new building. The roof stayed put all right, though we roared out the chorus of Clementine enough to deafen us, so everyone was happy. Then we sang the Star Spangled Banner to finish and thought we were done.

But the Welsh had to have the last word, breaking into their national anthem to make sure no beams were loose. All but little Pat, who was asleep in Bessie's arms, got their tongues round the language to the last Parhau and there was much cheering and kissing and shaking hands to follow.

'God bless you, my lovely,' said Auntie Sarah, 'and keep you at one with your Daddy and Granny Watkins who for sure have been with us this night.'

2

We got the windows fitted and the bunks in place before Alec left us.

'I'll be back next weekend, Mom,' he said, 'so don't kill yourself trying to get everything done without me.'

Zeb was still with us, attending to the finishing touches, so he took the smaller room and we moved the boys' stuff into the bigger one, where they spread out their personal treasures and had a big closet in which to put their clothes. I left them to squabble over who had the top bunks and where to put their toy box while I went indoors and reclaimed the room that had been mine before our cousins arrived.

'Say, ain't it just too great, Mom, having all this space to ourselves? I shall put my desk back by my bed and have my very own books right here on top the chest and.....'

'Hold on a minute, child. I aim to give the whole place a thorough clean now I have room to move, so don't you get carried away with your plans until we have done.'

Then she launched into an orgy of sweeping and scrubbing, washing drapes and beating rugs, that lasted well into our summer recess. I was clean wore out just seeing her carry on from morning till night in this manner, not to mention having to do my share of the chores. Dan took charge of some of Alec's jobs meantime, and Freddie and Idris were banned from setting foot in the house lest they bring dirt onto clean boards.

She sure left us no time to languish over absent brothers

or parents. Indeed I wonder now whether that was her intent, to keep so busy that neither she nor we could mope. When at last she was satisfied that the homestead was in tip-top order, there was creosoting and painting of fences, exercising horses, inspecting the cattle and riding the boundary to keep us out of mischief. She borrowed two quiet ponies from the Barkers for Dan and Idris for a spell, so we could all go together into the forest and up the mountain, taking food sacks for a long day's ride.

'And a couple of baskets for huckleberries, Berta May,' she would say amidst our preparations, and we never came back without filling them.

'I never seen these before,' said Dan. 'We get bilberries out on our mountains this time of year though. Wonder whether our Mam have got any without us to pick them?' He sighed, looking east across the valley and the peaks of Idaho as if wishing he could see right over to Wales.

We chased ground squirrels and marmots round the tree roots till they went to ground and we lay on our backs watching buzzards swoop and stall.

'I got a dandelion clock,' shouted Idris, 'I'll tell you what the time is.' We heard him blowing and counting.

'Are you having a wish for every breath?' asked Mom. I guess she knew what they both would wish for most.

Then we got a letter from Auntie Sarah, inviting us all to visit and stay over for a night or two. She had a plan for us, she said, and if Momma were too busy to stay, she could come back to collect us. We should take some blankets.

'I cannot think where she aims to put you,' she said, 'but she is welcome to entertain you for a couple of days if she wishes. I need to see Uncle Henry anyway, to show him this strange letter I got last week. Make sure you pack some clean underwear and a nice cotton frock, Berta May. I better attend to the boys' bags myself or they'll be trailing through town in their winter pants. I wonder will you need your swimming costumes?'

Mystified, we bid our horses farewell, scrambled into the car and headed for Newport. The roads were baked hard, dust flying with every passing pick-up and grass along the edge beginning to turn brown.

It was pretty hot in town, not a breath of air stirring the

87

two trees at the front of Auntie Sarah's house, but we found her out back sitting in a shaded corner; and there on the grass patch where I had used to play ball was a green canvas tent, pegged out neatly.

'Welcome to your new bedroom,' she smiled. 'Danny got it from the Scouts who were selling them off now they have got new ones. We thought you boys could camp out here tonight.'

'And me. I wanna camp, too,' I protested.

'All right, tom boy,' she said. 'Now let's have a drink while I tell you why I want you here.'

'There's to be a Grand Summer Concert on the last day of August,' she told us, 'to raise money for sending comforts to those poor soldiers out fighting for freedom's sake.'

'Ooh, can we go?' asked Idris.

'Better than that. We can be in it,' she continued. 'They are asking everyone who can perform in any sort of way to offer their services. I even heard that someone famous may be coming and I thought we Watkins should do our best to help. After all, we Welsh are renowned for our singing the world over and we have enough of us here to make a little choir. And then with Cassie's voice to help, we could sing some songs from the shows.'

'And Danny could play his accordion,' I said.

'And I can walk on my hands,' said Idris, jumping up to demonstrate.

'We could put on a half-hour turn between us,' agreed Momma. 'So you've collected the team together for rehearsals?'

'That's the idea. With two or three whole days together, we can practice as much as we like. Bessie says she'll make our meals, though we want her to sing as well, of course, and then when we are tired, we'll all go down for a swim or an ice cream. Now, what do you think of that?'

It was a novel idea and a welcome change, we all agreed.

'Can I go round to see Auntie Bessie now?' asked Dan.

'Yes. I need a word with Uncle Henry when he comes in for dinner,' said Mom, 'so take them all with you and play with the girls. What time do you want them back, Sarah?'

'One sharp if they want to eat, and tell Bessie rehearsals

start at two please, and be careful crossing the road.'

So we went visiting in town without Mom, skipety-hop along the side walk, two blocks round the corner and over the road, while the adults chewed over the latest problem.

3

She had received a letter from England. It had come from a woman of whom she had never heard, a woman who lived in some town called Canterbury which it seemed was in a dangerous situation.

'We are in the direct flight path of the German bombers,' she wrote, 'and would be first to be over-run if the enemy should invade England. It is not for myself that I write but for my grandson Frank, who is all I have left in the world and the last of our family.

'I am an old woman now and can barely remember your father, my younger brother who left home after a family quarrel. It must have been about 1906, when I was away in teacher training college. I came home to find him gone and was forbidden to make any attempt to contact him.

That is all water under the bridge now, but in desperation I have been trying all avenues to trace him and at last have been given your name.

Please, dear niece if such you really are, can you give shelter to my grandson for the duration of the war? He is twelve years old, an intelligent, musical boy of great promise doing very well at the Grammar School. I will pay all expenses of his travel, will send money for his keep if that is possible and will, I promise you, see that in the fullness of time you are amply recompensed.'

'Dear me,' said Uncle Henry after reading it. 'Another one.'

'But I have never heard of her,' said Mom. 'I thought I had no relatives on my father's side.'

'Did he ever say what part of England he came from?'

'I suppose he did, but I can't recall. However, the few papers he left had this photograph with them, and Mrs Taylor has sent its double.'

She showed them the faded brownish snap, a picture of a girl dressed in white frilly clothes standing at the knee of a

89

woman who was holding a boy in a sailor suit.

'The very same,' they agreed. 'She must be telling the truth.'

'In that case, it is my duty to offer the boy shelter,' said Mom, 'though whether an intelligent, musical young man from Canterbury will like sleeping in our bunkhouse is another matter.'

'He can always borrow Danny's tent if he prefers,' laughed Uncle.

'Say, don't those Earls and things send their sons to Grammar School? Are we about to host a noble lord, you reckon?' I heard her say when we arrived back for our dinner.

Our concert troupe took shape. Auntie Sarah was musical director, pianist and choir-mistress, but when it was suggested that we might perform a dance, it was Bessie who took charge and taught us the steps. Everyone had the chance to come up with ideas and after we had finished our first session of rehearsing, little groups of two or three went away to practise their own turns. I came across Dan behind the fruit bushes, throwing three stones in the air at once.

'I saw a clown juggling in the panto once,' he told me. 'Used to be able to do it, I did, but I need some tennis balls.' We went off to see if Auntie Sarah could provide them.

When Laurence came in, he offered to be Stage Manager and said he could find all the props we needed. We had another quick run through a few songs in the evening, but the next day we would get down to serious work.

Yet Auntie Sarah managed to make it not too serious. We had a lot of merriment and fun between singing choruses and solos. After dinner, we went to the river to bathe near the old ferry landing, towel robes under our arms and sandwiches in baskets. Then it was back for a quick run-through the items in which the youngest children were to appear, before bedding down in our tent.

We four had got little sleep the first night, for we giggled and talked so long that Uncle Henry came out to threaten to take us indoors, but the second and third nights, we were quite wore out.

'This is harder than doing chores for Mom,' I sighed as we tried for the fifth time to perfect a simple square dance which all eight of us children were to perform.

'Not to worry,' smiled Bessie, 'by the time you come again, even Pat will have it off perfect.'

'Until the twenty ninth then,' we called, waving goodbye as we left.

'Don't forget to practise,' said Auntie Sarah, 'and tell Mom about the dance.'

'I'll tell her,' said Uncle Henry, who was driving us home.

4

The weeks passed quickly and pleasantly with not too many quarrels between Idris and me. Mom made sure we had no time for mischief, but although she gave us plenty of chores to work, she also devised ways of amusing us. I was sent to ask could we borrow the Barkers' ponies again and one fine morning early, we packed food in our bags and set off to find where Mr Withers lived.

'But mind, you go no further than the pass. If you don't find Lon at home, just eat your dinner and come right on down.'

'Ok Mom,' I said, urging Storm into a trot.

'All right, Auntie Cass,' said Dan, serious under the responsibility of leading the expedition into new territory.

'No galloping now. I want you all safe back. And Idris, you go nice and steady.'

He nodded, clinging to the pommel for all he was worth. Horsemanship was not his best skill. None of us was surprised to hear him say at the gate out of the meadow, 'I'm going back now. I'm not going up that mountain without Auntie Cass, so there.' And he plodded slowly back towards where she stood in the yard.

'Good. Now we can get along much better,' said Freddie heartlessly and the three of us set off at a canter. It was a good day for going up the trail, some light clouds high overhead and a breeze keeping the air cool. We passed Sutton's meadow, had a look at the cattle and quickly counted them, then pushed on up the steepening slope under tall tamaracks. Sheltered from the direct sun, our horses went at a good pace, twisting this way and that until

91

suddenly the trees thinned and the ground levelled some.

'Hey, take a look at that view,' shouted Dan, reining in to stand facing West. Ahead of us, a vast area had been logged clear of all trees and we could see right out over the sunlit valley below.

'My, I wish we could go on and see what's down there,' Freddie sighed. 'I never been over that side the mountain.'

'Well we ain't going there today,' I told him. 'You heard what Mom said. Now where is Mr Wither's cabin?'

Turning through a hundred and eighty degrees, we could not fail to see it. Squat and grey and sturdy, it stood back a-ways from the trail with its open door facing south and an irregular plot of flat ground fenced around it. There were tools and blocks of lumber in front the barn door, from which we could hear sounds of singing.

'Anybody home?' called Dan. The old man appeared, axe in hand. It took him a minute or two before he recognized us.

'Hi, how y'doing?' he shouted then. 'C'mon in. I'm real pleased to have you drop by. C'mon now, tie up your hosses and visit awhile.'

He was pleased to have visitors, he could not do enough for us and we spent the rest of the morning with him. He showed us how to shape logs for building a cabin in the old style so's they fitted together neat at the corners and how to make shakes for the roof. Then we ate our sandwiches sitting on his porch, while he fried eggs for himself, talking all the while about the way his parents had established their homestead and telling tales about the old times. By the time we left, the sun had gone right round over the western valley and it was a hot afternoon, sure enough.

'Now you-all come back soon,' he said when at last we got to leave. 'And thank your ma for the jelly and canned fruit and tell her I'll be down to pay my respects before the Fall. Durned if I ain't been alone on this old place so long I near forgot how to socialise.'

After that, it was soon time to return to Newport for the variety concert. We called ourselves the American Dragons and we nearly brought the house down with the applause we received for our performance. In fact, we almost filled the whole of the programme after the interval, for with Welsh songs and American songs, clowns performing (Dan and Idris), solo instrumentalists (Laurence and Danny), solo singers (Auntie Sarah), choruses from shows and dances, we were a complete concert troupe. The audience was ecstatic and we had to perform two encores before they would allow us to leave the stage for the entrance of the celebrity artist.

'WELSH FAMILY WATKINS STEALS THE SHOW' was the headline in the paper, alongside our pictures. 'Aged five to fifty five, their voices and varied talents brought smiles and tears to the eyes of the capacity audience which filled the school auditorium in Newport Saturday evening last. Stepping in time and singing in tune poses no problem to these children, nurtured in a musical tradition.....' and so it went on right down the page.

'We must buy some extra copies and send them to Wales,' said Mom.

'Can I send one to Mammy?' asked Idris.

'And Grancher,' said Dan.

'And Megan and Emmie and Lizzie. And Trefor and Bethan,' I added. 'If only Bethan had come, we'd have no need of a celebrity at all. When is Bethan coming again, Mom?'

'No idea,' she said. 'Well, if you must know, I think she is on her way overseas by now. Gone to entertain the troops, I think, like Vera Lynn and the others. That friend of hers, James, hinted that was what they were fixing to do, a year back when they came. She wrote Alec last week.'

'If she goes to Italy, she'll likely find Trefor. I wish Tref was here, Mom.'

'So do I, honey, but we just gotta get on without him. At least we got Alec still around.'

He was beavering away at his new job and talking of surveys and Power and Dams and Turbines on his weekends at home. He was part of a team that moved up and down river, measuring and making tests. With industry coming to life in order to make weapons for the war in Europe, it seemed electricity was needed urgently and the Pend Oreille was about to supply it.

School opened and Freddie enrolled, leaving Mom with the whole day to tend to the farm and homestead. We began to look forward to welcoming the next arrival, her unknown nephew from Canterbury, but she had mixed feelings about him. From the photos and reports she had received, he was not a sure-fire candidate for life on a mountain.

Auntie Sarah came up with a solution, by suggesting she had him live in town with her.

'After all, Cass, you took Dan under your wing when he could not settle in town. And with Laurence away to college, we have room enough for Frank. He'll be company for Danny and if he is as musical as his Grandmother says, we shall get along just fine.'

'Why Sarah, that sure is thoughtful of you. I have been a mite worried on account of his being so smart and all and our way of life a wee bit rough. But he can spend as much time as he likes with us, out of school.'

Chapter 7

Pearl Harbour hit the headlines on December 7th, 1941, when it was bombed by the Japanese. Three days later, America had entered the war and the lives of ordinary citizens were abruptly affected. There was talk of possible air attack on power supplies and factories, while the production of armaments was stepped up. On the Pacific Coast along the west of our state, all persons of Japanese descent were to be removed to government camps, whether they were U.S. citizens or not.

For the first time, we experienced the fear that our relatives had been enduring for nearly three years. It had become a World War and we were part of it.

'Why the name of all that's crazy do they need to know how many horses we got?' puzzled Mom, with a printed paper in her hand. 'Are they about to ration horse feed, too?' She had already had to furnish all the details of her family, in readiness for ration cards being issued.

'Maybe they want them for horse meat,' suggested Dan. 'Our Mam told me the Froggies do eat horses.'

'They'm not having our ponies to eat,' Idris shouted. 'Not while I'm here, they'm not. Shoot the varmints, I will, before they get to take Misty and Storm.'

Mom was laughing by now. 'But you don't like horses, Idris. Anyhow, it says they simply want to count the horses because while the war takes more and more machinery, farmers will need more horses to pull plows.'

'Guess if we got a plow and tore up the meadow, we'd get to keep our own horses and maybe more,' I said.

The arrival of one more English boy paled into insignificance against the national emergency. Frank Taylor had accepted with quiet gratitude the arrangements made for him and it was obvious he was just made for town life. I did attempt when we met, to interest him in farming. Dan tried, too, but all the boy wanted to do was to read or play the piano and he was delighted to know he could start straight in at High School. Laying in supplies for the winter as usual, Mom had been relieved to have him content and safe in Auntie Sarah's care.

'It never rains but it pours,' she moaned, throwing off her heavy jacket at the end of a wet February day when the old car had let us down outside the school. Expert farmer though she was, mechanical things defeated her completely and we had perforce to await the help of a passing truck driver before we crawled up the hill an hour later than usual.

'If the old girl dies on us, I don't know what we'll do, for I have no money for a new one.'

'Get us a pony, Auntie Cass, and we can ride to school,' said Dan. 'Do ponies cost less than cars?'

'Now you-all get the chores done quickly,' she said, making an effort to be her usual cheerful self. 'I left supper in the oven and we don't want it to spoil.' She sat down to read the only letter she had collected that day.

I came in from locking-up to find her looking shocked.

'What is it, Mom? Are we really short of money?'

'No honey, that's not what's upset me. It's this letter; it brings bad news. I don't know how to tell you.'

By then, the boys were in and pulling chairs to the table. She got busy serving the chops and mash and they failed to notice she was so quiet. Then she said, 'I have to tell you bad news, kids. I just heard Auntie Bessie's husband has been killed in action.'

'Oh no.' Dan's face went white and Idris was for once silent. 'Not Uncle Bob. What ever will Auntie Bessie do without him?'

'Does that mean Sheila and Mabel ain't got no dad?' asked Idris.

'Same as me and Freddie,' I said.

'Poor things,' sighed Momma. 'We better go visit them come Saturday, if the car will roll.'

It would not, but Mom rode into Cusick to get a man to come and fix it and we got to town after church on Sunday. The family all had sad faces, but sitting around and moping wouldn't bring Bob back, said Bessie.

'Nothing to go back for now,' she said, picking up her knitting. 'Sunday or not, men need warm feet - better the day, better the deed and some frozen lad will be glad of these socks now Bob can't make use of them. Go on, you girls, have a game of chinese checkers - enjoy yourselves while you can.'

I thought she was very brave. 'If they'll take Pat in school next September, I shall get a job and help the war effort all I can,' she added. 'There must be something I can do.'

Zeb had already gotten into action, one of many older men who had formed a sort of home defence unit. He had taken his turn patrolling the railway bridge at Albeni Falls until an official guard had been placed there. He was with the volunteers making plans for all kinds of protection against infiltration by the enemy and he got onto a committee.

'Natural Resources, that's what we gotta defend first and foremost,' I heard him telling Alec. 'No use hanging about until they got their secret agents in already. What we need is a network of loyal observers, properly trained.'

'Watch out, Zeb, they'll put you in charge of the lot if you show too much brain-power,' said Alec.

'Like you,' I chipped in. 'You got put in charge of concrete supplies, didn't you?' I knew he'd got a lot of responsibility with the Corps of Engineers, thanks to his clever ideas. They had sent him to work on the new dam, miles away at Grand Coulee before Christmas and he was now studying some new scheme nearer to hand.

'Sh! You never heard that walls have ears, Berta May?' cautioned Alec. 'Time you started to think before you speak, like it says in the paper. Look at this.' He picked out a crumpled newspaper from the basket next the furnace and spread it out, turning pages until he found what he wanted, a half-page warning about careless talk.

'HE'S WATCHING YOU!' proclaimed the poster, where a sinister black helmet was silhouetted against a white background. It was enough to send shivers down my spine.

After that, we began to see coloured propaganda posters around the town, at the Post Office and in the stores. In school, we were warned not to chatter to strangers and told how we could help to win the war.

'I wanna be a Boy Scout,' announced Idris in the middle of March when we got home. A sudden late season of snow falls had kept us away from school for a week and this had been our first day back.

'Why? You told me last Fall there was nothing they could teach you,' said Mom.

'Aw, he just wants to be a messenger,' I told her.

'They gonna need us to form a Unit,' he said.

'You got ears, or what?' I asked him. 'Miss Lucas said you're not old enough.'

'And to get waste paper for the War Effort,' he protested. 'I could do that, sure enough.'

'Had a talk we did,' Dan explained patiently. 'The Scouts are to collect waste paper and maybe them and the Camp Fire Girls will make some kind of force to carry messages. But only when they're twelve or more.'

'Seems like you got to wait awhile then, Idris,' said Mom. 'How about you get the chores unit moving on the home front first? We farmers have to produce more food than ever, come summer.'

'You could join the Scouts, Dan,' I suggested while we were in the yard.

'I might do that. But then, what about this 4H outfit? The guys over Tacoma creek, they all want me to join that. Reckon getting to Scouts would be too far to go, but Stoney 4H meets in our school.'

'I'm joining, soon as I'm nine,' I said, shutting the barn door, 'sooner if they'll have me. Hey, maybe we could make Idris practice riding and roping and have us a team to enter the rodeo at the County Fair. Needs three and Freddie's not old enough. Then they'd let us all in 4H when they got to see how good we was.'

That was easier said than done. Idris was not turning out to be a natural cowboy and even when school was out and there was hours of time to practice, he did not shape up real good.

'I'd far rather get a bike,' he stated. He brushed himself down after yet another fall and flatly refused to remount Dusty.

'If he can't do it, he can't,' said Mom. 'Sakes, let Freddie in the team if you want to win, never mind is he a mite small. But no more wild capers now for a spell. I have to go down to Barkers and I want no accidents while I'm gone. Why don't you three ride up and see have the cattle strayed, and Idris can come with me to help load the stuff Sue got for me in that sale she went to?'

It was mid-June 1942 and we had driven the cattle to Sutton's meadow two weeks before, when there were still Trilium and Lupins and Wild Balsam in bloom. After a dry, hot spell these were finished, the track had hardened and our horses' hooves clattered sharply on exposed stones. The animals were soon sweating with the climb.

All was in order, the cattle all within sight, but a rotted tree had fallen across the creek just below their watering place. Debris was collecting behind it.

'Better see if we can move that,' I said, 'or there'll surely be a deep pool soon.'

'Does that make a problem?' asked Freddie.

'Only if some brainless cow falls in and can't get out,' I said. 'Think we can move it, Dan?'

No doubt we ought not to have tried, but we took up the challenge. First, we attempted to move it by hand, then Dan had the idea of tying a rope from his saddle to the further end of the tree and getting Mature to pull. That horse had never been harnessed to a cart nor a plow, however, and flatly refused to work. Dan almost came unseated as she pranced and reared.

It was my Storm who finally shifted the log far enough to let most of the debris clear away, with a fair amount of heaving and pushing by the boys at the same time. They were pretty well soaked through and their boots were full of mud by that time and in the shade of the forest as we rode home, they both complained of being cold. I was damp around the legs and seat myself.

'Why, you look like you been in one heap of trouble,' said Idris when we all rode in. 'Auntie Cassie's gonna be real angry.' He grinned wickedly at the thought of our getting bawled out. 'Wait till you see what I got,' he added.

There was an assorted collection of items lying beside the vegetable patch, but we gave it but a glance, for our urgent need was to turn the horses loose and then change our clothes. Mom told us to hang them out on the line. She said she would ride up next morning with a saw to fix that old tree good and proper and 'Well done, you guys.' So much for Idris' gloating.

He had gotten a prize out of the odds and ends from the sale right enough. I went to look as soon as I was warm and dry and found him tinkering with an old bicycle frame.

'Only needs a new saddle and some brake blocks,' he said, 'and it'll be as good as new.'

'Needs a good clean,' I told him.

'Aw, give me a chance, girl.' He was turning nuts and taking bits off.

'You'll have it all in pieces if you go on like that,' I said.

'That's the idea, stupid. Got to strip it down to clean it. Then I'll rebuild it, see. You can keep your old horses; I like bikes.'

We had to admit, he knew what he was doing. When Alec came home, he was full of praise.

'Got a real mechanical bent, has Idris,' he said. 'If we'd only got that tractor we talked about, he'd soon be servicing it for us.'

'Well don't let him loose on the car,' said Dan, 'or we'll never get to Newport again.

2

Restrictions on one thing and another were making life harder for all and there was no question of our getting a tractor now. Mom had borrowed two strong draft horses to plow up half of our meadow a few weeks back and then we had sown oats and planted rows and rows of cabbages.

'No guarantee of a good crop,' she had said, 'but we got to do our bit. We'll get Zeb to come up and fall a strip of them tamaracks so's we can push a new meadow out that a-way.'

Storm, Misty, Dusty and Mature did not like being restricted and had broken through the temporary fence which we had put up. It was late June and time to be making a new one.

'Berta May, maybe you and Dan could give me a hand with a new rail fence, for we can't wait for the men,' Mom said. 'We'll turn the horses onto the trail for the day and Idris and Freddie can watch them while we get to work.'

So we put up a new length of split-rail zig-zag. Since our stock of rails was not enough, there was hours of sawing

100

and splitting to be done. Dan got real handy with the saw and axe, but my arms were not strong enough as yet to be much use with the tools. There was plenty to keep me busy however, fetching and carrying, stacking rails and then holding posts, too, and they had to saw some more.

'If only we had a chain saw,' groaned Mom, not for the first time. 'Zeb has been telling me for years to buy one.'

'But we couldn't get the gas to run it, more than likely,' said Dan. 'A fat lot of good it would be with no gas.'

'There's some sort of allowance for farm implements,' she told him, 'and I may be wrong, but I believe there are electric chain saws now. They can't cut our electricity supply, since it comes from our own creek.'

'May me and Dan go visit the Barkers and Wesleys, Mom, when we're through with this?' I asked.

'Dan and I, not me and Dan,' she said, hammering another post home with the sledge hammer. 'Sure you may. We'll be through by tomorrow evening, so how about I give you Thursday and Friday free?'

'No chores at all?'

'Not one.'

'I'll have time to ride clear over to Jimmy's,' said Dan. 'I wonder, shall I go down and call for Randy Wesley first or go right on over Tacoma by myself?'

'I'd be happier to know there was two of you,' Mom said, 'in case of accidents. With the CCC camp empty now, you could wait a long while for help. And again, Randy would like the company. Guess he's missing his two brothers since they got drafted into the army, or so I heard from Sue Barker.'

Of course, Idris wanted to come with us, then Freddie clamoured to be in on our day out, but Mom said she needed their help Thursday, but if the Barkers and anyone else cared to come visit with us Friday, she would make it a holiday for all. I was up and waiting for Dan at half past six and we cantered out before seven, our dinner packs and jackets stowed in saddle pockets. Down from the sunlit meadow into the shadowy forest trail we went, Storm and Mature picking their way carefully on the steepest gradient. To our left, we could hear the waters of the creek tumbling over rocky outcrops amongst thick timber. Here and there, shafts of sunlight lit the pale brown dirt; when we came to the little clearing near the plank bridge, where the trail crossed the Greywater, two deer were grazing. One of them had a fawn at her heels. Startled at our appearance, they leapt into the nearest thicket, white tails erect.

'Hi, Berta May, Hi, Dan,' called Sue Barker, out hoeing her corn patch when we came in sight. 'How y'doing?' Dan rode on, to find his friend half a mile down the road, but I slid out of the saddle and hitched Storm to the rail.

'May I visit with Babs and Chuck awhile?' I asked. 'Mom's given us leave to stay out the whole day and I brought my dinner with me.'

'Now that's real nice, honey. We could do with some company, for them two's getting quarrelsome with too much time on their hands. Go down the creek a ways, that's where I saw them last.'

Then I followed the twisty path past her fruit bushes and a handful of apple trees, to the steep-sided cutting where the creek ran behind the farm land. I soon heard voices and called, 'Chuck! Babs! Hi there!'

Babs' black curls were first to appear above the bank. Her cotton dress was smeared with mud, her feet bare and wet. Chuck had stripped off his shirt and rolled up his coveralls above his knees.

'Hi, Berta May. C'mon down and see what we caught.'

We had a glorious hour then, clambering about the rocks, poking around to see what we could find and generally disturbing the lives of the water creatures. Babs had caught a salamander and put it in a tin can but we could not get another, no matter how we tried.

Tiring at last of our games, we went up to the house, leaving a watery trail as we went.

'Can we have some cake and orange juice, Mom?' asked Babs.

'Take them wet things off and lay them over the deck rail while I get you something,' said her mom. 'Here, rub yourselves dry with this towel and put these on.'

She threw a handful of clothes out of the screen door and we all scrambled to find pants to fit us.

'How do I look?' I asked Babs. I had a pair of her navy

blue panties, Chuck's old school shorts and a frilly little blouse.

'I feel like a pirate,' I said.

3

That was a day of furious fun and adventure, when we played pirates and gangsters and explorers, read comics and then got out some board games. Two more friends dropped by from neighbouring homesteads and Mrs Barker said she had never know a day go so quickly. I told her Mom's message about Friday, so we got it all fixed up for Chuck and Babs to come for breakfast.

It was seven before Dan appeared to ride home with me, having had the time of his life with Randy and Jimmy.

'Tell you what, Berta May,' he told me, 'when I get back home, I shall get Dad to start keeping horses. Do you know, Jimmy's pop has twenty eight.'

'Breeds them, doesn't he?' I ducked my head to avoid a low branch and reined in Storm, for he was getting too far ahead for me to hear Dan's voice.

'Yes he does. He showed me all his new foals and his yearlings and said Jimmy will fetch me over when they're breaking them.'

Mom said Jimmy's folks had done well for themselves out of horses and had a good name for their stock and it was they who had started Stoney 4H.

'I'm joining, come September,' said Alec.

Next morning, we rushed through the chores, since visitors were expected for breakfast, then Mom and I got mixing batter and Dan was set to cut thick slices of bread. By eight, the house was filling up and the first hot-cakes were on.

'Make them good and big, Auntie Cass,' said Idris, 'I'm hungry as a hunter,' but she made him wait until Babs and Chuck, Randy and Jimmy had gotten their plates filled first.

'Pass the maple syrup,' she told him, 'and Freddie, get that plate of hot bacon off the furnace will you, and put two pieces on all the plates.

I was serving the hot-cakes as fast as she cooked them

and Dan was ladling canned fruit out of a jar, but at last it was our turn to sit and eat and my, what a feast we had. I think we must have put away fifty cakes between us, not to mention mountains of hot toast and lashings of syrup.

'That should keep you going a few hours,' said Mom at last, looking at the wreckage on the table and counters.

'Thank you, it was delicious,' said Jimmy. 'We must help you to do the dishes.'

'Why, Jimmy, that's real nice of you,' she smiled and I could see he'd gone right to the top with her in popularity. 'Why don't you and me get started at the sink while Dan and Berta May take charge of the table? Many hands make light work and we'll be done in no time.'

Twenty minutes later, she shoed us all outside, saying she could do the rest herself and why didn't we get on with our expedition. For Dan and I had decided to take everyone to the lake. It was but a small lake, half a mile upstream from the homestead, just above a waterfall. It was shallow and safe for playing and we wanted to try making a raft on which to cross it.

Old lumber, ropes and empty oil drums had been put ready and Dan had a sack of tools, too. There was a bulging back-pack of food. We lined up our team and gave each a load to carry, the bigger boys having the planks while the four smallest of us got a drum to roll.

'Lead the way, Berta May,' shouted Dan, for I knew the route better than he did and the line began to move.

It was a very noisy convoy that snaked along the bank of the creek, following a barely discernible footpath. Momma had told me it had been an Indian trail, which came clear up from Calispel long before the Withers men made a route for the road. It linked our house with a ruined log cabin which had stood by the lakeside for eighty years or so. Who had lived there, I did not know, or what had happened to make them leave.

Alternately rolling my hollow drum and clutching it in my arms while I passed between rocks, stopping to push aside fallen branches and to make sure the whole party was keeping together, I led them to our lake. Its surface was partly covered with water lilies, already in full bloom, and ducks were quacking from the safety of the fringe of reeds.

We lay our loads thankfully on flat ground and Dan took charge of operations.

Two hours later after many capsizes, a small raft was afloat. True, it would support only two passengers at a time, but by perseverance and determination, Dan and Randy had succeeded where the rest of us would have abandoned the project. They set off on a journey across the lake.

In the meantime, some of us had found our way around it on foot, with much merriment and not a little splashing. Some had taken to climbing, having discovered some old gnarled fruit trees, while others had built a den under an overhanging rock. Babs and I had discovered a huckleberry patch on the furthest bank high above the lake and we swore to keep it's whereabouts secret.

'We'll come back in August, just the two of us,' I told her, 'and we'll fill two cans each and won't our Moms be pleased?'

'Hey, look,' she said, 'that's your Mom down there. What's she doing here?'

'Come to see no-one ain't drowned, I s'pose,' I said and hollered, 'Mom! Mom!' Seeing the rest of them gathering round her, we thought maybe we were missing something, so hurried down and back around the lake. A good clear path had been worn by now and we arrived at the same time as the raft landed.

'Hurry up,' said Idris, 'she won't open the tin until everyone's sitting down. C'mon, Auntie Cassie, we're all here now. What have you brought?'

'Fresh meat pies,' she said. 'Only one each, but that should keep the wolf from the door. I'm glad to see the bears didn't get you, nor the sharks.'

'Too noisy, bears ran away,' mumbled Randy through a mouth full of pastry.

'You like a ride, Mom?' asked Dan and she said of course she would.

Then Freddie and Babs got onto the raft with her and she paddled that old boat across and back. Next, Chuck and Jimmy took it out and after that, Idris and me. I was certain I had got the hang of steering and paddling after seeing everyone else in action, but there was more to it than I thought.

'Sit still, Idris,' I shrieked, gripping the plank on which I sat for all I was worth.

'Paddle, girl, paddle! Never get anywhere if you don't paddle.' He thrashed about with the flat piece of wood and we spun round in a tight circle.

'Take it slowly!' shouted Mom.

I lowered my paddle over the side and took a long, careful stroke. The raft swung to the left.

'Paddle your side,' I told Idris. He made three or four swift strokes and we turned rapidly to the right.

'Go slow!' I ordered, again dipping my paddle.

'We'll never get there before Christmas,' he complained.

'We'll surely drown, the way you're acting.'

Arguing and splashing, we made our noisy way. All ducks had disappeared. It was a miracle neither of us fell in. A mischievous breeze sprang up while we were at the furthest point and made our journey back yet more lively. Steering seemed impossible and at the very moment when we seemed set to float into the landing safely, a sudden gust of wind caught our stern and we swung violently about. Idris, already standing up ready to jump ashore, lost his balance and slipped right over into the water.

It was barely knee-deep, but he was soaked from head to foot as he crawled onto the bank. Everybody crowded round him, laughing and quite forgetting me, still battling single-paddled to get the raft lined up for the shore.

'Hey, you-all going to leave me out here till Thanksgiving?' I hollered as loud as I could. Mom looked up from rubbing Idris with a towel and shrieked, 'She's drifting down the lake again. Do something, Dan, can't you?'

'Catch this!' shouted Jimmy and a coil of rope unwound itself in the air to hit the raft plumb in the middle. Thank heaven for the practice he'd had, I thought, grabbing the loop and holding tight while he and Dan began to haul on their end.

'Heave, heave, heave,' they chanted as the distance between us grew smaller.

'Welcome home, Ma'am,' said Randy, making a mock bow as I stepped ashore. 'We sure are pleased to have you back in the United States of America and we hope your voyage was a smooth one.'

'Mine wasn't. I'm sticking to my bike after this,' said Idris, sinking his teeth into a beef sandwich.

We ate every scrap of food out of the pack and were still hungry. Dan and Jimmy hid the raft amongst bushes well above water level and we swore ourselves to secrecy, not only about its hiding place but about the lake itself.

'Let's call it 'The Summer Sea',' said Babs, and we'll come back every summer.

4

Soon after that, Alec came up for the weekend. It was some weeks since he had been and he said he was sorry to have stayed away so long and were there many jobs to be done, because he'd called in at Newport and Zeb had said he would come and help out.

'But I see you folks have got most things under control,' he said, walking round with us and admiring the neat rows of cabbages well weeded and the yard as tidy as ever.

'Sure have,' boasted Idris. 'Busy as beavers we been and no kidding, we never had a day's rest the whole darned vacation.'

'Idris!' said Dan and Freddie together, while I gave him a great shove and told him he'd get his tongue cut out for telling lies.

'Guess I'll take that with a pinch of salt,' laughed Alec. He no doubt knew which of the four of us was least likely to overwork and who had been down to the Barkers' place on his bike four times in the past two weeks.

He had brought a new saw for Mom, one that ran off electricity. He told her how to use it and he laid down the law to us about not touching it.

'Never!' he said, his face real serious. 'This is not a toy and is definitely for adult use only. But I wouldn't let Zeb get too carried away with it, either' he advised her. 'It's not meant for felling full-grown timber but you will save a lot of time and effort cutting up posts and fire wood.'

They put it in a strong chest in the store and locked the lid. Then he went to check on the water pump and the turbine that supplied our power. He told me to bring a pitch fork and help fish debris out from behind the little dam he'd built and Idris tagged along, talking mechanical things.

'I'll give him this, he has a natural bent for machinery,' said Alec later. 'He fixed that bicycle up real good and knows more about gears than most kids his age.'

'Pity he don't know nothing about horses,' I grumbled, thinking of the rodeo.

Chapter 8

Whether Trefor's letters were subject to a stricter censorship because of his being officially engaged on Communications for the armed services, we never knew. From the time he was first posted abroad in 1940, we received little mail from him, to the extent that Mom spent months believing that he had been captured by the enemy. After the exodus from Dunkirk, he had been in Britain for some weeks, but even at that time, his letters were not the newsy scripts like we had from Megan and others, which was surprising considering that he had earned his living at home by news-writing.

'And now he's been to Italy and then Africa and goodness knows where else,' said Mom, 'and who cares if he's alive or dead? And when he writes, I swear some-one has cut his letters by half.'

'He must be on very important business, Auntie Cass', said Frank gently. 'They have to be careful not to let the enemy obtain information or even know where it comes from.'

We were visiting in Newport. Mom had promised us a trip out, for she said we'd worked hard enough these last months. When she read in the paper that the Jungle Book was showing at the Rex, we packed up and headed south, though Dan decided at the last minute he'd rather join Jimmy on a camping trip. Auntie Sarah had received mail and papers from Wales recently, so they were having a ball of anxiety over coffee.

'I know, Frank. I try not to worry so, but now and then it gets to me, not knowing. See here in this paper - a list of men known to be held prisoner and others killed in Africa. Letters from men in the Far East and thanks for gifts sent from home, but not a word have I had from Trefor for nearly a year.'

None of us was used to seeing Mom disheartened, but she had kept her worry to herself for too long and needed a shoulder to cry on.

'Frank,' said Auntie Sarah, 'could you take Berta May

and Idris and Freddie round to see Bessie for a while? And take that bag of clothes Cass just brought for the girls and the books they wanted to borrow, will you? Be back for dinner at half twelve.'

'Of course I will, Auntie,' said Frank and shepherded us out at once, closing the door quietly behind him. Though the clothes he wore were less formal than the grey suit in which he had arrived before Christmas, his manner remained strangely stiff for a boy. After all, I thought, he was the same age as Dan, but acted like he was a grown man. No, a gentleman, I reflected as he held open the yard gate so that I might leave before him.

'You like it here?' I asked.

'Oh yes, it is very pleasant and your family has made me feel welcome. After all, I was a complete stranger and had no claim upon you, but Auntie Sarah and Uncle Henry could not have been more hospitable had I been their own son.'

The only place I had heard a voice like his before was on the radio when Alec or Mom was listening to news bulletins. It was English through and through and the words he used were like those of newscasters, too. I looked up at him in fascination.

'How's High School?'

'Tolerable. I think it true to say I have adapted well to the system, strange though it seemed at first, and Danny was of great help to me when I first arrived. My grandmother is delighted to know that my musical studies are progressing well.'

'Oh well, you're in the right place for that,' I said, 'with Auntie Sarah and all. You play the piano then?'

'Yes, I do, and the violin. I hope to specialise in that field and had expected to become part of a Junior Orchestra in England. At the current rate of progress, I shall be old enough for the Halle before I return home. That is, if there is any home to return to,' which reminded me that he, too had his worries.

'Is it very bad over there where you come from?'

'Terrifying. One hears the bombers going over night after night and does not know when one will fall on one's head. So noisy. And what they have done to London is appalling. We used to go up to London once a month to concerts, Grandmother and I, until it became too dangerous. Poor Grandma, I hope she is well. You can never tell, you know. People are so brave, they rarely write about the worst of their fears and troubles. After you, Berta May.' He held open Bessie's back door and ushered us inside.

After an hour of playing noisily with Sheila, Pat and Mabel in the garden, we had a cool drink and a cookie. The girls tried on some little frocks which Mom sent because I had outgrown them.

'That's one of my favourites,' I told Pat, who had chosen a pinafore dress with striped cotton skirt, red bib and white blouse trimmed to match. 'Mom says she'll make me another when she gets the time.'

'You look like a real American now,' said Bessie. 'I never saw anything like that in Wales. We'll take your picture and send your Mammy so she can see you.'

'Me too,' said Mabel. 'I look real nice too, don't I Momma?' She was wearing my old green gingham trimmed with lace.

'You look cute,' Bessie agreed, 'and you sound as American as Berta May.'

'Very smart,' agreed Frank, 'but it is time we returned for lunch. Freddie has to go to the hospital at two, but I gather we shall all meet at the Rex later.'

Still somewhat lame and needing the support of a brace, my brother was to have a further operation and Mom hoped it might be done while school was out.

'Would you like to look at my photographs?' Frank asked me after dinner. 'It won't take long.' I could see Auntie Sarah smiling and nodding her head so thought I had better say Yes.

He had just a wallet full, some of them as old as those in Auntie's box but mostly fairly recent. Some showed his grandmother's house, a huge brick building with a high wall around it and a wrought iron gate in front.

'But they've taken away the gate and the railings, to use the iron for making weapons for the war,' he sighed. 'See, this is London the day after the first incendiaries fell,' and he pulled out a folded newsprint photo. I stared in disbelief

111

at the scene of devastation.

'That used to be a street of shops and theatres,' he said. 'Now this is the only one I have of me and my parents. They died before I was two, you see, in 1931.'

'My Poppa died when I was little, too,' I told him. 'Have you seen Auntie Sarah's box of photographs and things?'

'I showed him a few of them,' she told me. 'I thought he might like to see the others next winter - something to do on dark evenings. But if you want to look now, Frank, Berta May can help me show you.'

He would probably have liked that, but at that moment Bessie and the girls arrived so we all went out together. Despite his formality and the difference in our ages, I was feeling a new friendship towards Frank.

'Say, why don't we ask Momma can you come back home with us and stay a day or two?' I suggested. We were on the sidewalk opposite the seed merchant and he was carefully walking at the outer edge lest harm should befall me or Sheila. That was the way they did things in England, he had said.

'How very kind of you, Berta May. Do you not think it would be too much trouble for her?'

'Trouble? Mom don't make trouble out of one more mouth to feed and there's a spare bunk out with the boys.'

'Ain't no need for you to worry about them none,' I added, seeing that he was unsure of his welcome.

'But did she warn you how rough and ready life is outback?' Mom asked him later when we put the idea to her. 'I sure would love to have you visit, but it won't be no garden party, you know.' I could see her eyeing his neat short pants and white shirt. 'Do you have any coveralls or old pants?'

'I can kit him out with the right clothes,' laughed Auntie. 'Into the wilds of Greystone Valley, is it, to complete your education? Take your violin and you may have pleasant surprise.'

Put like that, it was a challenge he could not resist and I gladly relinquished my front car-seat to him after the show, wondering what Dan would say when he saw we had a visitor.

He always said a lot less than Idris, of course, but after he had told us every last detail of his camping in the forest, he made Frank truly welcome. In fact, the two older boys settled down so amicably that I felt quite left out. It was not my idea of fun, to be looking at an old school atlas and finding where the troops were fighting. Nor even to be swapping news about how the war was affecting their respective homes - they had the Free Press spread out over the table and were combing through it, Dan explaining with little drawings where his parents' farm lay and where the rest of the family lived.

'Had to plough up half our land for food, they have; potatoes all up the valley and wheat and barley everywhere. And trying to feed the stock on kale and oat straw if you please, in place of hay and oats.'

'But I thought it was all coal mines in South Wales,' said Frank.

'Rubbish, man. Coal mines we have got, yes, and iron and tin plate factories but not everywhere. Farmers we are, see and feeding the whole nation by our work. And Dad and Grancher having to manage without me.'

'But look what a good job you're doing for me,' interrupted Mom, 'and what a fine crop of vegetables we've grown. I tell you, Greyroofs has done its bit for the food supply and your folks would be proud of you. Now clear this table or you'll get no supper and then off to bed with the lot of you. We have work to do tomorrow.'

Dressed in old denim pants and a checked shirt, Frank looked a different boy the next morning when we went the rounds, but remembered his beautiful manners at every turn.

'No need to say 'Excuse me' to the hens,' shouted Mom after a while, seeing him gently trying to shift them from under the wagon. 'Just stir them with the broom and shoo them through the gate as if you mean it.'

'We gotta finish creosoting the rail fence today,' said Idris, giving him a pot and a black brush. 'You start by the barn, I'll go over the other end and we'll meet in the middle' - there was no please or thank you or standing on ceremony from Idris; but I liked the way our new cousin behaved and secretly vowed I would have those other boys treat me with respect in future.

'And what else?' I asked at dinner time when Idris told me he wanted more potatoes.

'Nothing else. Just Potatoes.'

'Potatoes please,' I said primly, just as I had heard mothers teaching their children.

'Potatoes, please then,' he said. 'You want one, Frank?'

'No, thank you, Idris, I have eaten sufficient.'

We had more than a few laughs at the long words he used and sometimes we were hard put to it to understand him, but he was a good sport and took our teasing well. Wickedly, Freddie and Idris invited him to take a ride up the track with them and were all set to put him on Storm until I came on the scene.

'Get off my horse,' I shouted, just as they were showing him how to mount. 'You can't ride him.'

Startled, Frank jumped away and Storm began prancing in alarm. 'I am so sorry,' he said. 'I did not wish to offend you.'

'Spoil sport,' said Freddie, showing off by cantering away down the meadow.

'Can you really ride?' I asked.

'No, but I would like to learn.'

'Then wait till I get into long pants and I'll give you a lesson,' I told him. 'Storm would have thrown you before you'd gone twenty yards. Just wait till Mom gets her hands on those two. She'll make them scrub the stables from one end to the other.'

2

For a city boy, he had good horse sense and he learned quickly, but it would take a few more visits before he was competent enough to ride the mountain. When he left us, Frank's thanks were sincere and we were equally sincere in hoping he would come again, not the least for the musical evenings we had enjoyed at his hands.

'Now just you mind what Zeb tells you,' Mom told Idris sternly as she loaded the car. 'Chores first and play later and no riding that bike up the mountain alone. Berta May, see you keep an eye on the duty rota I pinned up in the kitchen and when Alec comes on Saturday, get him to have a look at the pump.'

'OK Mom,' I said. 'Good luck, Freddie. Come back soon, Frank.' We waved, Zeb and Dan and I, until the car disappeared into the woods. It was time for Fred's new operation, from which he desperately hoped to return completely sound of leg.

Of course it was Dan rather than our easy-going Zeb who kept Idris in order. Turned sixty five now, cousin Zeb was a weather-beaten bachelor, happy enough to dig and saw and paint and haul but with no air of authority. We kids could twist him round our little fingers and he had no idea how to control a rebellion of the sort that Idris might instigate.

On this occasion, however, all went smoothly. Idris and I were both turned eight years old now and it was months since his last outburst of temper. Seemingly, he had accepted Greyroofs as home and was too busy trying to beat me in school to have time for mischief, but I know Mom was never quite sure whether he would blow his lid one day.

The fences were all done, the cattle inspected, and loads of cord wood hauled from the forest for winter fuel within four days. Then Alec arrived to spend the weekend at home and I went mad with joy to see the letters he brought.

'I emptied the box on the way up,' he said. 'Look, here's one from Trefor.'

'Oh boy, let me open it,' I shouted, quite forgetting to be glad at seeing Alec himself. I slit open the envelope, disregarding the fact that it was addressed to Mom.

'Berta May, you should have left it,' he chided. 'Look, here's one for you from Lizzie.'

'But I don't want one from Lizzie, I want to know if Tref's OK,' I cried, almost weeping in frustration.

'Come on then,' he said. 'Let's just have a quick read to make sure and then Mom can see it as soon as she comes home.'

'You can take it down town for her, when you go back,' I said, drying my eyes on the back of my sleeve. 'Read it to me. Alec, please.'

'Dear Mom and everyone,' he read.

'Sorry I have not written for an age but I have been

unable to get letters out for security reasons. Now on leave for two weeks, so will write every day to make up.

I am in very good health, so if you have worried, stop now. I cannot pretend life is much fun, but I have not been in great danger and am one of the lucky ones. I got your last parcel of socks, etc. Also, I know Sam was pleased with his and Lizzie with hers.

I nearly met with Bethan in Italy, but got posted again the day before she was due to arrive so I had to leave a message for her. I cannot tell you where I have been but now I hope to be in Britain for a spell on a special assignment.'

And so it went, light, unimportant chat about this and that, but the main thing was, he was safe.

'Tell Berta May and Freddie I will write to them next, so to look out for a letter. I mean to visit the folks in Wales next week. Your ever-loving son, Trefor.'

'Oh my, will Mom be happy now?' said Alec, hugging me and battling to disentangle himself from Idris.

'If he's written to our Sarah, she will have heard by now,' Zeb said, handing glasses of root beer around. 'You didn't stop on the way through town?'

'No. I came by way of Sacheen, to cut off the corner. Now what jobs have to be done?'

'The pump,' I told him. 'We're not getting a steady flow of water now the creek is low.'

'Right, I shall do that at once. And I want to take a look at the generator. I think I could put in a better one before next winter, give you more current. Time Mom had some electrical gadgets in the house to make life easier. Who's coming to help?'

When it came to following Alec around the farm, I could beat the boys hollow, for I'd been doing it for years longer than they had. We soon had things fixed, he and I. After supper, Zeb came up with an idea for Sunday,

'What say we go fishing tomorrow?'

'Good idea. Where?'

'Conger Pond,' said Dan and I together.

'Sullivan,' said Idris.

'Too far to go on horse back and I need a ride,' said Alec. 'Conger it is and an early start then , so off to bed now while

Zeb and I pack food.'

'And if only we had a refrigerator, we could have taken twice as many,' said Alec at the end of the day. We had all succeeded in catching several trout, which were in our saddle bags, but could have had more, so good had been the day.

'I shall give it top priority to get things seen to before Christmas and then I will buy the fridge as a gift for the household. Just think, fresh trout in the middle of winter, not to mention salmon. A nice change from beef and rabbit, don't you think?'

'And ices in summer,' said Dan.

'You can't beat a nice joint of beef,' said Zeb, 'though a bit of fish or game do make a change, right enough.' We turned our heads towards home as clouds began to build over the western forest. 'A change in the weather coming, I reckon. Good thing we have no cereal to harvest, barring the patch of oats.'

By Tuesday, Mom and Freddie were home, jubilant at having heard of Trefor's safety and thankful that the operation was over. There were almost daily letters after that, we children taking turns to ride down and collect the mail because we could not bear to wait for it.

'Dear Berta May,' I read, sitting on the porch in the sunshine mid-week.

'I have come home to Wales for a rest as I have two weeks' leave. It is wonderful to see everyone and to be able to thank people for their kindness, not only our family but all the people of the valley who keep sending parcels to the troops. These wonderful people have also been holding concerts to raise money, just like you did last year. Are you having another this summer?'

'I like to have your letters and hope you will keep sending them, even if you get no reply for a while. Sometimes I am in places where I cannot write to you, but your letters get to me. I like the drawings you made and I am glad you and Idris are getting on well in school. I hope you will give my kind regards to Miss Petersen. Is she teaching your grade now?'

I read it over and over and before the next morning, had written a reply to him. A few days later, we got picture postcards from Wales and some letters from Auntie Megan and Emmie.

'Mom, are we doing a concert like we did last year?' I asked. 'Trefor wanted to know. We ought to be going to Auntie Sarah's to practice.'

'I clean forgot to tell you, in the excitement of hearing he was safe. The concert this year will be end of September and yes, Auntie Sarah wants us to perform. She says, can you and the boys work up some ideas and go down for a day before school opens, to have a practice?'

That gave us plenty to do for the rest of the vacation, between harvesting fruit and so on. The few wet days we had, the bunkhouse became our practice room. Some of our ideas were pretty wild, but with help from Mom in the costume line, we got our act together. It was essentially an extension of Dan's circus act, with juggling and rope twirling, acrobatics and general horse-play, but we also got into tune for a few popular songs like 'Lay That Pistol Down' and 'I'm a Yankee Doodle Dandy' which we had heard on the radio. I spent an unusually cold and windy afternoon designing the cover for a theatre programme in which the American Dragons featured prominently. After filling in a few missing numbers when I next saw Auntie Sarah, I would send copies to Trefor and Bethan, I thought.

At the same time, we were spending as much time as possible on horseback, for although the county fair had been abandoned because of the war, there was to be a Community Fair at Cusick on September 6th, Sunday. With Freddie's leg in plaster, he was out of our team, but Dan roped in Randy and we called ourselves the Stoney Ranchers.

All homesteads and farms and camps must have been deserted that day, for the fair ground was packed with people. There were kids' contests and a bicycle parade, so even Idris got to show off and although our team did not win the rodeo, we got some of the loudest cheers from the crowd.

118

'And please may I join 4H?' I pleaded with Jimmy's mother when Mom stopped to congratulate her on her son's having won first prize. 'I do so want to get on with things and Dan will be coming next month, so I'll get there safe enough.'

'Well that's real good to know you're that keen, Berta May. I will do my level best to fit you in.'

'Now get along over with the boys and wait for the pony races to start, Berta May, while Mrs Jones and I take in this Victory Garden. Seems like I could have entered my cabbages, had I only known what the competition was.'

'Won't be much ground left for trees, time we have dug up all they want for.....' I heard as I hurried away. Storm and I were entered for the weaving race.

4

There was no doubt about who would be star of the show this time. As soon as we began rehearsing together, it was obvious that little Mabel would steal the hearts of the town. She was small and dark and usually very quiet, an angel in school and no trouble at home, but she had acting in her blood.

'Just like me when we lived on the Garn and your Bethan when she was a tot,' I heard Auntie Sarah say to Mom. 'Put her on a stage and she's in her element. We'll have no need of a celebrity this year.'

For Mabel was to be Shirley Temple. With her hair curled in ringlets, a short flouncy frock and shiny black shoes, she looked nearer four than seven years old and she did the 'Good Ship Lollipop', to perfection.

'Do it again,' we roared, when we first saw her prancing and dancing on Auntie Sarah's porch, but her mother was not wishing to have her overworked or over-praised. 'You can see it again at our dress rehearsal,' she said.

We only had one day to get everything polished and apart from blending the musical items together, they had to polish mighty hard to get our circus act up to standard.

It was Frank of all people who rescued it from mediocrity. Dressed as always immaculately and with never a hair out of place, he had performed his violin solo and his duet with great solemnity. Likewise, he joined in the choral items earnestly and it was with a shock that we saw him step forward while Dan was trying to improve his juggling.

'You need a partner,' he said and picked up three spare tennis balls. Which is how he came to be on stage, wearing his best grey suit and tie and a borrowed bowler hat, at the same time as us clowns.

As a comic turn, it was an immediate success, for here was the perfect English Gentleman apparently arriving by accident in a circus ring, only to prove himself a competent performer. He snatched Dan's brightly coloured bean-filled cubes from under his nose, juggled them at speed and then threw them back, at the same time bringing a further set from his pocket. The two of them then juggled the six between them, but while Dan grinned all the time, Frank's face was solemn and straight.

Then he got in the way of Idris's mad capering and my rope swirling, as a result of which I lassoed him, tied him up and towed him away in a garden truck. It went down a treat with our audience, who roared 'encore' when we finished.

The concert, one of a series of fund-raising events that fall, was an immediate success and the American Dragons again got a good press write-up. The outward-bound mail next week contained many cuttings, bound for Wales and other parts of Europe.

'I should like to see my grandmother's face when she sees that I have joined a concert troupe,' said Frank. 'Somehow, I think she may not be rushing to show her neighbours, though she will be proud to know I played my violin.'

'There's Bob would have been proud, too,' sighed Bessie, 'to see our Mabel in the limelight.'

5

So the year of 1942 drew to a close and winter set in with no apparent change in the fortunes of the war. There was near enough full employment, factories expanding, men and women flocking to take up work wherever it was available and more being spent on defence than had ever been allocated to welfare programmes during the recession.

We suffered no real hardship at Greyroofs, though austerity was our watch word and Mom would brook no wasteful habits.

'Just think of those poor children in Europe,' she would scold Idris if he grouched about his diet. 'They'd be only too pleased to have what you spurn and I guess your Grancher would hate to hear you complain.' That always did the trick. He cleaned his plate at once.

'I think there's a scent of hope in the air,' I heard the adults remark one to another during the Spring and Summer. 'Did you read the leader in the Press last week?'

'From what I hear, the Nazis have reached their peak and we can beat them in the end,' said the Minister in church, 'but a lot more courage and fortitude will be needed in the coming months. Yes, and self-sacrifice, too, before the Allies achieve victory.'

I was sure something was brewing, for Trefor had not written since Christmas, not even a note of thanks for the woollen scarf I had knitted for him. Miss Petersen had taught all twenty of us in Grades three upwards to knit, saying she was sure all the children in Europe would be glad of a nice warm scarf or bonnet and we were honour-bound to spend the dark winter evenings making things to send. A good-sized parcel went from out school before the end of April and we awaited with interest an acknowledgement.

It came in a big brown envelope from the Headmaster of Garndiffaith School, enclosing letters from the children to whom the gifts had been given. How proud and pleased we Watkins felt, to know it was through us that a little warmth and happiness had crossed the ocean.

'Some of the children are those who came from Birmingham at the outbreak of War,' wrote the teacher. 'They rarely see their parents and some of them have lost fathers and brothers on active service. All our children wish to thank you most heartily and we hope you will continue to be our friends in the future.'

So I picked up my needles again, no matter was summer approaching.

'See here,' said Dan one evening in July. 'They want folks to spend their holidays at Harvest Camp.' He got his head down study the latest paper.

'A holiday that is Healthful, Patriotic and Cheap,' he read. 'In order to harvest the increased acreage of cereal crops, now 70,000 more than pre-war, Monmouthshire needs an army of extra workers. They pay twenty eight shillings a week for their keep, but get paid a shilling an hour for their work. Wish I was there, I do.'

It was a long time since he had been heard to wish he were home, but I had to agree it sounded a good way of spending the vacation, for there were places for boys and girls.

'You fix up the trip and I'll go with you,' I said. We fell to building castles in the air.

He was thirteen now and Mom's right hand, a fact I was perfectly ready to acknowledge though I always considered myself to be second in command when Alec was absent. Zeb had taught him a bit of carpentry and he was learning to be quite a knowledgeable woodsman as well as a horseman.

'When the time comes for you to go home,' Mom said, 'we shall miss you terribly.'

'Will it ever come?' he asked with a heavy sigh. 'Not that I want to leave you, Auntie Cass, but I sure would like to see the valley.'

'You will, honey, you will,' she comforted, putting her arm around his shoulders. 'President Eisenhower is over there on a visit right now with his wife. Something is brewing and we're going to win.'

Chapter 9

Some events in childhood remain alive in memory for ever; some years are recalled almost in their entirety, while others seem to have slipped by so rapidly that little of their content can be brought to mind. Thus it was with the last two years of the war, when home and school, work and leisure swept us along, our own little crises of far greater importance to us than were tragedies elsewhere, as far as we youngsters were concerned.

When they told us our school was to close, our indignation was as enormous as if the whole world had turned upside down.

'Go to Cusick? I don't want to go to Cusick,' I wailed along with the rest of the Stoney scholars.

'Consolidate? Would someone please explain the meaning of consolidate?' asked Mom, talking with a crowd of other parents who'd collected for a meeting.

'They surely cannot mean to bus these little kids nine miles to and fro every day of their lives. It don't make no sense,' said Sue Barker.

'This school was good enough for me and it sure is good enough for my kids,' shouted Jimmy's dad.

'This school has sent heroes to fight for us,' said another. Davises, Wesleys, Storks, Jones, Barkers, Watkins and every other family from miles around crowded into the old wooden school house. It was a stormy meeting.

We protested and threatened to boycott our classes, but once Miss Lucas and Miss Petersen were gone and the building was locked against us, there was nothing for it but to get on the bright yellow bus each morning at seven thirty. Progress had decided that a big new central school was better for our education than had been all the little scattered Grade Schools.

It was a novelty to travel with so many other children and to be in a class where they were all of the same age as myself. I made new friends, some with fathers working at Cusick mill, one who lived with her grandparents while her mother was serving as a doctor with the army. My horizons

123

were extending. It was decidedly interesting to have the use of a gym and other special rooms for cooking and metal work, but Stoney School had given us all a good start and we just hated to see it close.

Our 4H continued to use the building and I was getting on real well with my hand crafts and farm skills. Mrs Jones was preparing us for taking part in demonstrations and I sure wanted to get a blue ribbon before Idris could win any Scout badges. We two were in competition all the time. Soon a Campfire Bluebird Group was started for little girls and the ladies of the valley got together for sewing parties, so the old schoolroom kept right on serving the community. Home and local happenings were the focus of our lives, with national and world news impinging but lightly, thanks to the love and care of our family.

I realise now, how fortunate we were, how privileged to be amongst the survivors and how little true sympathy we children had for those who fought for our freedom. Our imaginations could not envisage the horrors inflicted upon thousands in far-off lands.

When the news came in 1944 that the Allies had landed in France and were at last driving the enemy back from its conquered territory we shared the sense of relief and hope that our elders expressed. The older boys followed the progress of the advance, vowing to add their strength to the armed forces as soon as they were able to enlist, but most of us simply wanted to hear the word Victory.

It came at last after another year of war and the news was a few hours old when I found Mom and Zeb opening a bottle of home-made wine at 7 am on the morning of May 8th, 1945.

'Go and wake the boys, Berta May and tell them to come and celebrate. We've won the war!' said Mom.

I hammered on the bunkhouse door like I'd never done before.

'Wakey wakey,' I shouted like I'd heard on the radio. 'Get up, you lazy lot, Mom's getting drunk in the kitchen.'

'What?' Dan's head shot off the pillow. 'What's up? You ill or something?'

'Go away,' muttered Freddie.

'WE'VE WON THE WAR,' I shouted and marched out

singing, 'I'm a Yankee Doodle Dandy.' They were after me within seconds and we all got to drink wine for the first time in our lives, singing and cavorting around the place like wild horses.

'When can we go home?' asked Dan.

'Will Trefor be coming back soon?' I wanted to know.

'I'll have the bunkhouse to myself, when you're gone,' mused Freddie.

'Now sober down and eat something, do,' said Mom at last, 'and don't count your chickens before they're hatched. The Germans are beaten, but we still have to finish off the Japs, so I guess there'll be no going home yet awhile.'

'Aw, Auntie Cass, won't take no time for our boys to finish the job off,' boasted Idris. 'Guess I'll start packing my bags come Friday.'

'You better get dressed and start out to school first,' she told him, 'and hope your teachers don't smell your breath.'

But neither our teachers nor anyone else was likely to attempt to curb our exuberance that day, for one and all were in jubilant mood. 'Take the rest of the day off,' we were told at dinner recess, 'and have a holiday tomorrow too'. We sang songs of triumph in the bus, all the way to the end of the dirt road.

'Now they'll have to keep their promise and grade the next two miles,' said Mom, 'so's the bus can come clear on up for you.'

2

By the time the excitement died down, we had letters from Wales and boy, were they celebrating?

'Listen to this,' said Dan. 'Auntie Megan says they had a party for five hundred people at Cwmavon chapel.'

'Five hundred?' queried Mom. 'That's the whole of Cusick. Are you sure?'

'Certain,' he said. 'And a sevice and a tea and at the Garn there was a parade and just look at this cutting from the paper.'

'Every street had a celebration,' he read. 'There were bonfires all round and at Talywaun Cross they had an open-air dance that lasted till 2am. Then they collected food and had a tea in Albert Field and two people played accordions on top of the Air Raid Shelter. Coo, I wish I'd been there. Must have been real wild. Hey look, I know that man.'

'Auntie Megan says some of the family is going on the air,' I told them, reading my own letter. 'The Garn Gleeman and the Ladies Choir and a Band is to be on the Forces Programme. Will your Pop be singing, I wonder?'

'Sure to be,' said Dan, 'and Grancher and Uncle Tom. I shall join the choir myself as soon as I get home.'

'You ent old enough,' said Idris.

'Fifteen I'll be, come August, and my voice is breaking so I'll be ready for the Tenors by the time we get back.'

It must have seemed a long wait for him until VJ Day came and the world was free of war. Meanwhile, the army in Europe was liberating prisoners and nations which had been under German domination. Unknown to us, one of the family who I suppose must be a sort of cousin of mine, had been captured two years earlier. Sam had disappeared after an abortive parachute landing over Belgium. He had spent an horrific imprisonment in one of the worst of the POW camps and was unrecognisable when he returned home, an invalid and a nervous wreck.

'Still,' wrote Auntie Megan, 'he is alive and will recover in time and I suppose we are lucky to have lost only one of the family during the war. We are looking forward to having Lizzie home and wondering how soon Trefor will be demobbed. Tell the children we can't wait to see them. There have been a few changes in the schools, so Idris and Sheila will have to sit an examination to see can they go to the Grammar. Varteg and the Garn is only for children up to 11.'

'Can't make head nor tail of that, I can't,' said Bessie. 'Anyway, I am none too sure I shall be going back. My job in the creamery keeps me and my girls fed and clothed and who knows whether I could get one back home? We might as well stop here.'

She had been talking of staying in Newport ever since her husband was killed, but neither Mom nor Auntie Sarah had thought she meant it. Nor were they sure she would be allowed to stay, but it seemed she was determined to find out.

Slowly, arrangements for Dan, Idris, Pat and Frank to leave us were made, papers stamped and tickets bought. The few other British children who had come to Pend Oreille County were to travel at the same time and escorts were promised. As the time drew near, I began to feel sorry that they were going. How empty the house would seem; how much extra work there would be for me and Mom and Freddie, without Dan's help; and school would never be the same again once Idris had gone, for all our quarrelling and arguments.

At the very last minute, Bessie could not see them go.

'Breaking my heart I was, see,' she confided in Mom on the last day when we went to see them all off at the station. 'Much as I do like it here and the girls all nicely settled and the place so friendly just like home, it's not the same, is it? On the Garn I was born and on the Garn I will die and oh, Sarah how ever did you tear yourself away?'

She wiped her eyes and busied herself with the luggage.

'Thank you all so much for all you have done - paying our bills and letting us have the house and so on. There'll be a welcome in Wales for each and every one of you, if ever you can get over to see us.'

We kissed the girls and Bessie, hugged Dan and Idris and Frank.

'I am very grateful to you,' he said stiffly, shaking hands with Mom and Auntie Sarah. 'I cannot tell you how happy I have been. I hope one day I may return your hospitality.' There were tears in the eyes of us all. As the train steamed out, I waved until I could see it no longer, my heart heavy and my lips pinched tight to hold from crying.

'I wish the war hadn't ended,' I said.

3

That not being a tremendously popular sentiment, I amended it to a wish that something new might happen to relieve the boredom that I feared lay ahead. If Auntie Sarah's house seemed quiet, there was a silence worse than Church round the corner, where only Zeb remained. Dolls and books were gone from sight, no socks or jumpers lay around and the furniture was deathly tidy. I hated it.

'Wait till Trefor do come,' comforted Zeb. 'He'll bring a bit of life into the place again.'

We motored home, Mom putting her foot down hard and the old car swaying round the bends and bouncing over rough patches.

'I sure hope they hurry and fix this highway,' she said, 'it's all well and good putting the speed limit up again to fifty, but the surface needs oiling real bad.'

Freddie and I said nothing. We stared out the window without seeing much and were so quiet that Mom accused us of sulking.

'Boredom is all in the mind,' she admonished. 'Busy people do not get bored,' and she must have spent the rest of the journey making plans to keep us occupied, for I'm sure there were never two more hard-worked children in all Pend Oreille than me and Fred throughout all that fall. With tending stock and preparing for winter, stacking firewood and mending tackle, our hands and backs ached before we even set out for school. Then there were lessons to do in the evening and letters to write, gifts to make for Christmas and costumes to create out of crepe paper. The latter were for us to wear in our church pantomime, a new venture which gave us hours of fun.

Yes, fun we had after all, with our neighbours and friends who were putting their all into making the most of the first post-war Christmas, so that boredom was forgotten and life was there to be enjoyed. We got down to town on fourth December to see a pipe band parade and saw Santa in the cafe in Cusick.

'And I guess it is nice to be just us four again,' I said on a Saturday evening when Alec had come just in time for supper. There was a cosiness about the old kitchen, snugly warm at the centre of our homestead while snowflakes drifted past the windows.

Mom smiled. She was stitching a collar to put on a shirt she was making, while Fred and I had got our paint boxes to make Christmas cards. She too was having more fun now her responsibilities were fewer and she had time for some social life.

'I only hope they are as happy over there in Wales,' she said. 'No doubt we shall soon hear how things are with them, but in the meantime I sure am glad we got that food parcel off in good time.'

'What did you send?' asked Alec.

'Dried goods, mainly - raisins and currants, beans and suet. Some candy bars for the children and a tin of maple syrup.'

'And I put some comic papers in, because Bessie said they could hardly ever get one,' I said.

'That should help out a bit,' agreed Alec. 'Has anyone heard from Trefor yet?'

'No,' Mom sighed. This was the one blight on our happiness, the lack of news from him. We knew he was safely back in England and had been given a medal for his wartime bravery, but remained in the army and had given us no idea of his plans.

'It's too bad of him,' said Alec. 'If he doesn't intend coming home for a spell, all he has to do is to say so and we shall know where we stand. I shall write and give him a piece of my mind. As a matter of fact, I would like to know myself, because of the house. We could let a part of it for a year or two if neither he nor Bethan is coming.'

'Bethan is back in Hollywood,' I told him. 'She's going to be on the movies.'

'I know. She never gives up trying and I'm sure the troops appreciated her entertaining them. Perhaps we'll yet see her on the screen.'

'I've finished four cards,' cried Fred. 'Guess I'll stop now. Look, Mom.'

'That's real nice,' she said. 'I like the picture of the forest. Would you like to sprinkle some glitter on the trees?'

'Yes I would.'

'You have to spread some of this glue first,' she said, taking the top off a little tube. 'Then sprinkle the glitter, just lightly, not too much.'

Then I glittered my cards too and we set them aside to dry. No matter how annoyed Mom was with him, I would be sending the best of mine to Trefor.

What Alec said to him, I have no idea, but a long letter to Mom arrived with the first thaw in March, along with newspapers and mail from Auntie Megan. There was a letter for me from Dan.

'Dear Berta May,   20.2.4€

We have had a bad winter and the roads were blocked in places, but nowhere near as much as we got in Pend Oreille I keep telling them. Mam and Dad can't get over how much me and Idris have grown. I think Grancher expected me to be still in short trousers.

I am working on the farm and they say your Mam have done a good job teaching me all the jobs, but I do a bit of work for a man up the valley as well to earn a bit extra. Food is still rationed here but with our hens and rabbits we do all rite like you do.

Our Idris passed the scholarship exam to go to Abersychan Grammar but Sheila didn't so she's at the British. They've got a new stitherum of a name for it but who cares? Mabel did her Shirley Temple act at the Christmas concert and brought the house down. Mam says she's a show off. Auntie Bessie got a job at the plastics factory down Cwmavon in the old brewery where they used to make clothes. She's got her name down for a council house but will have to wait her turn but Lizzie is letting them live with her.

There's some new factories opening. A big one making nylon and taking on a lot of workers, which is a good thing, but the munitions laying people off because they don't need weapons anymore. There was a big strike about it last December.

Well now I am going to rite to Frank and tell him about the open cast up Blaenavon, an awful mess they have left and will they ever put it rite? He has to sit some awful hard exam soon - rather him than me, but then I'm not the brainy type. Probably be Prime Minister one day he will. I think his gran's been bad this winter.

Love to Mom and all. Dan

P.S. We got three ponies on the mountain. Tell you more next time.'

By the time I had worked my way through that and puzzled over some of the items, Mom had finished reading Trefor's letter. She was sitting perfectly still and looking sad.

'What is it Mom? What does Tref say? Is he OK?'

'Yes, he's OK honey, but we won't be seeing him yet

130

awhile.' She smiled, shook her head and tried to sound cheerful.

'Trefor's decided to stay over there,' she said. 'He thinks he can make good as a journalist and wants to try life in Wales, at least for a year or two. Fact is, Berta May, our Tref is Welsh through and through and his roots are pulling him home. I cannot blame him, but I wish it were not so.'

'Oh Momma, how could he? We need him so.' I was near to tears.

'I know, honey. But that is where he was born and where his own Momma lived and died. Your Pop used to say, 'I think Trefor will go back some day, if Leonie will go with him.

Well, she didn't go and it took a war to send him, but it seems he means to stay. I am sure he will visit us when he can.'

To tell the truth, Trefor was already more of a happy memory to me than a real person, for I had been only five years old when he left. I doubt whether Freddie could even recall his face, but I think Mom had always seen in him a younger version of Pop. She was truly sad to know he would not return and for her sake I too was dejected.

Mercifully, Alec was firmly established in his engineering job and although he travelled extensively around the state, his home base was Greyroofs. To his great joy, although the end of the war had come before some of his plans to harness the power of the Pend Oreille by building more dams and generating stations could be accomplished, there was still the need for them. He was deep into measuring water flow and other technical stuff and earning a good salary. We could rely on Alec.

4

'Is she ever going to stop growing?' wailed Mom more than once during the next couple of years, trying to fit me out with new shoes and clothes for school. Both Fred and I had become very tall for our ages and were for ever needing the next size up.

'They sure don't take after me,' she would add, looking at her well-rounded figure against our athletic slimness. We were lucky. To be slim was to be beautiful, according to our magazines and the movie stars whom we worshipped in our teens, though I would have liked better to be a peroxide blonde than a brunette. Sport figured high in our best activities, both in school and out, and both of us were playing in teams during that time. The only thing Fred could not manage was football, because he might damage his leg if things became too rough, but in swimming, tennis and horse riding, he was equal to most. Mom spent a good deal of money on our equipment and our travel, but grudged not a penny.

There came chances too to get away to camp in summer recess and Mom was all in favour of our doing this. We got to Priest Lake and out west to Skagit valley and over into Canada and I just loved the water sports. It was in summer camp I met my first boyfriend, whom I thought the handsomest person after Clark Gable. For two whole weeks I tackled canoeing and rock climbing and rafting no matter how scared I might be, for I desperately needed his admiration. I spent hours washing and tidying myself each evening, hoping to be chosen as his partner for games or dancing and went home wearing a dreamy smile, certain that every mail would bring me a letter post-marked Seattle.

Alas, our friendship had meant nothing to him and I wasted the remainder of the vacation in love-sick listlessness. I also wasted half my allowance on postage stamps and missed out on several fairs because I had no heart to socialise with my old friends. When Fred and Mom came home with prizes, I was secretly green with envy, but too proud to admit it.

I took solace in reading romantic poetry, committing verses to heart and reciting them aloud whenever I was alone. Curled up on my bed one wet afternoon, I took from my desk a packet which had lain under my notebooks and pens for years. I began to read Trefor's diaries and poems.

In the diaries, I soon lost interest, but the sentiments he had expressed in verse were of immediate appeal to me. Written while he was a teenager and very much in love with Leonie Petersen, they brought tears to my eyes. I had never suspected that my brother Trefor, he of the dancing dark eyes and mischievous grin, could write with such feeling. I began to make fair copies of my favourite ones, in italic script for display on the walls of my room.

'You gonna mooch around next week, too?' asked Mom, 'or will you come down to the coast with the us? Auntie Sarah told me there's a train excursion Wednesday and I thought we all might go. That is, if seeing the ocean and spending two days in our company is not beneath you?'

She was, naturally, becoming exasperated with my languishing on the deck all day while my chores remained undone.

'Guess I might as well,' I sighed. 'Nothing is likely to happen here.'

'Then jump to it and get started on this list of jobs so we can all go off with a clear conscience.'

Reluctantly, I tied up my hair, put on denims and tee shirt and joined her and Fred in the yard. It was not long before I was back in the old routine and more or less enjoying it, but I took good care with my appearance on the day of the excursion, lest there should be any young men worth cultivating on board the train. There was just the outside chance that I might come face to face with my heart-throb in Seattle.

We had visited Spokane city already on several occasions and thought it a huge place, its hotels, shops and offices towering over us and its river criss-crossed with bridges, but Seattle was another world. I was truly pleased to be able to see it.

Streets climbed steeply from the waterfront, to be intersected by avenues which ran parallel to the bay. The waterfront itself was a hive of activity, with docks and cranes, merchant ships and ferries and all the sounds and smells of seaside life. We took a cruise around Puget Sound and wished we might have had a whole vacation in which to see the coastal resorts. Our brief shopping spree, culminating in walking the length of Third to reach the train station, just whetted my appetite for a longer visit.

5

In my next letters to Trefor and Dan, I enclosed both

postcards and photos, for we had taken our Kodak with us and had two whole films of snaps. I knew they would like to see all of us enjoying ourselves but I especially wanted them to admire the picture of me. Nearly as tall as cousin Laurence now, I fancied myself quite stunning in my summer shorts and sun top on board a ferry boat. Someone had likened me to Grace Kelly, which had boosted my ego a lot. I was sure Mr Right was just around the corner.

From that time on, I was in and out of love a hundred times, but in general life in school and home went fairly smoothly. There was a spell in the winter of 1948 when none of us could get to school, for the whole town of Cusick was under water. The Pend Oreille was in flood, riverside properties from Newport to Metaline were damaged, some of them entirely swept away and their occupants made homeless. There was a lot of hardship for weeks though most of the kids thought it great to have no school.

'The worst thing they ever did, closing Stoney School,' moaned more than one mother. 'That was never flooded, nor did it ever fail to open, barring exceptional storms. Miss Lucas saw to it.'

Miss Lucas, now retired and gone to live in Spokane with her brother, had taught school from the late twenties, when the teacher was not only expected to instruct, but to act as janitor and to make hot food for her students in winter. Our little community owed a lot to Miss Lucas, but even she had been unable to stem the tide of progress. With the dwindling numbers of children now living along the creek, the old schoolroom would never again ring to the sound of infant songs.

My sixteenth birthday was coming over the horizon. There was going to be tough competition for the best grades in end-of-year exams and I had determined to graduate with straight A's. Not a little of this determination stemmed from letters recently received from abroad, where Idris was boasting that he would be getting distinctions in something he called School Certificate and Frank was almost graduated through University. I got the impression they thought their system superior to ours, for all they had done well enough while they had been with us, so I set about showing them I was no dumb blonde. Well, they knew I was no blonde but neither was I dumb; and considerably more adult in appearance, I thought, remembering the snaps of the boys in their strange school uniforms.

Math was not my strong point and I needed to concentrate on that, lest Idris beat me hollow, but I was reckoned to be a high flyer in English and Social Studies, while in practical work I had no problem for my hands and eyes were well co-ordinated. With good grades at the end of Junior High, I would have a wide choice of classes next semester. I might even switch to Newport Senior High, in order to specialise, but first I must get those grades.

Then into our lives came two new characters and suddenly there was friction and bad feeling where there had been love. Mom shielded me from the hostility as best she could while I was studying hard, but it hit me all the worse when I surfaced from my books.

There was of course no reason for us to expect Alec to remain single for ever, but we were all taken by surprise when he brought home a young lady and announced his intention of marrying her. She was no great shakes in the beauty line, but Gaynor was well-groomed, well-educated and well-endowed with self-assurance. She was city-bred and about as far removed from the type one would have expected Alec to marry as it was possible to imagine.

'Welcome, my dear,' beamed Mom, pushing a stray hair out of her eyes as she straightened her back. 'Excuse me not offering to shake hands, won't you, but as you see, we are cleaning the yard and all in need of a tub'. As indeed we were, having been sweeping and swilling since dawn.

'Don't mention it, Mrs Watkins.' Gaynor remained on the far side of the gate, shocking pink shoes safely out of reach of mud. Her voice reminded me of Doris Day.

'Sorry to catch you unawares, Mom, but we just came up on the spur of the moment.' I could have killed Alec at that moment for bringing her out of the blue. I knew I did not look my best in stained denims and old red shirt.

'My word, this sure is a cute little old ranch,' she said. 'Just like something out of the Westerns.'

'Take Gaynor into the house and make coffee, while we clean up a bit,' suggested Mom.

Conversation proceeded in a stilted manner. Alec wanted to know how I fared in my exams. Mom asked when they would be getting married.

'Next Spring, we hope,' he answered. 'Luckily, the people renting the house will be gone by then and we can move in. I have written to ask Bethan and Trefor to let me buy out their share.'

'But we shall retain my flat in the city,' said Gaynor. 'I could not bear to bury myself in the outback the whole year round.' From the tone of her voice, we knew our whole life-style was beneath her.

They left after an hour or so. There had been no mention of their staying over.

'Well, she's hardly the type to sleep in the bunkhouse, is she?' said Mom.

'She's awful,' said Fred, who had hardly spoken a word since the arrival of the pair. 'I can't think what Alec sees in her.'

With that sentiment we all were in agreement and the succeeding weekends did little to alter our views, the last straw being when Mom heard Gaynor had been married before.

'Divorced!' she exclaimed on hearing the position when Alec next arrived for a weekend.

'It was none of her doing,' he said gently. 'The marriage lasted only two years and then the scoundrel deserted her. That was five years ago. Gaynor is free to marry again.'

'In my opinion, a marriage is for ever in the sight of God, except in the case of bereavement,' sniffed Mom. 'Had my Fred lived, nothing would have turned my head away from him.'

'But you lost him and married Pop and a very good job you made of your second chance,' he calmed her. 'Could you have happily stayed here alone for ever? Give us a break, Mom. I'm not getting any younger, you know.'

'I know, I know and I hope you will be very happy. I am old fashioned and must try to get on with Gaynor.'

'We want Berta May to be our bridesmaid,' he said. 'Will you, Berta May?'

I was immediately interested, picturing myself in yards of net and chiffon. Perhaps there was something to be said for

136

this idea, after all.

The biggest bone of contention, however, proved to be the house in Newport. Left jointly to Alec, Trefor and Bethan by our Pop, it had lately been occupied by tenants, with Zeb having the basement as usual and Alec staying overnight now and again. To his astonishment, his plans met with opposition.

In early August, who should arrive in town but Bethan herself, visiting for the first time in years. She had come to lay claim to her property, for it was not to her liking that Alec should buy her out. And she had with her a boy of ten.

There ensued a family row whose details I can only imagine, since I was neither present to hear it nor informed of its precise content. I only know that it was the first of many, for Bethan had come to stay. Knowing Alec, I could hardly believe that he allowed his temper to get the better of him, but Zeb said he had heard shouting. He arrived early one Monday afternoon.

'Seems she has decided to quit the stage and get some training after all this time,' he told us. 'Fancies herself as a nurse. Then she wants to settle in Newport and be one of the family as she puts it. So she aims to keep the house and if Alec wants to marry he can buy another for himself. And my word, did the feathers fly when she came face to face with that Gaynor? No love lost there, I can tell you.'

'Two of a sort,' said Mom. 'You reckon I should go and have a word with Bethan?'

'Not if you value your hide,' he said. 'Keep out of the way I would, till things calm down a bit. Thought I might bed down in the bunkhouse for a few nights, help you out with hauling lumber or something?'

'Glad to have you. We three been pretty busy but we got way behind somehow.'

'But who is the boy, Zeb?' Fred wanted to know.

'I don't rightly know. A war orphan, I think she said, who she promised to bring up. Has a foreign look about him, but I've had no chance to talk with him because of all the arguments.'

'Perhaps Sarah can pour some oil on troubled waters and get things settled,' said Mom.

She must have worried some, as to how she would

manage with Alec no longer likely to be helping out and me off to college sooner or later. Hale and hearty though she was in her mid fifties, she was going to have her hands full.

Chapter 10

My visions of myself wearing acres of net were doomed to disappointment as the bride declared she was too old at thirty five for a traditional white gown and anyway divorcees did not dress thus. That being so, she and her attendants were to have silk suits, hers in cream and theirs in pink.

My immediate reaction was to rebel. Hearing that the other bridesmaid, Gaynor's cousin in Spokane, was delighted at the idea, did nothing to lesson my chagrin and I declared I would rather die than have my classmates see me in pink silk. Senior High School students with shoulder-length hair did not consider silk suits the 'in' thing. Denims and shirts were the norm for both boys and girls but if one must dress up for a wedding, one expected to do it in style.

In view of the example being set by the principals in the affair, they could hardly blame me for being so pig-headed. As far as I could see, all the adults concerned were being equally so and my little rebellion was a mere fire-cracker compared with the explosive arguments going on between them.

'Why must you be so obstinate?' asked Alec. 'You were always a little madam, but used to be able to see reason.'

'You have no idea what reason is, yourself,' I retorted. 'The only reason I can see for Gaynor to want to marry you is to get her hands on your money. I do not call it unreasonable to want to dress in fashion,' and I leaped into the saddle and rode on down to 4H meeting.

When I saw the swatch of material, however, and felt the rippling silk in a deep dusky pink and looked at the pattern for the suits in a style straight from the pages of Vogue, I shrugged my shoulders and said I supposed I would have to agree. A visit to a dressmaker was arranged. Secretly, I thought I would look quite well, so expensively dressed.

My adult relatives, however, continued to pursue their selfish ways and Fred and I used to raise our eyebrows whenever the word 'house' was mentioned, for we were tired of the subject.

'If it weren't for the fact that Gaynor is such a snob, I would say Alec ought to have first call on the house, for he has made more use of it, paid the bills and kept it in good repair,' said Mom to Auntie Sarah. She and Uncle Henry had driven up to visit us.

'I know what you mean. Bethan seems to be expecting too much, but at the same time, there is something equally grasping about Miss Gaynor.'

'Mrs Gaynor,' Mom corrected. 'Not that she lacks money herself, but it must be she who is making Alec so obstinate. He never used to be so.'

I listened no more. 'I'm going to saddle up. I have to be in Cusick by half two.'

Obstinate or not, it was in the end Alec who yielded. Bethan and her adopted son Luke got to stay in the house, while Gaynor's apartment in the city would be home for her and Alec.

'I shall look round for a cabin or a vacant lot where I can build,' he told us. 'I only need something small, for vacations or an overnight stop when I am working down valley. Gaynor will still be employed by the travel agent so will need to be on the spot.'

The next thing we knew, they had decided to bring the wedding forward a couple of months to March, but it was up to the bride and her family to put all the arrangements in hand. We were involved merely in getting my suit made and in choosing a wedding gift.

2

With the turn of the year, we were as usual into the worst of the winter and both Mom and I had a nasty bout of 'flu' which cost me some time off school and left her feeling listless and unlike herself. Neither rest nor tonics seemed to bring her back to normal, so poor Fred had more than his fair share of farm chores to do. That was hard on him, as he was trying real hard in school and hoping to make as good grades as I had done.

'Wow, was that ever a hard ride,' he said one evening. coming in covered in snow and throwing a pile of mail on the table. 'If it snows all weekend, I doubt the trail will be passable, come Monday.'

He took off his jacket and I got a hot drink for him, while Mom sorted the letters.

'Hello,' she said in surprise, 'this one is strange.'

Most of our mail from Wales now came by air, the flimsy blue envelopes being at once recognisable. Packages and newspapers came surface mail, but it was a long time since we had received a bulky, old fashioned envelope of the type now in Mom's hand.

'Well, open it and see what it is,' I told her and passed a table knife across. She slit it open. She read the large typed pages with a frown. Then she exclaimed, 'I simply don't believe it!'

'What?' we both asked. 'Tell us Mom. Is it bad news?'

'Sad news, not bad news. In fact, it is a stroke of good fortune, but I'm real sorry for Frank.'

'For heaven's sake, will you tell us then?'

'Let me get my breath, I'm so surprised I can hardly speak. Now then, I am sorry to hear that Frank's grandmother died in December and that poor boy is now all alone in the world except for us. We must write at once. I wonder will he keep that great big house to live in all alone?'

'Mom, he's turned twenty one now, he may be married for all we know. He hasn't written in an age.'

'Yes, yes, I know. Now this is the bit that took my breath away. She has left us some of her money. Her lawyer says there is three thousand pounds for me. Also, three thousand each for you, 'To be used for the purpose of education or educational travel,' it says here.'

'Wow!' For a moment we too were dumb-struck, staring at each other with open mouths and startled eyes.

'How much will that be in real money?' Mom asked. We did a few calculations on the back of the envelope. About four US dollars to the pound, we thought, so that came out at twelve thousand dollars each.

'And there is a thousand for Auntie Sarah in recognition of her kindness to Frank during the war. That must have been one very rich old lady! And to think I never heard of her until she wrote me.'

If anything could have aroused Mom from her

listlessness, that was the very thing. Both she and I felt better than we had for a month. Had we not been snowed in for a spell, we'd have been rushing down to see the folks in Newport, but as it was, we got hours of pleasure from the thought of all those dollars getting into our bank account.

'We're rich,' Fred said over and over again.

'No you're not. You only get your money for your education,' said Mom. 'I'm the one who is rich.'

'Well, at least I get to do the things rich folks do.' He whistled the whole day long until I threw things at him. My imagination was running riot with foreign travel and I wished I could get some brochures from the city.

Getting there for the final fitting of my wedding outfit involved Mom and me in a hair-raising drive up through the pass to Spokane while another snowstorm was under way, but we made it in safety. After the tedious hour at the dress-maker's, we had lunch and spent a couple of hours shopping.

'Just think', said Mom, 'when the money comes through, I shall be able to afford a few new things for the house. We might even get a telephone installed.'

'I shall go to Wales,' I announced.

3

To say Mom was alarmed at hearing my proclamation was an understatement, for she at once feared I would stay overseas as Trefor had done. I assured her that I was merely thinking of an educational trip. I thought of many others during the next few weeks, but Alec's wedding was looming large and our main anxiety was, would late snow prevent our getting there?

It was a fashionable affair, no matter if I thought the bride less than attractive. Her family and friends from the coast appeared to have spent a great deal of money on their clothes and their gifts.

'Perhaps Alec has done well for himself, after all,' muttered Mom, 'though all this finery may be rented, of course.'

We presented a fairly respectable turnout ourselves in my opinion, Uncle Henry in tails and topper, Laurence,

Fred and Danny likewise, Mom and Auntie Sarah in new-length rayon suits with picture hats and even Zeb so gentleman-like that I would not have recognised him if we'd met in the street. Bethan's avant-guard short skirt raised a few eyebrows.

'To the Bride and Groom,' we raised our glasses.

'To absent friends,' we concluded the toasts and then we wondered whether Trefor and Dan and others would be thinking of us at that moment.

'Not a chance,' said Fred. 'They'll be sound asleep in bed.'

'Sure to have stayed up an hour to drink Alec's health,' said Zeb. 'You can depend upon it.'

There were cards with comic greetings and a telegram or two, which Joe Walker the Best Man read out slowly with a bit of prompting from Alec. Then a waiter handed him a piece of paper.

'Just in the nick of time,' said Joe. 'A cable all the way from Wales.'

TO ALEC AND GAYNOR GREETINGS AND LOVE FROM ALL WATKINS.

'My word, that sure was a kind thought,' said Mom.

'Trust Trefor,' said Auntie Sarah. 'He knows how to do these things.'

'Wish we could send them a parcel of this food,' said Mom.

'They still have sugar and butter rationing according to what I heard.'

'If it says it in the Free Press, it has to be true,' said Uncle Henry, 'now Trefor is on their staff.'

'We've had a bundle of papers this week,' said Mom, 'but no time to read them. I aim to be real lazy for a day or two now and catch up on all he's written.'

Well, to hear her, you might think he had composed the whole paper, but it sure did add interest to the news, knowing he had been on the scene and written things down. She and Fred and I took off our wedding finery round about half eight and prepared to put our feet up.

'I can't think how women can stand these high heels all day long,' I groaned. 'My feet feel as if they've marched a thousand miles.'

'Pride must bear pain,' Mom laughed. 'You still want to work in the city?'

4

Since we had never seen the valley from which the Watkins had come, we could hardly envisage what the creation of a new town there would mean, but it was interesting to follow Trefor's story through the months when the planners in Wales were working on their plans. Our own town of Newport had around a thousand inhabitants, Ione only five hundred, so rolling them together with all the settlements that lay between the two would hardly make a place as big as they planned to build around Cwmbran.

'They must be desperate for housing,' said Mom, 'to think of taking all that good land.'

'And then they have to drown a lot more in making a reservoir to supply the town with water,' added Fred.

'More jobs than workers, it says here,' I read. 'The factories need workers and the workers need houses and the houses need water. That's progress for you.'

The last thing we were thinking of at that moment was that some of us might get to see that new town before so very long. The dreams and vague plans I had made were to be put into operation some time in the distant future, I thought, when I was through college. I would be twenty two or three by that time and perfectly capable of travelling abroad.

Then by the next mail came another surprise.

'Dear Mom, Berta May and Fred,' wrote Trefor. His letter was typewritten.

'I cannot have my older brother beating me in every way, so am writing to tell you my wonderful news now you have got over his wedding.

Last October, I got engaged to Doris, whom I had met soon after coming out of the forces. She lives near Newport and works in the Council offices.

We kept it quiet for a bit, but have now decided to get married at the end of July as I have the chance of a little house if we put a deposit down now.

144

She is a darling and I know you would all love her (snap enclosed) and just wish you could pop over and meet her.

You will all be getting an invitation of course, Alec and Gaynor as well. I can't tell you how much I am hoping that some of you can come, although I know what a great expense it would be and what a long journey for a short time. When I tell the rest of the family, which I am going to do after allowing time for this letter to reach you first, I know they will all offer accommodation to any or all of you.

And by the way, in case you have not heard of it, this is Festival of Britain year over here. There are lots of things going on, especially in London which you are bound to visit if you come.'

Then the letter continued with news of his work and of the family, but we were into a hectic discussion about ways and means. Three months earlier, it would have been out of the question for any of us to go. Thanks to our recent bequest, the trip was a possibility. Each in our own way, we spent hours working on various schemes during the next month.

'The time has come to make up our minds,' Mom declared at last. 'Sunday after church, we all sit down and thrash out details, see if we can get things cut and dried.'

It seemed she had been beavering away behind our backs, talking to our teachers and ministers and even to Gaynor, who knew a lot about foreign travel through her work. We had a real council of war Sunday morning and all tossed our ideas into the pool for consideration.

What came out was a plan for Mom and me to attend the wedding. Fred was adamant that his commitments with school and summer camp, where he had volunteered to work for a month, were more important to him this year than a wedding in Wales.

'Sorry if I sound unfriendly,' he said, 'but after all, I can't even remember Tref and would rather save my money for the future.'

I, on the other hand, was more than a little interested in Mom's proposal for me to make an extended visit, travelling in Britain and possibly France, with maybe the chance to enrol on a course of study for a semester. I was astonished at her having the courage to suggest it. Suppose

I should decide not to return, like Trefor had done?

'No chance,' she smiled. 'He was born in Britain, you were not. Makes all the difference when it comes to residency. I checked all that.'

'But you will come with me? Trefor sure does want to have you there, Mom, I know he does.'

'I'd like to. Depends on whether I can get Zeb to take over up here. It would be for several weeks, see, even though I'd only have a short time in Wales.'

Air travel was only for the very rich and the business world in 1951. Ordinary folk still travelled by train and sea, a journey of at least ten days from where we lived and a toil of an undertaking to get only a couple of weeks with one's family.

'We must think of the journey as a big adventure, just as important as the wedding,' I told her. 'When can we start making reservations?'

'As soon as I have made certain Fred's arrangements are all fixed and Zeb is willing. I wonder whether Alec has decided to go?'

Zeb was willing. He would have loved a quick visit to his old home himself, but that being out of the question, was only too ready to assist our going. In fact, he and Mom decided that it would be a good excuse for him to move into our bunkhouse on a permanent basis. Bethan and he were not getting on well together in the town house.

Alec would not be at his brother's wedding, his work on the dam in Box Canyon being at its peak. We suspected that his wife had little inclination to mingle with those of the lower orders, to which band she made it obvious that our family belonged.

Nevertheless, she was of great help to Mom in making our reservations, ironing out some snags and smoothing our passage. Much as I still disliked her, I was grateful to her for the gift of some stylish clothes with which she had finished. Three of the dresses fitted me to perfection and the others I packed in the expectation that Sheila or another of the girls might like them.

We had written Frank, telling him of our plans. He said we must visit with him in Canterbury and he would show us London, if none of our family was able to come from

Wales, so it was arranged that we would fit that in first. We were ready to leave in mid-June as soon as school was out.

4

Mom was as wide-eyed and impressionable as me, for she had travelled very little in her life. As the train swept us away from the mountains and over the endless prairies, we were both intrigued at the new horizons before us. My daily diary was closely packed with details of scenery, people and the meals we had, but I was so glad I was not alone.

'Just think, Bessie came all this way with those five little children, back in thirty nine,' said Mom. 'How ever did she endure it?' For after a time the tedium set in and the fatigue, so that we neither wanted to talk nor to read. I pitied the young family who shared our compartment, the baby fretful, mother tired and father becoming tetchy with his infant girls. In the night, I wished they might move elsewhere.

Stations and cities, docks, hooters and cranes were behind us and we steamed out of New York amidst noise and bustle, just like on the movies. High above the grey water we stood to see the last of our country disappear over the horizon and then the boat was our home for five days. At first, we dared not move alone for fear of getting lost in the maze of gangways and decks, but within twenty four hours, all was familiar. Mom spent a good deal of time relaxing in a deck chair, but I made the most of every facility from swimming to deck quoits. There was a cinema on board and I saw every film they offered from 'Green Grass in Wyoming' to 'Spring in Park Lane.' I vowed eternal friendship with two boys and three girls with whom I had taken up, but as soon as we docked in Southampton I lost their addresses and forgot their names.

There was Frank waiting for us. We would have known him anywhere, we said. Very spick and span in a navy blue pin-stripe suit, he shook hands correctly and then relaxed to throw his arms round us both, a merry grin all over his face.

'Cassie, Berta May, I can't tell you how glad I am to see you.' His perfect English voice, almost forgotten, brought

147

laughter to my lips.

'Frank. We've missed you, I didn't know how much until right now.'

Somehow, we got out of the port and onto the train. It was about mid-day and the sun was shining, the fields yellow with cereals and the trees bright green flashing by.

'Boy, was I ever glad to see an end to that old ocean,' sighed Mom.

'Why, you were just loving it, soaking up sunshine,' I said.

'I was not so,' she contradicted. 'If I had to waste the time, I figured I might as well waste it in comfort, but I'd rather have been turning the hay.'

'I suppose we could find you a job on the farm if you wish,' laughed Frank, 'but I have quite a lot to show you. There will be no time to be bored for the next few days.'

How right he was. First, we went to Canterbury, where he was still living in his grandmother's old house.

'I am sorry it is so untidy and I hope you will not find it too cold,' he said, 'With me away in Oxford and such a small ration of coal for heating, I am afraid it is getting damp. I shall sell it eventually and buy a smaller place for myself.'

'It sure is a beauty of a house,' said Mom as we looked into all the rooms, 'but the upkeep must cost a packet. A house for a big family, this is. It must have been a worry for your grandmother.'

'Not until she could not heat it or find a maid,' he said. 'She had plenty of money for upkeep but could not get staff once the war started. It did her health no good, being alone all that time.'

'Poor lady,' said Mom. 'We are all indebted to her.'

'She would be very happy to know you were able to make good use of her bequest,' he said. 'Now, when you are settled in, come down to the kitchen for tea and we will make plans.'

5

On the first day, he showed us round Canterbury, a truly historic town with an ancient cathedral which was a day's work in itself to view. We walked miles through narrow streets and over stone floors, bought some cards to send home and returned exhausted to the house.

'Can you face London tomorrow?' asked Frank, 'or would you rather leave that for another day?'

'Got to see all we can while we have the chance,' said Mom.

'That's the spirit. We shall need more than one day there, anyway. It would be best if we took some sandwiches, I think, to avoid wasting time in queues for food.'

'Let me help you make them,' I said and we left Mom to have a quick sleep.

'Tell me all about yourself,' I said as we chopped tomatoes and sliced bread. 'Have you finished college now?'

So I got to hear about his course in Oxford and he promised to take me up there on a visit after Mom had gone home.

'I just can't describe it,' he said. 'You have to be there to understand.' He told me his plans and hopes.

'You got a girl?' I asked.

'Sometimes.' He laughed. 'I had one of whom I was very fond, but she took off with a Medic last winter. Left me high and dry, but I can usually find someone to take to the ball. Pity we'll be coming down next weekend and there's nothing special to which I can take you. You would go down well and it would boost my ego to have you there. I bet all the lads rave over you.'

I blushed. 'Not that I have noticed. My latest, he moved back east with his parents in May. I'm writing to two others.'

I was running up a lot of expense with all the cards I was sending, but that came to an end very soon, for our week of sightseeing left little time or energy for sending mail.

It was almost an hour's train journey to London and we passed through mile after mile of pretty country though not a mountain in sight.

'I thought it would be all streets,' said Mom.

Frank laughed. 'Most foreign visitors think that, in spite of all the pictures in the guide books. We shall be into the city soon enough.'

149

The approach to the capital itself was through a district of grey houses packed together in close streets where black cars fought red buses for right of way. Here and there was a glimpse of green, a playing field or a few trees.

'This is London?' I asked. 'Where is Big Ben and the Palace?'

'Ten minutes away,' he laughed. 'It's a big place, you know. Thirty miles or more from one side of the city to the other, so we shall not be in the middle for a few minutes yet. See that big open space? That's one of the bomb sites, not yet rebuilt.'

There were new blocks of flats towering over the old rows of houses and stations where quiet crowds pushed their way onto the train.

'Now look there,' ordered Frank, pointing to his left at a soaring needle-like structure. 'That's the Skylon. Down there is the Festival of Britain site where we'll be going the next time we come up. We are now crossing the Thames. London, here we come.'

We arrived at an echoing smoky terminal with grimy wrought ironwork supporting cracked glass roofs and I wondered whether it had been worth the journey.

'This is Charing Cross.' Frank told us, pointing to a memorial outside the station. 'It is the last in a series which King Edward the First erected to the memory of his wife Queen Eleanor. She died in the north and each cross marks a resting point of her coffin when he brought her to Westminster to buried.'

'When was that?' I asked.

'I forget the precise date, round about the twelve hundred mark, I suppose. Now we'll take a bus to Hyde Park Corner rather than take the tube, so I can point things out along the way.'

A wait in a queue and we were up on top of one of their two-decked buses, seeing London from on high. We passed Trafalgar Square, the National Gallery and Picadilly Circus and I was real glad traffic moved so slowly for we would have surely missed a lot had it run at speed.

'My, just look there. A real live English policeman in his helmet and white gloves, directing the traffic,' said Mom, as excited as a child as we stepped off the bus.

'Excuse me, young man, may I take your photograph?' she asked the guard at the gate of Buckingham Palace when we arrived after a walk through Green Park. 'Berta May and Frank, do go and stand either side of him will you? I gotta send this home for Alec to see.'

I shuddered in embarrassment. Our voices and clothes gave us away as American tourists, without her behaving thus.

'Mom, must you?' I whispered. Frank laughed and told me not to worry. 'The guards get used to it,' he said, 'but don't expect them to answer you.'

We ate our sandwiches in the park, walked on down to Westminster Abbey and spent an hour and a half in there. It was overpowering in its magnificence, even to my ignorant eye. I knew nothing about architecture; medieval, renaissance or perpendicular meant nothing to me, but the sheer majesty of the place was stunning. We bought the guide books and said we must come again after reading them. Foot-sore and hungry, we let Frank lead us back to the station. The lights were lit on the Skylon as we crossed Waterloo bridge.

Chapter 11

After that taste of historic London, Frank took us next day to the Festival exhibition on the south bank of the Thames. People were flocking there in their thousands, flags were flying everywhere and although the day had started out dull, it grew hotter as the hours passed.

We queued for admission to most things. They stand in queues most patiently in Britain and woe betide any excitable foreigners who try to jump their turn. There were French and others rubbing shoulders with us all day long and once I was sure I heard a voice like Dan's. I wanted to shout, 'Are you from Wales?' but thought better of it.

It was the electronic equipment in the Dome of Discovery that was attracting most attention and I took my turn at pressing buttons and watching lights flash. Television was already becoming fairly common back home, but apart from that I had little understanding of what was on display.

'I'm not of a scientific turn of mind, either,' confessed Frank when I said I had seen enough. 'How about getting a snack and then going along to Battersea Gardens?'

That was a refreshing change. First we had a breath of fresh air along the river side, then sat on the grass to eat our lunch. After that, we spent an hour in the pleasure park. I never would have expected Frank to have a taste for hair-raising rides but I was wrong. All three of us screamed and shouted in exhilaration as we were swirled and spun into dizziness. From atop the Big Wheel, we saw the whole expanse of the river, the ancient and the modern side by side along its banks and the masses of insect-size people scurrying about their business.

'Now I am going to be selfish,' said Frank when we left. 'I have no idea whether you like the same sort of music as I like, but as soon as I heard you were coming I got three tickets for tonight's concert in the new Festival Hall. I hope you will not mind.'

Far from minding, we were delighted, for we had read of this revolutionary design of concert hall and knew of the high standard of music performed there. It had never been our luck to hear a live symphony orchestra, so just being there watching and listening was a new experience. As for the music, it was something light by Mozart and we loved every moment of its magic. Then there was the William Tell Overture and Handel's Water Music and we came out onto the Embankment with stars in our eyes.

'Thank you, Frank, that was something I shall never forget,' said Mom, taking his arm as we set off over the bridge to Charing Cross Station. The lights were twinkling and reflecting in the river. Trains rumbled beside us and a lone plane crossed the sky far out to our right.

'It was a perfect day,' I agreed.

We were too tired to move on the next morning, so had a day's rest. Rain had set in but we agreed that, whatever the weather, we must put our best feet forward the next day, for that would be our last with Frank.

'And you must see the Tower at the very least,' he said.

2

Relentlessy, we tramped from one stone building to another, umbrellas up and plastic macks on. We peered at our guide book and listened to Frank telling us about gatehouses, drawbridges and vaults. In the White Tower we spent some time, moving from armoury to chapel, sword room to cannon room. Then out into the Crown Jewels in the Wakefield Tower. By the time we had admired those and shuffled along with the crowd to the exit, we were all pretty tired.

'If you've had enough,' said Frank, 'why not go out along the river front and take some photos? Then we'll take the tube into the city and keep out of the rain.'

Of course, Mom had to take snaps of the Beafeaters and then we saw a river boat ride advertised, so instead of riding underground we got to sail along the Thames right up to Westminster. There was a man with a loud hailer telling us what to look at as we cruised along and we saw Somerset House where they kept all the family records from way back as well as a glimpse of St Paul's Cathedral. There were pleasure boats and barges, little rowing boats and big

153

steamers going up and down and all across the river.

'When you come back after the wedding, Berta May, I will take you to Hampton Court,' said Frank. 'There is so much more to see but not enough time for it all.'

Next morning, he escorted us into London again, got us one of those black taxi cabs to Paddington Station and saw us onto the train for Newport, Monmouthshire.

'At least we shall not forget where to get off,' said Mom. 'Tell you what, Berta May, this touristing sure is hard on the feet. Give me my working boots in place of these shoes any day. I hope those new sandals I bought will be more comfortable. Do me a favour and wake me when we get to Wales, honey.' She kicked off the offending shoes, settled into the most comfortable postion she could find and went to sleep. I was pretty drowsy myself.

'You missed a lot of nice farm land but nothing worth shouting about,' I told her when I decided at last to wake her. 'We are about half way there and I got a cup of tea for you from the guy who came round, so drink it while it's hot. I think the next stop is Bristol.'

We went through a tunnel not long after that and then there were hills to our right and flat ground on the left. 'Newport, Newport. Passengers for Pontypool Road, Abergavenny and Hereford change at Newport,' a guard went all along the train making this announcement. We collected our things together, pulled on our coats and took our suitcases off the rack.

'This is it,' I said as the train slowly steamed across a mud-bank river and into the station. 'We are in Wales and the sun is shining.'

3

Trefor had been unsure of whether he would be free to meet us, but had assured us that several of the family would be at Pontypool Road, just half an hour along the line towards the north. We collected our big trunk from the guard's van and stood back as the train pulled out. Other passengers quickly went their way and no-one paid us any heed.

'The train now standing at Platform Three' screeched a

voice from on high, 'is the one forty five to Shrewsbury, calling at Pontypool, Abergavenny, Hereford,....'

'That's the one,' we both said at the same time.

There being no porter in sight, we took one handle of the trunk each and struggled over to the platform behind us, then returned to fetch our suitcases. Just as we were manoeuvring the load into the nearest carriage, a young man ran along the platform and skidded to a halt by my side.

'Auntie Cass, Berta May, sorry I'm late But I went to get some things for Mam and it took longer than I expected.' He was helping us while he talked, heaving the trunk aboard and slamming the door. A whistle blew and we sank onto the seats.

'Idris, I would never have known you if it weren't for your voice,' said Mom.

'I never thought of you coming,' I said. 'Why aren't you at college?'

'School,' he corrected me. 'Grammar School until eighteen, then college. And anyway, why aren't you?'

'Just like old times,' laughed Mom, 'you two arguing already. By the by, Frank sent his regards and hopes to see you soon.'

'Good. He's going to show me round Oxford. I'll be going there next year if I can get a Senior Scholarship.'

'Where are we now, Idris?' I asked. 'This is a pretty valley. Is it the one where you all live?'

'No, this is the Usk. We shall be seeing the Afon Lwyd in a few minutes and then you'll be able to see the mountains. Look, over there above the trees, that's the start of them. There'll be a big new town here within a year or two, you can see where they are starting work now.'

'We read about that in the paper,' said Mom. 'The night of Alec's wedding, that was.'

'How's Alec then? I'd like to see those dams he's working on.' After a few minutes catching up on news, we felt the train losing speed. 'Here we are, Pontypool Road and the end of the line as far as we are concerned. I think Dad will be here with his van and the reception committee.

Sure enough, there was quite a crowd awaiting our arrival and I felt shy of meeting them. For the whole of my life, I had heard about them, written to them, sent photographs and had known six of them well during the war years. Yet here I was, momentarily shaking at the knees at the sight of them.

'Mom!' Trefor broke the ice and stepped forward to throw his arms round her. I looked up at him, dimly remembering the dark hair and twinkling eyes that I had so loved when I was an infant. 'Welcome to Wales,' he said.

Then they all shouted their welcome and we shook about a hundred hands, or so it seemed, for everyone on the platform had come to join in the excitement. Apart from Trefor, Dan and Idris, I had no idea who was whom, but they were all so friendly and welcoming that I was happy to be there. Mom just could not let go Trefor's arm.

In due course, we got into a car with two ladies and a girl, who said she was Pat though she'd grown so I hardly knew her.

'Come in front with me,' said Emmie the driver, 'And our Mam can get to know Auntie Cassie while I point things out to you as we go. Not our car this. We got a loan of it from Lizzie special, like, not to make you ride up the valley on the back of Bobbie's lorry.'

'Is that how the rest of them are travelling?'

'All but Tref. He'll be on his motor bike and probably Idris riding pillion.'

'Now, look at that hill to our right. Top of Pontypool Park that is, you can just see the grotto if you know where to look.'

'And there used to be a tower up there, the Folly as they took down in the war to stop the Germans using it as a landmark,' said Auntie Megan from the rear.

'Park gates on the right now. We're coming into Ponty and not a lot to see apart from shops. There's the Clarence Hotel. Town Hall just round the corner on the left.'

A grey towered building with a clock on top stood a little way back from the road. Emmie concentrated on her driving until the town centre was passed.

'It looks a big place,' said Mom.

'What, Ponty big? Just wait till you see Cardiff.'

'They're building a lot of new houses up the hill there at Trevethin,' said Emmie. 'Our Bessie thinks she might get one, now she's got a job at the nylon factory.'

'She'd be better off to wait for one up Varteg,' said Auntie Megan. 'Look, there's our hospital.'

'Why, it looks like a fairy tale castle,' said Mom. 'They sure do build in the most unlikely places.' We were watching the valley become narrower, the houses clinging to the hill sides while the road followed the river upstream.

'We're taking you up to our Bobbie's first for tea,' said Auntie Megan. 'Old Idris and Jane just can't wait to meet you but he wasn't fit to come to the station and there's Sam has to be watched. A bit of a squash it will be to fit into their place all at once but we can sit in the garden and all get to know each other.'

So then we started going up hill quite steeply and they continued telling us the names of the places, though to us it seemed like one long town without a break. Suddenly, we caught sight of a big mound of black soil. The beautiful green mountains were beyond, but this artificial hill blocked our view.

'Pit waste,' said Megan. 'Going to clear it soon, they are and make the British safe. All sorts of plans for it, they have, but what they give with one hand they d'take away with the other. Talking of open cast over Lower Varteg now, like they done at Blaenavon. Over there on your left that will be, and look, Berta May, I nearly forgot to tell you. Right over there up the hill, that's where your Dad lived on Craig Ddu.'

Which was all very interesting but confusing and I was sure I would never find my way around here. We drew up in a narrow lane in front of a low white cottage, where an old man and a lady stood at the gate.

'Welcome to Penylan,' said Uncle Idris, holding out his hand to Mom. Auntie Jane hugged and kissed me.

'I never thought you would come,' she said with tears in her eyes. 'If I drop dead tomorrow, I will die a happy woman to have had the joy of meeting our Rob's wife and daughter. Come in now, do and I will brew the tea.'

When all the family arrived, we must have been about fourteen in number and we sat in the garden for two hours or more getting acquainted. It was a peaceful spot, with woodland below us and a panoramic view of the mountain over the far side of the valley.

I had more or less learned all their names before Auntie Megan suggested that we move along to her house. Sheila, Mabel and Pat were now in their teens and we had lots to talk about. Fashion and hair styles figured pretty large in our conversation.

'I brought some dresses for you,' I told them, 'but they are at the bottom of the trunk. I'll get them out as soon as I can. Are you able to get clothes any easier now?'

'Yes, when we have the money,' said Sheila. 'I like your trousers, Berta May, they're very stylish.'

'I'd like a pair like that,' said Mabel. 'The only trousers I've got are what I had for helping Grancher with the harvest and I wouldn't be seen dead in them for walking around.'

'Nor I wouldn't,' agreed Pat. 'We better be moving, Mam's got to drive you down to Auntie Megan's and then take the car back to Auntie Lizzie. See you again. Bye, Auntie Jane.'

'I'll be over to see you on Saturday with Doris,' said Trefor 'and we'll take you to see our little property, Mom.'

4

By way of a very steep drop down a narrow tarmaced road, we came to the valley bottom and thence along a dirt road to Auntie Megan's farm house. It was a long narrow building of white-painted stone, with cute little windows set up in the roof to light the bedrooms. It stood about fifty yards above the narrow river and black cattle grazed the meadows round about it. Behind rose the valley side, forested with trees in their full summer green. We heard the clatter of the rail wagons somewhere above, yet the only railroad lines we could see were between us and the river.

'Welcome to Cwmavon,' said Auntie Megan. 'I'll just go call Tom and get him to help carry your luggage. Tom! Tom!' She bustled into the house.

'What a lovely place,' said Mom.

'You really like it?' asked Emmie. 'We were worried you would find it too quiet, but Bessie and the girls said you

158

were used to being a long way out of town.'

'It's just like home,' Mom said, 'except we're a mite higher up and don't have no railroad running through the property.'

'We have two,' laughed Emmie, 'though how much longer trains will run, I don't know. The top line only carries coal and this line down here has only a couple of trains a day.'

Uncle Tom had appeared, a wiry grey-haired man not as tall as Mom but about as weather-beaten, a farmer without a doubt.

With his help, we got the cases and trunk indoors.

'But you'll never get that trunk up our stairs,' he said. 'Have to unpack it down here you will, and carry your stuff up bit by bit.'

'First let me show them their room,' said Auntie Megan.

Emmie was anxious to leave, so waved good bye and drove away.

'She'll be back for supper,' said Auntie Megan, leading the way up a twisting stone stairway which started beside the living room fire place. 'Mind your head, Berta May, you are so tall you could hit it on a beam. Emmie and her hubby and Pat d'live in that cottage down by there, so they are all coming in to see you later. Now this used to be our boys' room. I hope it will be big enough for the two of you.'

'Your boys? I'd forgotten you had boys,' I said.

'Older than the girls they are and adopted after the first war, see, long before you were born. Off and away to war they had to go in '39, but mercifully spared and now both doing very well in their jobs. Arthur in the north and William in the midlands - meet them at the wedding you will, they're both coming.'

'I shall simply never get this family sorted out,' sighed Mom as we started to unpack. 'I just think I know who's who when another couple of them pop up to confuse me.'

'Never mind, relax and just enjoy yourself. Which closet do you want to use?'

'I need the bathroom before anything else,' she said, kicking off her shoes, 'and then a nice long lie on my bed. Take whichever of the closets you like best.' Little did she know she would have to cross the yard to find the lavatory.

It took me all of an hour to carry my clothes up those stairs and then there was no room to pack them all away, so I dragged up the empty trunk and replaced my winter clothes in it. Coming for a whole year had meant bringing an awful lot of things, but as Mom said, I did not want to waste my inheritance on buying everything new.

She slept while I was busy and then we heard a car arrive and voices down below.

'Guess we'd better wash and dress,' I told Mom, 'company has come.'

They were so very friendly, these relatives of ours, and their neighbours too. Some of them dropped in that evening, others came during the next few days and each with an invitation to visit with them.

'Though how we are to fit in half of the things they say we are to do, I fail to see,' said Mom later. 'If we ever needed another twelve hours adding to the day, now is the time. Phew! I could sleep for a fortnight.'

5

The girls were pleased with the dresses that I had brought and we had a great time trying them on when they came over on Saturday. Sheila and Pat were already finished school and working, one in a shop and one in a plastics factory. Mabel was at the same school as Idris and studying hard for exams. School was not out until almost end July so I got to see them in their green blazers and all, their uniform as they called it. It sure looked funny to me, boys and girls of my age all dressed alike walking down the street, carrying leather satchels over their shoulders. As for Mom, she was all for stopping the bus so's she might take snaps of them.

Trefor brought his fiancee Saturday too, and we took to Doris like we had never taken to Alec's Gaynor; but truly Doris was a real nice-natured young woman.

'I am very pleased to meet you,' she said politely to Mom, 'and so glad you could come for our wedding. It would not have been the same without you, not for me nor Trefor it wouldn't.'

Now that was real nice, I thought. Mom was quite

overcome at the way everyone treated her like one of the family just as if she were Tref's real mother and I was mighty relieved to find it so, for I had been telling her for two months they were not likely to pin 'Wicked Step-Mother' on her lapel. She and Doris hit it off at once and were soon laughing and chattering as if they were old buddies. We all piled into Uncle Tom's pick-up to go and look at the house Tref was buying, me and him and the three other girls bouncing around on a layer of straw in the back and singing 'She'll be coming round the mountain' - their idea of what all Americans sing.

Twenty minutes and a few bruises later, we were standing in the front room of the tiniest, darlingest house half way up one of those steep hills that abound in this district, where you felt your feet must be set on the roofs of the next row down.

'This is the lounge,' said Doris proudly. 'We've stripped off all the dark old paper and done it with this new emulsion paint and next we shall hang our curtains which are striped pink and gold.'

'Why, you sure got this place fixed up real good,' said Mom at once. 'I like your colour scheme and what a nice view you have from here.'

'That's the Lasgarn Woods,' said Trefor. 'Presented to the public in 1943 while I was overseas, by a Miss Edmonds who had owned property here. A good place for a walk.'

'Come through to the back now,' said Doris.

We went into a larger room with furniture already in place and a square of carpet on the floor. A small kitchen could be seen beyond, with a cooking stove and cupboards on the walls. Everything was light and clean but there were no pictures on the walls. I hoped they would like the one we had brought as our wedding gift.

'We got most of this furniture from my parents,' said Doris, 'but for our bedroom and the lounge we're having new.'

'And our Dad made things for the second bedroom,' said Pat, 'and Auntie Jane made the curtains.'

There was a tiny garden out back, with a gate into a lane which ran along the rear of the whole long terrace.

'I shall be able to keep my bike safe out there,' said

161

Trefor.

He was obviously very happy and very much in love with Doris. I thought them a well-matched pair and just knew they would have years of fun together. We started talking wedding plans.

It was to take place at the end of the following week at a church down valley in Newport where Doris lived. By all accounts, the ten o'clock train along the valley line was to be more or less taken over by family and friends and after the service there would be a reception in the church hall.

'Say, what's the right thing to do with our wedding gifts?' asked Mom. 'Do we take them to church with us, give them to you today or what?'

'Generally, people give them beforehand so's they can be opened and displayed,' said Doris. 'My mother has put a big table in her front room and we have started spreading them out there, with the cards.'

'A good thing I asked, then,' said Mom. 'Do you plan on coming back up to Megan's today?'

'We've a few jobs to finish here first,' said Trefor, 'but we could pop up after we finish if you like.'

'Then you can collect the ones we brought. Sarah and Alec sent theirs with us but I have a little more money to spend on you if there is something you really need.'

'Well, one of the first things Berta May needs to do next week is to come down to Newport and try on her dress, so Doris can tell you what she wants and then you can go shopping. Doris, when does your mam want Berta May to come?'

'Monday morning as soon as possible. Our Mair and Gwladys have had theirs fitted and all finished, so if there's any alterations to be done to yours, she has all week to do them. You'll look gorgeous, I know you will.'

At last, I was to have my wish and wear a proper bridesmaid's dress and I could hardly wait to try on the full-length pale blue taffeta with flocked nylon overskirt.

'You can count on it, I'll be there by the first train,' I said. 'Now, can we help you for a while?' and Doris's face lit up.

'Would you, please? I have to unpack some boxes in the kitchen now and the curtains at the front need hanging. There really is a lot to do. Trefor, will you set up the step-ladder for Berta May?'

She soon had us all working, Sheila and I doing the drapes, Mabel and herself sorting crockery while Mom lined some drawers with clean white paper. Trefor roared away on his BSA to collect some tacks and other items from the hardware store in town.

'What are you doing tonight?' asked Sheila as we worked.

'I don't know. What is there to do around here?'

'On Saturdays, we mostly go to the pictures. There's 'Mother Wore Tights' on at the Pavi and everyone we know is going.'

'That old movie still around? I saw it when I was about fifteen.' Her face fell and I realised I had been untactful. 'No offence meant. I'd sure love to come with you.'

'I've seen it before, too, but Mabel and Pat haven't and nor has my boyfriend.'

'Oho, so there's a boyfriend. What's his name?'

'Simon. An apprentice at the steel works, he is.'

'But you won't want me tagging along, will you?'

'Too much of a crowd to notice one extra - I told you, everyone I know is going.'

She omitted to say that half of them were going for the sole purpose of meeting this strange cousin from the States or that they had prayed for weeks that there would be an American movie showing, just to make me feel at home.

'We have to be there by half past five,' she said, 'to make sure of getting in. So don't let our Gran push you into anything else.'

It was something of a rush to be ready, for we were late for tea and I had to try on half my clothes before I found something I thought suitable for Saturday night out. Mom said she'd be glad to have a quiet evening at home with Auntie and Uncle, but from what I heard afterwards, it had been anything but quiet. All the other aunts and uncles, cousins, in-laws and neighbours seemed to have been to Cwmavon to take part in the reminiscing and family updating.

As for me, I got a tremendous welcome from the teenagers. We stood in a long queue to wait for the 'second house' to start, but our section of the queue was somewhat ragged, for they clustered round me and my cousins, asking questions, showing off a bit or just staring. I felt a bit like an exhibit in a zoo, for I knew my striped pants and sloppy-joe were a bit out of the ordinary to their eyes.

I found myself sitting between Mabel and a plump girl who told me she was Sheila's best friend, not counting Simon.

'But that won't last long,' she added. 'He's just the worst flirt this side of Newport.'

'She's jealous,' whispered Mabel. 'He went out with her for two weeks. She's sweet on our Dan but he takes no notice of her.'

Dan had come too, but was sitting in the back row with a red-head whose name was Doreen. A student at the teacher training college, said Mabel and 'he knows which side his bread is buttered.'

Personally, I was quite stupidly envious of Doreen, for I would have liked to share the evening with Dan. I did not wish another girl to push me out. Meanwhile, the news bulletin was over, the big movie about to begin.

'This is the moment we've been waiting for,' sighed Mabel.

She was in her element. I had forgotten until then how happy she had been to tread the stage back home in war time and in spite of her high academic ambitions, she still hankered after a singing career. Her enjoyment was infectious and the whole row of us was tapping our feet and huming 'Burlington Bertie' and 'Chewing Gum' in due course.

Then we made a hasty exit and ran to catch the last bus up the valley, for even Sheila at eighteen was not keen on either walking home or facing 'our Mam' if we should miss it.

Chapter 12

At ten the next morning, Trefor arrived and disturbed our leisure. We had done the dishes, I had given Uncle Tom a hand with the milking and Mom had said she was looking forward to a restful day until it was time to go to chapel along with the family.

'It's a glorious day and the only chance you'll get to let me show you our mountains,' he said, kissing first Mom and then me. 'Put your strongest shoes on and your trousers and we'll go up the Snail Creep and over to Craig Ddu.'

'You can't expect your mam to walk all that way,' protested Auntie Megan, 'and what about dinner? I got a joint of lamb all ready for roasting and I don't want it to spoil.'

'Then I promise to have them back by two,' he said. 'Could you have dinner a bit late for once?'

'Oh, go on then, I won't spoil your fun. Only not a minute after two, see?'

We got away then within ten minutes and he led us along the lane to the village before starting to ascend a steep track up the side of the valley. All the time, Trefor was telling us about the place, who lived where, what they did for a living and where the old tracks went. We hardly noticed being out of breath, though Mom did stop once, saying, 'My, all this travelling is making me unfit. Time I did a day's work on the farm and got some of this flab off me.'

We had left one chapel at the bottom and saw another near the top, built of grey stone like the school that stood beyond it and the rows of cottages nearby. It was a different world up here above the woods and I imagined it could be windswept and cold, but I found the clean fresh air invigorating.

'This is Varteg,' said Trefor, 'and I must point out over there, the row at the top of the hill is where Uncle Henry used to live. His sister and brother want to meet you while you are here.'

'More family to remember,' laughed Mom. 'We got a gift to give them, from Henry and Sarah, when we meet.

165

Where to now?'

We had come to a tarmaced road but we simply crossed it and carried on uphill. Clear to the top of a rocky pitch and onto the shoulder of Varteg Mountain we went, to the summit of Farteg Fawr and from there we had some distant views. It seemed strange to Mom and me, having a sort of rough open meadow way above the trees, but it made for good visibility. There were sheep grazing everywhere as we picked our way between clumps of sprouting heather.

'See the glint of sunlight on water? That's the Severn and you can see England on the other side. They say here, if you cannot see the Severn, it's raining and if you can see it, it's going to rain. Now just a little way and we'll be able to see the Beacons.'

So then we looked to the North and North West, where lay further mountains and three prominent peaks in the distance. Though nowhere near as high as our ranges back home, they were impressive and had a beauty of their own.

It was something of a rush after that, to cross the valley where the Ffrwd brook ran and scramble up a field path to find the place where my father had lived as a boy, high above the woods. I was real glad to see it and so was Mom, for before he died, Pop had written about it and drawn sketches of the woods and of the valley below. I recalled the words of the song I had learned at his knee.

'I Wish I Were Back In My Valley,' I hummed quietly and Trefor took my hand.

'There's something in the blood that makes some of us want to come home,' he said, 'but your valley is over the ocean. You'll be wanting to go back to it before the year is out.'

'I know how you feel,' said Mom. 'I shall be glad enough to see the Pend Oreille when the time comes for me to go home, though I sure am having a good time while I'm here.'

'Now you two must remind me,' I said, 'when we get back to the farm, I have a package for you, Tref.'

'The wedding gift?' he asked. 'I thought you were taking it down to Doris's as it was a bit bulky for us to carry on the bike?'

'Not a gift,' I laughed. 'Something you charged me to look after when I was five years old. Can you have

166

forgotten? I took real good care of them, like you said.'

'My diaries? Bless you, I had indeed almost forgotten. They'll make strange reading now.'

'I read your poetry through and through a year or so back. I thought it was positively soulful,' I told him.

'She was having a major heart-break at the time,' Mom said.

'And I used to look at your diaries now and again, to remind me of you when I thought I might forget. But your writing was so almighty bad, I gave myself a headache in the attempt.'

'But she copied out some of your poetry real neat and put it on her wall,' Mom told him. 'It's good.'

Then we tramped at a good pace back to Cwmavon, where the roast was ready and the table laid for dinner.

'That was real kind of you, Tref,' said Mom, 'to think of taking us out. The exercise sure did me good and I could eat a horse.'

No matter that sugar and butter were still rationed at that time, the folks in Wales made some fine wholesome meals for us. It took the rest of the afternoon for Mom to sleep off her hike and her dinner, then we all got ready for chapel.

'I hope you have no objection to coming with us,' said Auntie Megan, 'but people are looking forward to meeting you. Next Sunday, our Idris will be wanting you to go to his chapel up Varteg, because they're having a Festival of Britain weekend.'

2

Up and down the valley, it seemed there were plans for various festivities, so it was a good time for visiting and there was no chance of our being bored. We went to Newport by train on Monday morning early and found where Doris lived on the Chepstow Road. Her mother's house, built of red brick and one of a long row facing the main road, was bursting at the seams with wedding paraphernalia.

There were gifts displayed on a table in the front room and we laid our parcels there to await opening. Boxes and suitcases stood in the hall.

'Doris's clothes and so on,' said her mother, 'waiting to go up to their house. Come upstairs now, and see the dresses.'

My word, I thought they were swell. Doris was to wear a long white silk one, with a short train, a waist-long veil and a coronet for head-dress. Her two little sisters and I were having pale blue taffeta, with the latest thing in flocked nylon for the over-skirt and sleeves.

'We had to cut out some of the fullness,' said their mother, 'because we could not get enough material, but I think they are pretty enough, don't you?'

'I surely do,' beamed Mom. 'Berta May has been longing to wear a dress like this for years, haven't you, Berta May? Doris must have chosen the style just for you.'

By this time, I was stripping off my skirt and blouse, eager to slip the dress over my head. They helped me. I flicked back my hair and looked at my reflection in the mirror while they were zipping me up. Not bad, I thought. The colour quite suited my colouring and the fitted bodice flattered my figure.

'A perfect fit,' they declared. 'Do you like it, Berta May?' I think Mom would have killed me on the spot if I had dared to break the heart of Doris and her Mom by saying No.

'I just love it,' I nodded, 'but I wish I had remembered to bring my shoes with heels. The skirt is touching the floor.'

'I was a bit worried about the length, but Trefor said you were tall and sure to wear high heels. Here, why not try these ones of Doris's and see how it hangs then.'

They were far too tight, but lifted me high enough to see that the skirt would not trail. Apart from needing a stitch or two at the top of the zip, the dress was finished. I was reluctant to take it off.

'I can't tell you what a relief that is.' The two mothers went downstairs and left me to get dressed. 'I was hoping not to have a lot of last-minute alterations to do. Got enough work to get through this week as it is and the girls so excited and all. Have a cup of tea, will you, before you go into town?'

That town was pretty far removed from our own little Newport, both in character and size. A city, we would have called it, yet it had none of the shining newness of our cities. Set beside the tidal River Usk, its buildings were old, its streets close-packed and crowded. Buses and cars fought pedestrians for possession of the narrow thoroughfares. There were shops of every description along the main road, but the selection of goods was far smaller that at home. Just as in London, we saw here and there spaces where bombs had destroyed buildings and nothing had as yet replaced them. Some new shop-fronts were of plate-glass and aluminium, but there was a lot of old-fasioned stores. Finding a place to get a light lunch was most difficult and the food we had was poor.

'Say, they've a long way to go before they catch up with us,' said Mom. 'I thought the recovery would have gotten further than this.'

Nevertheless, spirits appeared to be high and our relatives seemed to feel that a new era was about to begin. They talked at length about the factories, the prospects for employment and the hundreds of new houses under construction.

'Like living in a palace,' someone had said about their new, modern council house and Trefor had reported that a survivor of Dunkirk had been given the key to the one thousandth of the houses. Everyone wanted to modernise their homes or to knock them down and rebuild.

'Not a trace of the old village there will be, come the end of the fifties,' predicted Uncle Idris when we went up to spend an afternoon with him. 'Knocking the place about something dreadful they are. Not that I would say a lot of the old houses was fit to live in - I could tell you a few tales about the damp and the draughts, and your father had to treat many a child that was sick owing to the stinking hole they lived in. But wholesale destruction it is, down by there see, and the council did ought to stop and think. Destroying our heritage they are, all in the name of Progress.'

He was a dear old man and I could listen to him for hours, while Mom talked to Auntie Jane. He wanted to know every detail of our life back home and that of Auntie Sarah and her family, too.

'Never thought she would have it in her, I didn't, to emigrate like she did and set up in foreign parts, and I could have sworn they'd be back within the twelve month,' he said. 'And as for our Mam and your Dad going after them, well it near broke my heart to see them go.'

'Thirty year ago that was, and it seems like yesterday. But what am I doing, talking in this dreary way to a young lass like you? Real proud to have a Yank in the family I am and as for that Mom of yours - well all I can say is, our Robbie was a lucky fellow. Be chasing her myself I would, if I didn't have Jane to keep me on the rails.'

Auntie Jane had her hands full, I could see, not so much in keeping Uncle in order but in caring for their son, Sam. He was the one who had gone through the war in a prison camp and had come home to remind them for ever of the horrors he had endured. The same age as Trefor, he had the face of an old man and the faltering speech of a little child. For six years, the family had nursed and cared for him, slowly coaxing him back to some semblance of normality, but I doubted he would ever resume the life of a working man. Poor Auntie Jane, she was always cheerful but I guess life had been hard for her. She and Mom had things in common.

On Saturday, I was taken to Newport by Lizzie, who drove me in her car while Mom went with the rest of them by train.

'It is good to have you to myself,' she said. 'I feel I know you quite well through your letters, but have not had the time to see much of you as yet. I expect they told you I had just got a Practice of my own?'

She was in her mid forties, very brisk and business-like and putting on a bit of weight or so she said.

'I used to be as nimble as a mountain sheep,' she told me, 'but now, I drive everywhere, I'm not as trim as I was. Your mother now, she's pretty sturdily built, but not much surplus fat in spite of her age.'

'She rides a good deal and works pretty hard on the farm - heavy work, some of it,' I said. 'Builds up muscle instead of fat.'

'I'm hoping to write a paper one of these days,' said Lizzie, 'on exercise and health, if I can ever get it done. Hope I'm not boring you. Tell me what you're going to do during twelve months.'

'To be honest, I could do with some help,' I told her. 'I applied to a few colleges for courses, but at seventeen, I am too young. I must make up my mind soon. Have you time to talk to me? You may know more about that sort of thing than the aunts and uncles do.'

'Of course. I must set aside an evening next week. Now, we are almost at the house. I shall drop you here and go on to the church. You'll be taken in one of the official cars.'

There followed an hour of girlish talk and laughter, culminating in Doris appearing just in the nick of time, radiant and pink-faced, groomed and made up and correctly dressed on the stroke of eleven. Two big black cars drew up outside the house.

'Bridesmaids please,' called Doris's father and we stepped out the door, beautiful and nervous.

I felt as if all the world must look at us. Indeed, a good many heads turned as we walked to the porch of St Paul's Church, small bouquets of cream roses in our hands. I wondered whether Mom was already inside, whether Trefor had arrived and whether Idris had been persuaded to wear a suit. We chattered and shivered as a chill breeze swept across the road, then saw the other big car arrive. Doris was dismounting, her father helping to arrange the train of her dress and we heard the strains of the organ within.

It was a huge building, the inside even more magnificent than the outside and I thought we walked half a mile just to get to the spot where the minister was waiting. A far cry from our modest church back home and from the grey chapels up the valley, its walls soared high above, its roof was invisible. I told myself not to stare around. I concentrated on not falling over my own hem or the white silk train ahead of me.

Doris turned round, gave me her bouquet to hold and the ceremony began.

3

In spite of its size, the church was pretty nearly full, all the old school friends of Doris coming to swell the crowds of relatives on both sides. The bells rang out as we walked away down the centre of the building and out into the sunshine, just like I had seen on the movies of Princess Elizabeth's wedding. My, how I wished Gaynor could have seen this right royal procession - there was no getting away from it, this beat her wedding into a cocked hat.

Then there were photographs to be taken, a man with a camera telling us to stand just so or to group again thus, and some of us including Mom had our own Brownie boxes so Doris and Trefor got snapped from all angles. Only a sudden shower of light rain stopped this going on all day, but then we were bidden to move into the church hall next door to avoid getting damp. There, tables were laid for fifty people and the reception began, laughter and chatter throughout the echoing old room until we were at length told to sit down.

'About time too,' said Trefor. 'I'm starving.'

'You're supposed to be nervous,' said his Best Man, Dan. 'I can tell you, I shalln't be able to eat a thing until I've finished my speech.'

Yet within minutes I saw him tucking into a good plate of roast beef and yorkshire pudding, for to my pleasure I was sitting on his left hand. We had chance for talking and reminiscing in between being pleasant to other guests.

'I suppose you'll be next to get married,' I said.

'Not a chance. Got to make sure my girl is the right girl first I have, then get the money together. Think I may go after a job down the nylon.'

'And give up farming? You can't do that, farming's your life.'

'Farming's in my blood all right, but farming don't pay. Not enough to support all us lot up Penylan, it don't. I got to get another income, see.'

There were toasts and jokes and telegrams were read out, just as at Alec's wedding, including messages from Auntie Sarah and Uncle Henry, Bethan and Alec. Unknown to me, Dan had got the picture which we had brought as our wedding gift and he held it up for all the guests to see. It was a painting of the Pend Oreille from the bridge at Usk, the river winding into the distance with log pilings stark against the lowland meadows. Then the forested slopes of the lower mountains led the eye ever upwards, to find one prominent peak snow-capped above.

'They are thinking of you in the other valley today, Doris and Trefor, and wishing you every happiness. I know you will agree, part of your happiness is due to their love and neither you nor I will ever forget that. Raise your glasses please to the people in Pend Oreille county.'

I felt a lump in my throat and I saw Mom dab her eye, but the next moment we were joking and laughing merrily.

'They'll be lucky if I don't steal that picture from them,' said Dan.

'I'll make sure to get one for you when you get married,' I laughed.

'Could be your turn first,' he replied.

The little bridesmaids were tired of sitting still, as were some other children amongst the guests. There began to be some movement about the room while the tables were being cleared and I joined Pat and my cousins in a group at the far end of the room. They were plotting how best to infiltrate confetti into the luggage of the newly married couple, who were about to leave us.

'Catching the four o'clock train they'll be,' whispered Mabel. 'I had it from Doris's mam. Why don't we all go down the station and see them off? At least we can throw confetti at them if we can't put it in their cases.'

'Where are they going then?'

'Cornwall.'

'Right. Let's go. Coming, Berta May?'

'Why, I just can't walk down Main Street in this gear, can I? I need to get into some regular clothing. I'll go ask whether Lizzie can take me over Doris's place so's I can change.' I saw them all grinning and knew I had said something odd.

'Commercial Street, not Main Street,' said Pat. 'This is Newport, Wales, remember.'

At that moment, Trefor and his bride were leaving and we all shouted farewells. Doris turned at the door and shouted, 'Who's going to be next then?' and threw her beautiful bouquet out into the room. All the young girls rushed forwards as if to catch it.

'Go on, Berta May, it's coming in your direction,' shouted Dan, but I was not quick enough. Pat leapt nimbly into the air and got her left hand round it. We all cheered and she blushed scarlet. Emmie groaned.

'She's only fifteen, don't put ideas into her head.'

I went to look for Lizzie, but she had been commissioned to take the younger bridesmaids and their parents home. I had a long wait.

'They'll all be disappointed anyway,' she smiled when at last I got my ride. 'That was a red herring started by Doris herself, for she guessed there would be mischief afoot. I put her and Trefor on the train to Glasgow at three forty.'

Since there was therefore no need to hurry, we lingered to look at the gifts and got to know Doris's people better. It was nearly seven before I was reunited with Mom and Auntie Megan back at the farm and we sat down for a lazy evening. Cheese sandwiches and a tumbler of beer were voted an ideal supper to complete that happy day.

4

On Sunday we joined in the Festival service at Varteg chapel and I got my talk with Lizzie on Monday, before Mom and I set off to look at a bit more of Britain.

'Now, what do you really want to do with your life?' she asked.

'Now there you have gotten to the heart of my problem,' I told her. 'I do not have a burning ambition to be anything in particular. I like sport and outdoor life and may even take up forest management after I get through college, but first I have to graduate from high school. They have allowed me a year out so's I can travel, but I want to study something truly British that we don't have in the States.'

'Like visiting our art galleries and museums?'

'That sort of thing. I got good grades in Literature last summer and my teachers suggested I might take the chance to visit Shakespeare's birth place and see some of his plays at the theatre.'

'What about music?'

'Not too hot, though I like a bit of singing.'

'Drama?'

'You mean, join a troupe of actors?'

'Not necessarily on stage. You could learn a lot about

174

Stage Management. I'm really just thinking aloud.'

'I appreciate that. Tell me, how could I get to know about traditional fabrics and the way they were used?'

'Goodness me, I can't answer that. It sounds like part of an art college course.'

'The trouble is, I am too young for colleges and universities and don't have the entry grades. Trefor got married a year too soon for me.'

'No need to worry. We shall find just the thing for you. I shall ask my contacts and someone will come up with just the very idea.'

So Mom and I went off north to look round Birmingham while the rest of the family returned to their working lives. Not much impressed, we then took a train across North Wales, spent two days hiking in Snowdonia and visited some ancient castles. We steeped ourselves in the past at Conway, Caernarfon and Harlech and it struck us for the first time how young our own history was.

'Just think,' I said, 'they know exactly when these stones were put together and what lives the people lived. We can only guess what the States was like at that time. Even the Indians cannot tell stories from so long ago.'

'Berta May,' said Mom on the way back in the train, 'why don't you just try to trace our own family history? Why, between the Watkins and the Taylors, I reckon you'd have enough to keep you busy.'

'And enough to write a book by the time I'd finished,' I said, 'but I have no idea how to begin.'

'Well it seems to me that you'd have to work backwards,' she mused. 'Start with all you know and all you can pick up from the living and then start looking for records of the dead. Speaking of which, I think I shall die of hunger before we get to Newport. Don't they have no restaurant service on these trains?'

Feeling soiled and travel-weary, we made our way up the valley, wishing a modern shower unit awaited our arrival at the farm. Luckily, the kitchen boiler had been lit and there was a tank full of hot water, so when Auntie Megan saw the state of us, she said she would put the tin bath in front of the fire and we could take a tub.

'Pity we couldn't have got the bathroom in before you

came,' she said for the hundredth time. 'Come next summer, we'll have the spare room converted and an electric immersion heater installed.'

Tracing the family history was not something I had thought of doing, but after talking to the local vicar and learning something about the parish records, I warmed to the idea of taking up the idea. Moreover, Auntie Megan and the others were full of enthusiasm and I knew how pleased Auntie Sarah would be when I returned home with a complete family tree.

'And you'll still have time for a bit of culture,' agreed Lizzie. 'I have been speaking to the English mistress at the Grammar School and she says you would be allowed to attend Sixth Form classes if you wished. They take the pupils on visits to see Shakespeare's plays and to the theatre in London sometimes and that would be good for you too.'

'Yes it would. I think I should like to take a class. What do I have to do to enrol?'

'Get Idris to take you over to the school before they break up for the holidays and you should be able to arrange it all.'

'And I still would have time for the history?'

'Goodness yes. You'll have no exams to sit, after all. And if you have to go to London to look for records in Somerset House, I expect Frank will look after you there. Yes, a very good idea and much easier to put in hand. I know your mum was worried at the thought of you wandering all over Britain alone.'

'But this could take me just as far. You never know what I may dig up or where it may lead me.'

'True. Grandma Watkins came from West Wales, you know, and Grandpa from England. I only wish I were free to join you. None of us has ever had time to do this sort of thing.'

With that decision made, Mom and I set about enjoying the last few days of her holiday and allowed the family to take us out and about. We went on a coach outing to Hereford and another to the seaside at Porthcawl. There, we swam in the ocean when the tide came in and ate fish and chips from paper packets. We had our photos taken

176

strolling along the promenade, all eight of us with ices in hand, and played crazy golf till tears of merriment were running down our faces.

At the other extreme, they took us to see the 'Messiah' in Pontypool Market Hall, an event of great moment for the valley. None of us was in Frank's class when it came to music, but we Watkins did know a thing or two about this piece and the traditions associated with it. To our surprise, the audience broke into applause at the end of each section of music. At last, the conductor was unable to restrain himself any longer and he requested silence until the end. This had a bad effect on some of us younger people and I am ashamed to say that Mabel and Idris and I were near to disgracing ourselves by laughing. We were prompt, however, in standing for the Hallelujah Chorus, unlike some of the big-wigs who had not been prepared for this.

After that, it was a concert on home ground, where the Garndiffaith Male Choir was giving a concert. With Dan, his father and grandfather taking part, we were of course expected to go. Totally unexpected to us was the welcome we were given in the opening speech. The village to a man knew who we were. My father, we were told, had been sped on his way to America from this very hall and it was a pleasure to all to meet us.

'My word, wait till I tell the folks we were VIPs,' said Mom after the press photographer had taken a picture of us. 'I feel like the Queen of England.'

It was a wonderful concert, the music varied and uplifting. As for the final Amen that came at the end of a piece whose name I promptly forgot, it brought shivers up and down my spine. I was proud that this was part of my heritage and was near to sentimental tears when they sang 'I Wish I Were Back In My Valley.' I savoured every moment of it, to tell Auntie Sarah.

'Now mind, Berta May,' said Idris as we fought our way through the crush at the exit, 'you have to come and see me play. Some of us do other things than sing, you now.'

'Play what? Have you taken up the fiddle or something?' I asked.

'Not he,' laughed Trefor, folding his reporter's notebook in which he had made lots of notes, 'he's talking about playing rugby. Mom's lucky to be leaving before the season starts. I fear you'll have to stand and freeze while he chases the oval ball, come winter.'

Mom's final weekend came and a farewell party was arranged, to be kept secret from her until the last minute. Bobbie took her and me with Sam and some of the young folk to a Festival Fair in Pontypool Park and we mingled with the holiday crowds for a few hours. There was a fancy dress parade and many games and competitions, a fairground and shooting alleys. In spite of it being cold and cloudy, the whole town was having a really good time.

Then we got into the truck and returned to Varteg, where the hall was decorated with flags and full of friends and food. Trefor and Doris, back from honeymoon, were there too. They had even hung up the Stars and Stripes with a 'Good Luck, Cassie', banner beneath it and a cheer went up when we came in.

> 'For She's a Jolly Good Fellow
> She's a Jolly Good Fellow
> She's a Jolly Good Fellow
> And So Say All of Us.' they sang.

Well, that was some send-off and Mom was as proud as could be to know they thought so highly of her. They put on gramophone records for dancing and played team games and competitions that we had never seen before. After we had eaten, a man arrived to play the piano, so there was a sing-song and more dancing. I saw Bessie go up and whisper something to him, then she came across to me.

'Li'l Liza Jane,' she said.

It was a good few years since we had done it, but the memory was still green and it took but a minute for the eight of us to form our set and kick up our heels like we had done in 1943. Bessie, Sheila, Mabel, Pat, Dan, Idris, Mom and I did a demonstration dance, possibly the first American Square Dance to be seen in Varteg, I thought.

After that, we had to teach three more sets how to spin and chain and dosey do, which they did until they were out of breath.

'More, more!' shouted some of them. 'Teach us another

one.'

'You've started something now,' shouted Uncle Idris, applauding strenuously. 'Wanting more of that we'll be. Stay a while longer will you, Cass?'

However, that was not to be. Time had run out and she must be away home to tend the farm and homestead, leaving me to begin my year of educational travel.

Chapter 13

There was no fear that I might feel lonesome once Mom had left, for the schools were out for summer vacation and there were festivities in all directions, to which my cousins wanted to take me. Weekdays, I was escorted by Mabel and Pat whose idea of a good day out was a shopping expedition or a trip to the fairground. Sometimes we went swimming in the open-air baths and I was glad to have the chance of some vigorous exercise. They seemed impressed by my performance and said they wished I were in their school team.

'Could we have a game of tennis hereabouts?' I asked one afternoon when they wanted to know if there were anything in particular I wished to do.

'We could hire a court in the park,' they said, 'but you have to book in advance.'

'Let's see if Idris will come too, then we can play doubles.'

'Can we get enough rackets?' They began to count the members of the family who had one which could be used. We finally got four together, two of which were somewhat elderly. I had never used one with catgut strings and an unbound wooden handle.

Of course, Idris was set on proving his superior skill and was reluctant to take his turn with the oldest racket. The other girls were inclined to give in to him, but in me he found the same old opponent as in childhood. Overall, he and Pat beat me and Mabel handsomely, but I challenged him to a singles match and we immediately booked the court.

At weekends, Dan and Sheila joined us and sometimes we went further afield, taking train or coach outings to Cardiff, Swansea, Hereford or Bristol if there were nothing in the valley to amuse us. They had to count their pennies, however, and I was not overly keen to spend all my money in the one month, so some of our amusements had to be less costly. The walks we took on the mountains, the days spent helping on the farm or painting the front room walls for

Auntie Megan were equally enjoyable.

I won my tennis game very narrowly and Idris challenged me to another, but the weather broke and we did not play again. Never modest, he reminded me frequently that he was in the school's rugby team and that I must watch him play.

'A spot of rain won't stop that,' he said.

It was nearing the end of August when Trefor and Doris came to see us and proposed an expedition over the mountains. He was of course pretty well-informed and his job took him around the county a good deal and Doris was on the spot in Newport to pick up the news.

'We've both got three more days holiday to come and there's an excursion train going on the twenty fourth to Brecon,' they told us. 'The fare is less than half the normal, so what we want to do is, go with the trip but not come back with it.'

'Not come back? Then what are you going to do?' asked Pat.

'Join the YHA and stay in a hostel overnight, then set off to walk home.'

'Walk home? You can count me out then,' said Auntie Megan. 'Never heard of such a thing I didn't.'

'Look,' said Trefor patiently. 'All who want to can come home on the train but those who like hiking can stay with me and Doris. We're off to the station on Monday to book. We shall have to hurry and join the YHA because you have to be a member to use their hostels.'

Then he had to convince Auntie Megan that the accommodation provided would be of a decent standard and that he knew the way home. In the end, there were twelve of us wishing to go, five of us willing to hike home. Dan was annoyed at not being able to join us because he would be at work.

I wished I had my old comfortable farm boots with me and thought I had better buy something stronger than the summer shoes I was wearing, for I had already found how rough the moorland heather could be. Pat and I went in search of walking shoes or boots and spent a frustrating day, for the shops simply did not stock what we needed.

'Perhaps you could get some in Brecon,' suggested

Auntie Megan. 'In the mountains there, they maybe sell that sort of thing.'

'Taking a bit of a chance though, to leave it as late as that,' said Uncle Tom. 'Need to be walked in, do boots.'

At length we ran some to earth when we went to Abergavenny on market day and although I had to wear three pairs of socks inside to make them fit, they seemed to be strong and comfortable. Wind-cheaters and plastic macs, borrowed haversacks, vacuum flasks and long pants were slowly accumulated as the day drew near.

'You better take plenty of food,' said Auntie Mabel, cutting round after round of bread on the evening before we left. 'Do you get those dozen eggs on to boil now, Berta May, while I spread the marg. There's a good fruit loaf in that tin and a pound of cheese in the larder.'

'I don't know whether I can carry all this,' I protested .

'Fit it in somehow you will and any way, our Trefor do have a big enough bag to take some of it. Oh dear, I wish we did have a telephone so you could ring us up every day and tell us where you are.'

'But I don't think they have phones on top of mountains, do they?' I laughed. 'Don't worry, Trefor will bring us home safely.'

'Mind you, he may have to carry us,' said Pat who had just come in. 'If we get blisters or sprain our ankles, that is.'

That gave our dear auntie something new to worry over and she got out her medicine chest to search for the plasters and bandages. I could hardly lift my pack when we set off for the train next morning and Pat had to take a canvas bag with food, for her mother Emmie had also packed supplies.

It was an entertaining and educational experience as well as a beautiful ride, for the train went from Newport to Cardiff, picked up passengers there and then headed north towards the mountains. Trefor had brought maps with him and made sure that I understood the lie of the land, following the route up the Taff valley through the heart of the coal-mining area. One industrial town came after another until Merthyr Tydfil was reached, but behind the terraced houses and the pit-head gear there rose the green and brown mountains.

After Merthyr, the gradient became steeper and the

speed reduced as we came through Pontsticill and into hills with conifer forests newly planted. Then there was a tunnel and a new panorama opened immediately after it. To my left, a deep valley with a stream swiftly flowing and beyond, mountain slopes more rugged than any I had seen before in South Wales. Even on this clear summer day, the summit was hidden in a light mist. We could hear the squeal of brakes as our train ran steadily downhill now, on a curving line high above the river valley, until we came at last to level ground, crossed the river Usk at Talybont and turned towards the West.

The Watkins contingent had more than filled one compartment, but we younger folk had made sure we were together, just Auntie Megan, Auntie Jane and Uncle Idris sitting with us while Bessie and the others were further along the coach. As excited as small children, we laughed and chattered throughout the journey, lowering the window at stations so as to see further and closing it in a hurry when clouds of thick smoke came our way.

'I never been to Brecon afore, have you, Jane?' I heard Auntie Megan asking.

'Once, yes. I came with our Sarah when she was singing in a concert.'

'Got around a bit in them days, didn't you. Fancy, a journey like this just to sing a concert.'

'At night it was, too, and coming back in the dark the two of us were and never thought nothing of it, did we?'

'Safer then than now it was. You couldn't do it nowadays - never know who's around, you don't.'

'Tref's mam it was as came this way, wasn't it?' I pricked up my ears.

'Louise? Why so she did. Near forgot about that, I had,' said Auntie Megan, lowering her voice. 'I wonder did anyone ever tell him? A brave girl she was and no mistake.'

I could see Pat's eyebrows rising and feared she might break in with a question, so I shook my head and put my fingers to my lips. Trefor and Doris were in deep conversation at the other end of the compartment.

'You can see where he gets his spirit of adventure from,' agreed Auntie Jane.

Once arrived, we shouldered our packs and prepared to

leave our elders, whose first thought was to find a cup of tea. It was none too easy to get away from them, but Trefor showed determination.

'All right you four,' he said to us. 'Nothing to eat until we get to the Ffrwdgrech Falls, so how about putting your best foot forward?' and we waved goodbye saying, 'See you on Tuesday.'

'Only nine miles to do today,' he told us as we tackled the first steep lane out of the town. 'Just to get used to it. Tomorrow will be longer and harder.'

'We're not going over the top of those, are we?' I asked. Pointing at the range of mountains ahead.

'Not exactly over the top, but we shall get to the summit tomorrow morning. Don't worry, you'll manage easily enough.'

We got into our stride, stopped for lunch beside a waterfall and continued up the lanes. Our destination for Saturday night was a hostel with one of those unpronounceable Welsh names and it lay to the east of the highest peak. Llwyn Y Celyn, the first Youth Hostel I had ever visited, quite took my fancy.

By the time we reached it, I had realised that my brother Trefor was using his family to further his career, but could not object to his doing so, since he had brought me on this exciting venture.

2

'I can't stay with the Press for ever,' he explained, 'Yet I don't want to leave the valley. So I'm trying to get into another sort of journalism. Sold a couple of short articles to magazines I have, and now I'm going to try my hand at travel writing.'

'Good idea.'

'Glad you think so. There should be a growing market for that sort of thing, now international travel is easier.'

'Have you thought of selling your stuff to US magazines as well? Alec's wife told us hundreds of Americans are starting to travel in Europe.'

'Yes, but I have to take one step at a time. Hey, Idris,' he called. 'Take the stile on your right. We're nearly there.'

The hostel was full of travellers, mostly hikers but a few cyclists. In the girls' dormitory, we three found neighbouring bunks, made up our beds and went to the wash room to clean up. Then we took our packs of food into the members' kitchen where we all got to work on cooking our sausage and potatoes. It was fun to be free of conventional behaviour and to get to know our fellow travellers.

After a slightly singed supper, I went into the sitting room, accepting the boys' offer to wash the dishes. A game of dominoes was in progress between a German girl and a coloured woman from London. I soon got drawn in and took my turn to play.

'Are you a student, too?' asked the German.

'Yes, I am when I'm at home, but I have got a year off to travel,' I replied.

'Lucky you. Is this not the most beautiful of countries?' Her English was very correct but heavily accented.

'Sure is. What part do you come from?'

It was a friendly evening and we knew we would see some of the young people on the mountains the next day. I slept well on my top bunk, but Pat and Doris said they missed their feather beds. We were heading up Pen Y Fan by ten in the morning after doing our share of the cleaning.

'That's one good way of getting to meet people,' I said. 'I shall do some more of this while I'm in Britain.'

'Don't you have hostels in the States then?'

'Oh sure, but I've never used them.'

Pat was less happy, her new boots rubbing her heels and her borrowed haversack uncomfortable. The day had dawned cool and damp and the way ahead was alarmingly steep.

'Stop and change your socks at once,' Trefor told her, 'before you get a blister, and let me have some of your heavier things.'

We all had a drink from our water bottles and then soldiered on towards the summit, passing a sort of monument. At last, we struggled up the last hard climb and collapsed in a heap on top.

Just look at that view,' said Doris. 'It was worth the walk to see that.' Clear across to the horizon, the landscape to the north was bathed in sunlight. Green woods and yellow fields, dark hollows and white farm houses lay below us, with the town of Brecon just in sight. Distantly, hills faded into a blue haze, but yet more ranges dimly showed themselves far beyond.

Trefor laid the map on the ground, determined to work out which mountain was which, while the rest of us opened packets of sandwiches.

'If you ask me,' he said, pointing, 'that very furthest peak, the one almost hidden in the clouds, could be Cadair Idris.'

'Who cares?' asked Pat. 'It's a good view and that's all that matters,' but Tref went on scrutinising both map and horizon, occasionally jotting something down in his notebook.

'The Eppynt, that must be in the middle distance. Do you know, Berta May, that whole area is closed to the public? Taken over by the Army in the war it was, and still used as a firing range.'

'He gets hot under the collar about that,' warned Idris. 'Don't encourage him, Berta May.'

'Too right I do and it's about time some more of you woke up and started fighting for your heritage before the whole country loses its language and its identity.'

'He'll be writing articles for the Welsh Nationalists next. You'll have to watch him, Doris,' laughed Idris.

'Have you eaten everything or has anyone got a sandwich for me?' Tref folded his map and held out his hand.

'Tref,' I asked quietly. 'Did you know your mom walked to Brecon once?'

'Mom?' he said. 'Don't be silly, Mom never came here, though I wish we had found time to bring her.'

'Not my Mom, your own Mom. Louise, was that her name?'

'Yes. What have you been hearing then?' He wore a worried frown. 'I sometimes wish the aunts would stop reminiscing, you never know what they'll drag up next.'

'Nothing nasty. Ask Auntie Jane, she said your mom was a brave woman and no wonder you had a spirit of adventure.'

In spite of our having been too hot earlier, there was a

cool breeze which soon drove us off Corn Du. We hurried to the trig point on Pen Y Fan and thence descended steeply, angling across the northern face of Cribin to take the shortest route towards Brecon.

'It's a pity not to complete the three peaks,' said Trefor, 'But tomorrow we have a long way to go and I don't want anyone collapsing on me.'

It was astonishing how happy and light of foot we felt, to be going downhill after lunch. We left the open moorland, joined a dirt road which soon became a tarmaced route. By four o'clock, we were in the town and looking for a snack bar.

'Hostels are not open before five thirty,' said Trefor, 'so's it's no use arriving early.'

Nor was it of use searching for tea in Brecon. It was Sunday afternoon and the town was silent, shops, cafes and public houses closed. We must needs walk on to Groesffordd and wait for the hostel to open, slaking our thirst with the last of our water and cold tea. Trefor busied himself writing notes about our trip while the rest of us lay on a grassy bank.

None of us was unduly tired, nor had we blistered feet. After hot drinks, food and a wash, we felt we could cheerfully cope with whatever lay ahead.

'How far tomorrow, Tref?' asked Idris.

'About twenty seven miles to...'

'Twenty seven!' Pat and I jumped out of our chairs.

'Wait a minute,' he laughed. 'Twenty seven miles from here to Cwmavon, I was going to say.'

We relaxed. 'That's better. Where's the next hostel then?'

'Ah, now just between you and me, there isn't one. We may have to sleep out on the mountain.'

'What?' Pat sat up again, but I had noticed the twinkle in my brother's eye.

'Well, it's a choice between the mountain and the pub at Llangattock. So I took a chance and booked beds in the pub.'

'Never slept in a pub, I haven't' said Pat.

'Nor I haven't' said Idris. 'Do our mam know?'

'No, I seem to have forgotten to mention it. Thought

there might be a bit of a fuss, so as no-one asked, I didn't say.'

We spent the evening talking to other hikers and discussing routes. The woman from London was there and we swapped addresses, though I hardly thought it likely she she would get to Pend Oreille county.

Our route on Monday lay at a lower altitude, roughly along the Usk valley by way of Llangorse. Over a mountain then and into Tretower, where we saw a ruined castle with a round tower standing within a bigger octagonal one. We sat on the hillside above, looking down at the strange structure and I tried to take a photo while Pat was sticking plasters on her heels. We arrived at Llangattock about six and found our way to the inn.

Trefor had booked a meal for us and it was good to have the cooking done with no effort on our part, for after three days walking we had to admit we were pretty tired. The landlady served our supper in a small rear room away from the bar and we devoured her shepherd's pie at great speed. Then there was something they called Spotted Dick, with custard sauce. It was solid and filling, satisfying even Idris.

'We'll have to go shopping in the morning,' I said. 'We finished the fruit loaf today and have no bread or anything left.'

'Well we must be ready as soon as the shop opens,' said Trefor. 'We've a long way to go and a few hills to climb.'

There was still an hour of daylight left, so he and Doris went to look around the village. Pat, Idris and I said we were too tired, but sauntered slowly over to the canal bridge. It was a picturesque place and I took a few snaps. 'I hope I can buy some picture postcards tomorrow,' I said. 'I got a couple from the warden at the last hostel but would like some more from here. I must write home before I go to bed.'

At the village shop, we bought bread, cheese, sliced meat and chocolate bars, but no picture cards were available. By ten, we were climbing uphill and finding our big breakfast lying heavy in our stomachs. We came to an old quarry where sheer rock walls rose high enough to block out the mid-morning sun and then followed a former railroad track.

'No, it was not a passenger route,' explained Tref, 'only a mineral line for the quarry. Anyone want to stop for a rest?'

'I want to stop for ever,' sighed Idris. 'You're a slave-driver our Tref.'

'And you're just a weakling, our Idris. I don't hear the girls complaining.'

'Let's get to the top before we stop,' I said. 'We'll have a better view then.'

'Oh, you and your views,' Idris teased. 'Come on then.'

During the next half hour, however, clouds built up and the sun disappeared, not to be seen again that day. The views were hidden in mist. We hurried over the shoulder of the mountain through a light drizzle and at last had to stop and put on our waterproof coats or capes.

There was barely sufficient visibility for us to see the gorge below us when Trefor called a halt for dinner. Sitting in the best shelter we could find, the lee of a stone wall, we looked down at Clydach.

'Now keep your eyes glued to the far side, Berta May,' said Trefor, 'and you may be lucky enough to see a train go by.'

'A train? You mean there's a railroad up there? You sure do build in the most unlikely situations. Where does it go to?'

'It comes all the way down from Brynmawr to Abergavenny, right along the side of the gorge. Look, there's one coming now. See the smoke in the trees down there on the left?'

We watched the trail of smoke run along the side of the gorge, rising steadily until it was above the tree line, when at last we could make out the engine and its two carriages. Munching our thick cheese sandwiches, we followed it until it disappeared into a tunnel.

'We had a ride on it, Mam and me and Auntie Megan,' said Pat, 'just after I came back home from America.'

'The only way for most people to get down from Brynmawr it was, till cars and buses started after the war,' Idris said.

We joined a lane that ran down into the gorge, crossed the river in the bottom and started to climb a narrow track up the southern side. Sometimes there was a stream on our right, sometimes we were high above it. The rain was now falling heavily and finding the leaks in our clothing. My neck felt damp and uncomfortable and Doris said her boots were as wet inside as out.

At length, we crossed the railroad but had a long way to climb before we were on more or less level ground.

'How much further, Tref?' asked Pat.

'About six miles.' We groaned.

'Straight on through Pwll Du and then we'll take a vote. If you want to get a bus from Blaenavon, we'll drop down and get one.'

With that promise, we found new strength to push on, though our boots became heavier by the minute. The wind was strengthening and clouds scurrying across the sky ahead, though the rain did not lessen.

'What do you think?' asked Trefor. 'Walk home or take a bus?'

At that very moment, a gleam of weak sunshine pierced the western cloud canopy and the sight of our own valley below gave us courage.

'Four to one in favour of carrying on. Let's stop and eat the rest of our food while it's not raining,' suggested Trefor.

Never had cold meat and thick chunks of bread tasted so good. We drained the last drops of tea from our flasks, shared the chocolate into five equal portions and shouldered our packs with determination. Less than four miles and we would be home.

3

It was a pretty bedraggled and footsore band of hikers that found their way down Llanover Road and into Cwmavon at about six o'clock that evening. All five of us were wet through to the skin, our boots and pants mud-stained and our legs weak with exhaustion and hunger, but our hearts were light.

'Now guess what our Gran will say as soon as she d'see Berta May?' asked Pat.

'Out of them clothes and into the bath with you,' said Idris in imitation of Auntie Megan. 'I do have put it ready in front of the fire and the water in the boiler nice and hot, see.'

'And Mam will make me strip off out in the porch and run up to the bathroom stark naked,' laughed Pat.

'Phew,' whistled Idris. 'Can I come home with you and watch?'

'No chance, you better be off up the Snail Creep and see what your Mam has to say. Probably throw you in the pond she will and tell you to wash the mud off before you set foot in the house.'

Laughing, we parted near the station, Trefor and Doris hoping to catch a train or bus home.

'Thanks for the trip,' I shouted back to them. 'I wouldn't have missed it for the world.' Then Pat and I limped slowly and wearily the last mile home.

I was pretty grateful to Auntie Megan for having gotten that hot tub ready. I soaked for ages, the aches and sores draining away, until I had to get out so's she could lay the table for late supper. Shaking her head, she listened to my account of our journey.

'There's a letter from Alec on the dresser,' she told me, 'and another from your Freddie and Zeb.'

'Dear Berta May,' Fred had started, 'I sure hope you and Mom are having a good time out there. I had a fine time in camp but it was real hot and some of the kids got sun burned.

The homestead is OK and we are setting out to get cord wood for the winter tomorrow. I saw Laurence in town and he said to tell you it sure is quiet here without you. Zeb wants to write some....'

With a guilty conscience, I read all the boys had to tell me about their summer back home. Alec had written at great length and I could picture all that was going on at the Box Canyon Dam site. I had sent them but a few picture postcards, hastily scribbled and mailed every few days.

'I must sit down tomorrow and write some long letters to them,' I said.

'If we sent an airmail, it might get there to welcome your mam home,' suggested Auntie Megan. 'I shall start mine tonight.'

Too tired to do the same, I resolved to spend the next day

writing. I knew my brothers would like to hear where Trefor had taken us.

'Back to school next week for the children isn't it, Megan?' asked Uncle Tom.

'Yes indeed. You'll be on your own then, Berta May.'

'But I'm to go with Mabel on the first day of term and get a time table for the English class,' I reminded her. 'And time I started making plans to start work on the family history.' I yawned. I was certain I could sleep until school opened.

They were truly pleased that I would be staying with them most of the time and we had worked out the delicate question of my paying for my board.

'Letters first, then I shall go buy lots of paper and start organising,' I declared, 'but first, a good night's sleep. Good night, Auntie, Good night, Uncle and thank you for being so good to me. I hope you didn't worry too much.'

Chapter 14

Dan was downhearted. He confided in me that his romance was foundering, indeed was almost dead.

'She told me last week she was going to apply for jobs in London when she qualifies,' he sighed. 'Said there's better prospects there and if I wanted to stay friends I better sharpen up my ideas and get into something with a future. I'm doing all I can to earn more money, driving haulage lorries when they can spare me from the farm, but she wants me to get into industry where the pay packets are bigger.'

I just hated to see him so sad. He was a good guy and we'd been pretty close when we were kids, and of all the people I had met since my arrival in Wales, he was the one with whom I would have liked to spend more time. It was Doreen had kept us apart.

'I'm sorry Dan, but do you think she's really the right girl for you? I'm sure I wouldn't want to marry someone who looked down her nose at me all the time.'

'She doesn't,' he protested, then sighed again. 'Well at least, she used not to. Got big ideas she has, since she been at training college.'

We were picking the last of Uncle Tom's apples in the orchard before going for a walk with Trefor and Doris. New plans were afoot for another hiking weekend soon and we expected them that afternoon.

'How you getting on with the family tree?' Dan asked. 'Uncle Idris said you'd been up a time or two to see him.'

'Slowly, but things are beginning to fall into place,' I said. 'I've written down all the names and dates of birth he and the others could tell me. The trouble is, once they start talking they get side-tracked and I spend hours hearing stories which are entertaining but not essential to what I'm trying to do.'

At that, he laughed. His eyes lit up like they used to do when we were sharing chores around the farm back home and I felt suddenly glad that his girl was deserting him. He was not meant for city life and the company of an ambitious woman.

'What you need is a long weekend on the mountains,' I thought, 'to blow the cobwebs away.'

'I hope we can fit our hike in soon,' I said. 'They want me to spend more time in school because they are putting on a drama for Christmas and I need to do a spot of travelling too. Now I know exactly where Grandma Watkins was born, I need to go down to Carmarthenshire.'

'Is Lizzie going with you?'

'Possibly, when she has a weekend off.'

'That's Tref's bike I can hear, let's take these baskets into the barn and get our boots on,' Dan said.

To his disappointment, the weekend when he was free for a few days, neither Trefor nor Doris nor the others could get away. Mabel and Idris, up to their ears in Sixth Form work, were limited to Saturdays and Sundays. Pat had found a job and could not have time off.

'Never mind,' I said, knowing how disappointed Dan would be, 'let's go together.'

'Where to?' he asked.

'What about the Wye valley? Trefor mentioned it and said there were hostels there. Is it a nice place?'

'I suppose it's all right. Pretty enough any way, but not really mountains. Rather go to the Beacons I would, if you don't care one way or the other.'

'Right. How do we get there? Train again?'

'Leave it to me. You book the hostel and I'll sort out transport. Tref said he'd lend me his big rucksack. You got enough waterproofs and things?'

For two weeks, I interspersed my school and family history days with making plans for our trip at the same time as trying to make arrangements for future research.

Lizzie's contacts were of great help, taking me to the County Records Office in Newport and explaining how to make searches up in London at Somerset House. I wrote to Frank and got a prompt reply:

Oxford, October 1951.

'Dear Berta May, Delighted to hear you have had a busy summer with your family and have seen a bit of Wales. I think it is a tremendous idea to do the family history and will help all I can. I hope you will be doing your mother's

194

side as well as your father's. Grandma had a family bible in which a lot of births and deaths were written, back to the 1820s I think. You are welcome to browse through it and anything else which might interest you.

Could you come up to town after I go down for Christmas, about the middle of December that will be? I shall then be able to accompany you some of the time. No, on second thoughts, come to Oxford first, a few days earlier and I will show you round, then we can go home together. I am taking part in an orchestral concert which you might enjoy. I will also get tickets for a couple of shows while you are here. I expect they will want you back in Wales for Christmas.

I hope you and Dan enjoy your expedition in the mountains. Tell him not to lead you astray amongst those Welsh sheep (joke - he and I got lost in the mist when I visited a few years ago - my fault; ask him.)

Auntie Cassie wrote me a long letter about her holiday and had obviously thoroughly enjoyed herself, but I fancy she is now quite content to be home. I am packing up a small parcel to send her for Christmas as a reminder of England.....'

2

'I shall have to be thinking of sending a Christmas gift to Mom,' I said to Dan as we strode towards Pen Y Fan on our first long day's hike. 'I can't think what to get for her.'

'Have a look round Brecon this afternoon when we stop to get bread and so on,' he said. 'Might find something here you couldn't get down Ponty.'

'Smart thinking. I'll do that. Hey, this is a pretty steep route. I need to stop for breath.'

We were approaching the mountain peak from the north. The morning, which had not been promising when we left the hostel at Groesffordd, was steadily improving. The clouds had lifted and thinned.

'Think it may be clear when we get on top?' I asked.

'Could be. I hope so, for I want to see the view.'

'Look, those three were at the hostel last night.' I pointed to a group toiling up the path towards us. It was Friday, we had three days ahead of us and already Dan's spirits were lifting. He had soon warmed to the company of other young people and taken part in an energetic game of table tennis in the hostel the previous evening.

'Hi,' I said as the three went by.

'Morning,' they replied one after the other.

'Better get on,' said Dan. 'Can't be much further.'

He was wrong of course; the summit was at the upper end of a long shoulder of land which rose in alternately steep and gradual gradients. We sat down to eat our lunch at the foot of a series of rock steps.

'I think that's the top, up there,' I said, 'but it's sure to be windy so we're better off here.'

The climb had been worth the effort, for the clouds were now well clear of the mountains and the view to the north was almost as clear as it had been in August.

'Perfect,' sighed Dan.

'You could never live in a city or work in a factory,' I said quietly. 'You're a mountain man.' He munched his way through a round of thick meat sandwiches, saying nothing. Then he put out his right hand to cover mine.

'Thanks, Berta May. I think I nearly lost sight of that. I belong to Penylan, not London.'

His profile was stark against the rock face; dark quiff of hair falling over his forehead; long straight nose; sensitive mouth that had always been ready to curve into laughter; weather-tanned cheeks with high bones.

'I wish I were a painter,' I said without thinking.

'Why?' He turned from his study of the sheep that grazed the further slope of the valley below us and looked directly at me. 'Want to paint the view?'

'Something like that,' I nodded, slightly confused at the sentiment which had come unbidden to my mind. 'Say, maybe I could buy a picture to send Mom? And one of those really truly English caps like you wear, for Fred.'

'Careful now,' he laughed as we tied our packs, 'don't let Tref hear you call us English.'

We were perfect walking companions, sometimes chatting, sometimes tramping for half an hour or more in silence and we covered some fifty miles during our three days on the mountains. The weather favoured us.

196

Saturday, we went out through a village called Llanfrynach, to do a long horse-shoe of a hike. Up onto one of those long north-facing shoulders, gradually rising to a peak which was the start of a rocky path all round the head of the valley, we came back by way of the next shoulder. Down through woodland and across fields to the village then and we trudged wearily back to our hostel, glad to know our beds were booked and our food awaited cooking.

'There's more people here tonight,' remarked Dan, levering open a can of processed peas. 'Bound to be busier over the weekend, I suppose.'

'There are fewer than in August,' I said, 'but that's only to be expected. Students are back in college.'

'You want two sausages or three?' he asked.

'Three. I could eat anything you offered me.'

'How about a chocolate then?' He pulled a small box from his food tin. 'Birthday present. I brought them in case of emergencies,' he said. 'Take your pick.'

'We shall spoil out appetites,' I protested, but immediately ate three soft centres. 'Let's save the rest to eat afterwards.'

But with eating and talking, playing cards and darts and resting by the big log fire, we got no more time together for sharing chocolates. I was sorry. It was a pity we must return home on Monday. I was wishing our weekend might go on for longer. I was loving every minute of Dan's company and trying to work out our precise relationship. Did he count as a cousin, a half cousin, a step-cousin or what? And ought I to feel guilty at loving him so?

3

I said no word about my feelings. All Dan said when we parted at the bottom of the Snail Creep where the bus dropped us late Monday afternoon in Cwmavon was, 'Thanks Berta May, you're a real sport.'

Then he leaned forward to brush the lightest of kisses on my mouth, grinned his merriest grin and set off at a spanking pace up the hill. I watched his pack disappear round the first bend of the track and whispered, 'Thanks, Dan.'

It was not surprising that I was seen to be somewhat pre-occupied during the next week. Concentrating on recording dates and on arranging my notes in order was difficult, with the ever-present memory of that kiss. I had been kissed before in school-boy fashion back home; I had been kissed expertly by my old flame of summer camp days; I had been kissed furtively and passionately by a friend of Sheila's who had become too fresh during Festival Fortnight in Pontypool. Dan's whisper of a kiss wiped all of those out of my memory.

Lizzie and I went off to Carmarthen, found a tiny chapel high on a hillside and searched for the grave of Grandmother's parents. Not only they, but five small children of theirs had been buried there. In the mid 1800s, when life was precarious and birth control unknown, many babies were born but only the lucky ones survived.

'Although whether they could be said to be lucky, facing a life of drudgery as many did,' said Lizzie, 'is open to question. However, Granny Watkins was lucky. She found Grandpa and he treated her well.'

I wrote a list of the names. We stayed a couple of days and got to talk to some local folk and to see some old registers from the school. Lizzie was good company and very eager to find out all she could, so she left no stone unturned.

'What nice people,' she said as we set off home. 'It makes me sorry I never had the chance to learn Welsh, when I hear them speaking. Granny did, you knew that, I suppose?'

'Yes, Auntie Sarah told me; and when Dan and the others stayed with us during the war, we tried to learn some songs for our concerts, but I never could get my tongue round some of the sounds.'

'It was funny when they came back,' she smiled. 'They all had American accents except Bessie and they couldn't spell properly. I bet Dan still writes 'nite' and 'color', not that he's had to write much since he didn't have to go to school when he came home. He's a nice lad. If I had married, that's the sort of boy I would have wanted, not a high flyer like Idris. What is Alec like? And Bethan? Tell me about them. I can hardly remember them at all.'

198

It was strange how the conversation came back to Dan time and time again. I found myself telling Lizzie how well he had fitted into on the homestead with Mom, Alec, Freddie and me. Then I made her laugh at the quarrels I'd had with Idris.

'You make it sound a heavenly existence,' she said. 'I feel as if I had been there myself.'

At that very moment, I caught my breath and almost sobbed, for a shaft of home-sickness pierced my happiness and I wished I were sitting in the kitchen at Greyroofs.

'And then there was Frank Taylor,' said Lizzie. 'That must have been a surprise for your mother.'

'It was, but as it works out, a useful surprise for me. He wants me to go up to London in December while he is out of college, so I can go to Somerset House as often as I want to. Did you never think of marrying, Lizzie?'

'Not when I was young. I was intent on becoming a doctor like your father and trying to help the people I knew to have better health and a better life. He was my idol, you know, and none of the young men I met could match him, so there was no danger of my neglecting my studies for romance. Then I settled down at the hospital, worked hard and when the war came, found myself unattached and free to offer my services. By the time it ended I was forty, dedicated to my profession and unlikely to marry even had I wanted to. I am something of a cynic where marriage is concerned.'

4

As the time drew near, I wanted less and less to leave Cwmavon, although I was making no further progress with my work there. Much as I had looked forward to seeing Frank, my heart wished nothing more than to stay within reach of Dan.

In the company of the family, we had fun and were part of the crowd, but now and then, we had managed to spend time away from them. He took me to the cinema twice, arranging to meet in Newport in the early evening and travelling home together afterwoods. We went to see 'No Highway' at the Pavilion, risking being seen by friends because I so much wanted to see that film after having read the book.

'Not that there is any reason for us not to be seen together,' he said, taking my hand as the lights went down. 'Can't a fellow take his yankee cousin to the flicks once in a while?'

How were we to know Trefor and Doris were sitting at the end of the row? Not that any of the occupants of the double seats at the back were aware of others in the cinema. Dan and I probably saw more of the film than did most, but were not above a kiss now and then.

'Well, fancy seeing you!' exclaimed Doris when we bumped into each other going down the stairs. 'Are you all here?'

'No, only me and Dan,' I said, trying to be nonchalant, but blushing to the roots of my hair. 'The others were going out somewhere.'

'You're going to have a long walk,' said Tref to Dan. 'Don't do anything I wouldn't.' He winked.

'Oh dear,' I said as we stood at the bus stop. 'Now the cat's out of the bag.'

'Tref won't stir up trouble,' Dan said, 'but we can't go on trying to meet in secret. We might as well tell them.'

'Wait until I come back from London,' I said. 'Maybe we'll tell them at Christmas. And by the way, what do you think Auntie Megan would say to inviting Frank to come for Christmas? I think he'll be alone otherwise.'

'She won't mind, but I will. I shall be green with envy, you and him in the same house. Let him come up Penylan and I'll come down Cwmavon.'

'I have to watch your brother play rugby before then,' I said. 'He wants me to go next Saturday. Can you come too?'

'You'll need someone for support,' he laughed. 'Wear every jumper and coat you can find and bring a brolly as well.'

There had been talk of the match all through the week, both in school and out. A good-sized crowd of supporters showed up to watch. It was after all not too cold a day, but after intermittent rain all week, the ground was slick before the game started. I watched in astonishment as thirty young

200

men and boys wallowed in an increasingly deep sea of mud. It was no surprise to see Idris tackling with ferocity, such was his competitive spirit, but he seemed positively to enjoy rolling in brown glutenous liquid.

'Mad,' I shook my head. 'Utterly, completely mad.' Yet before the match was over, I was drawn into enthusiastic support for the home team. I was screaming and shouting encouragement with the rest of the supporters.

'Great,' I said as we left. 'Mom's just going to love those photos I took.'

'Don't tell Idris you enjoyed it,' groaned Dan, 'or he'll have you watching him every week and I'll never be able to take you out again.'

Our parting was almost tearful, the evening before I left for Oxford, and I huddled into a corner of the compartment, hating the train that was taking me from my love. As for looking ahead to my eventual departure from Britain, I had closed my mind to the dreadful thought.

5

Oxford was a new world of churches and colleges, spires, arches and quadrangles. Thronged with hurrying students of all shapes, ages and nationalities, it was a wholly different experience, made most enjoyable by my having Frank to show me around. In spite of myself, I became more cheerful within an hour of arriving. He whisked me in and out of colleges, up and down streets and into ancient buildings whose size and grandeur quite overawed me. We had tea in an old-world tea shop, supper in an old-world inn and I watched him perform with an orchestra in an old-world concert hall that was stone from floor to ceiling. The next day, I met his friends, who spoke sentences that were almost beyond my comprehension, being so profoundly learned. I stood wide-mouthed at the sight of gowned figures tearing through the streets on rusty bicycles. As for my lodgings, a half-timbered house where the bed was of dark oak about a thousand years old, it was something out of Shakespeare. I lay on a thick feather mattress, thinking of Dan and feeling that I had stepped back in time.

Then off we went to Canterbury and I resumed my quest

for knowledge. A page or two of quarto paper was filled with the information I copied from Frank's Bible and more with that gathered from some of his grandmother's letters. London, we agreed, could not be visited every day, so we would try to do all we could up there on Monday, Wednesday and Friday. On other days, we would enjoy ourselves.

'You're very quiet,' he remarked as we sipped coffee in a side-street cafe after touring Canterbury Cathedral.

'Just thinking,' I smiled. 'I need to buy some cards and write them.'

'Just thinking of whom?' he asked. 'Come along, Berta May, tell Uncle Frank who you are dreaming about. You've had that far-away air ever since you stepped off the train in Oxford.'

'Oh, no-one important,' I shrugged, but felt my colour rising. 'Where do we go from here?'

It was perhaps as well that Frank had declined the invitation to spend Christmas in Wales, for I could not have hidden my feelings from him once we were back there. He said he would be spending the holiday period with some old friends of his family, who had been as good as parents to him since his return from the States after the War.

'They took me under their wing, having children of their own to keep me company, and were also very good to Grandmama. Since her death, they have been kindness itself, so you see I cannot refuse their invitation. Tell Auntie Megan I shall come to Wales in the Spring, if she will have me.'

After three long sessions in town, we had acquired numerous copies of Birth and Marriage certificates and traced both Watkins and Taylor families back to the late seventeenth century. We were sufficiently pleased with our progress to allow ourselves an afternoon's Christmas shopping.

Oxford Street was a-glitter, Regent Street quite brightly lit, though I gathered that things were but a pale shadow of times past. There seemed to be plenty of money about and I added to its flow by spending with unaccustomed freedom. I wanted to add a touch of luxury to the festivities in Wales and got a little something for each cousin, aunt and uncle. Mom's gift, I hoped, was already well on its way across the ocean along with Alec's, Fred's and Zeb's.

One good thing about having Frank's help was his ability to organise paper work. He soon showed me the best way of recording the information I had collected and a sort of reference system which made it easy to find names and dates. I packed up my files on my last evening in Canterbury feeling that at last I had made real headway.

'And tomorrow,' he said, 'we shall do the V and A and the Science Museum. You will be so steeped in culture when you go home that Auntie Cassie won't recognise you.'

I was sorry in a way to leave that corner of England, knowing that I would not see it again, for reasons of time.

There was much for me yet to see in other regions during the remainder of my visit and once the worst of the winter was past, I ought to travel to the North, Lizzie had told me. We hoped to spend a week in Stratford on Avon too, she and I together, during the spring.

6

Home to Wales for Christmas I then went and arrived just in time, for a period of heavy snowfalls was beginning and travelling was not the most comfortable of activities. I saw the light dusting of white on the hills above Pontypool as the train steamed up the valley and wondered how deep it was on our meadows at Greyroofs. Was the dirt road still passable, had Mom put chains on the car tyres yet, had she and Fred got in supplies as early as usual? I wondered whether there would be just the two of them for Christmas, then remembered that Zeb had moved in to stay. They would find it quiet without me.

It was quiet enough at Cwmavon, the snow muffling the sounds of the few vehicles moving up-valley. A hard frost came on Christmas Eve to put a crust on the drifts and thicken the ice on the pond. We crunched our way to chapel along with Emmie's family, helping support each other and treading cautiously where ice lay at spots whipped clear of snow. The service was both moving and jubilant and everyone at their most merry. The outing took over three hours to accomplish, but we knew that our roast turkey was all the time nearing completion in the old-fashioned kitchen range.

'Home reared and cooked to a turn,' said Uncle Tom, wielding the carving knife. 'You'll not come across a better, unless it be on your Mam's place, Berta May. I suppose you do have turkeys over there?'

'Sure we do. We eat one for Thanksgiving, too. Mom rears a batch in the yard and sells those we don't need.'

'Just like home then,' he said. It was indeed, even to the home-made wine. They just loved the gifts I had bought in London and I was delighted with the knitted gloves and neat new vanity case they had gotten me. There was a package from home to open, too. All I needed to complete the day was the company of Dan, if only for a few minutes; but it was not to be. Boxing Day was the time for family visiting and the snow had even put that in jeopardy.

'Though you and Pat might be able to get up there together if we don't have no more,' decreed Auntie Megan before bed time. I could not sleep. The whiteness of the ground was reflected on my ceiling, a hunting owl circled the farm, hooting. Tomorrow I would see him, give him the gift I had bought and see his dear face light up. The morning could not come soon enough.

With much sliding, pushing and laughter, Pat and I coaxed everybody up Shop Road to Varteg and along to Penylan.

'Though how we're to get back down without breaking a leg,' said Auntie Megan, 'I cannot imagine. The things we do at Christmas!'

'Come in, come in before you do freeze to death,' urged Auntie Jane. 'Never thought you'd get here, did we, Idris? Get along there, young Idris and give your auntie a chair by the fire. And put another log on. Where's our Dan to now?'

'Getting coal from the cot, Gran, like you told him. Come in the kitchen you two, help me pour a spot of winter warmth into a tumbler for Uncle Tom.' He beckoned to Pat and me.

We exchanged gifts and as I had hoped, I saw Dan's face light up on seeing the canvas haversack I had got for him.

'Berta May,' he said, 'you shouldn't of spent all that

on me.'

'It didn't cost a lot,' I said hastily, lest Idris suspect, 'I got it from an army surplus store. I thought it would be useful for hiking so's you needn't borrow Trefor's next time.'

A wonderful Christmas was that, my first away from home. There was little time for wishing Mom and Fred were here, between eating and drinking and playing Monopoly. From Uncle Idris to his namesake, all let their hair down, cheated abominably, shouted at their opponents and had a rip-roaring time. Dan was by my side and I was content.

On the following days, there were children sledging down the hills and building snow men, men and women taking short strolls in the fine fresh air and Dan and I meeting every evening on the Snail Creep. Then came bitter January, fresh heavy falls to close the roads and railway and a terrible time of unfriendly feeling between me and my kindly hosts.

For Auntie Jane had noticed. She had seen the long looks between Dan and me and had put two and two together. A short note from her to Auntie Megan sufficed to bring a rock-fall onto my shoulders.

At least, that is what it felt like, to be harangued night and day on the subject of cousins.

'Not seemly, it isn't, to be making eyes at your own cousin, Berta May. Dear me, I wish your mam was here to tell you. See, do two cousins marry, my lovely, there may be things go wrong with the children. Lizzie could tell you, she being a doctor. Not that I suppose you had it in mind to marry or anything, but one thing d'lead to another, see?....'

'A very nice young man is our Dan and you're a smart young woman and no wonder his head is turned. Never should have let you go off with him, I shouldn't. Youth Hostels indeed - I knew no good would come of all that walking. Duw, duw, how can I tell your mother?'

'No need to say a word, as far as I can see,' chipped in Uncle Tom when she paused for breath. 'No harm done, so long as they let it go no further. But your auntie's right in what she says, Berta May. Leave well alone and let Dan find himself a girl away from the family.'

'Going back home you'll be next summer,' she took up the attack again, 'and leaving him with a broken heart, I shouldn't wonder. It won't do, Berta May, I won't allow it.'

Having tried and failed to defend myself, I left the room and did not come down for supper. Conversation was stilted the next morning and, the weather preventing my going anywhere, I perforce buried my head in papers and books. The atmosphere was strained, Auntie Megan occasionally breaking into persuasive arguments and explanations, while I bit my tongue to avoid being rude.

'Sulking she is now,' I heard her tell Emmie. 'Won't say a word, though she must know she's wrong. I cannot think what we can do.'

'Nothing you can do, Mam, and much better if you stopped nagging her. After all, it's not the end of the world, cousins falling for each other. And they're not exactly cousins, are they?'

Good for Emmie, I thought, though she loosed on her own head a torrent of old-fashioned advice and hearsay. I put my papers together and went down the curving stair, smiling.

'Mind if I go over to see Pat?' I asked.

'Not at all, she's tidying her room as she can't get to work again today,' smiled Emmie.

It was not long before she followed me.

'Don't be too upset,' she counselled. 'Mam means well and she does have a point, I suppose. Her tongue runs away with her when she's worried. Just ride the storm for a few days and she'll calm down.'

Pat shook her head. 'It's none of my business and you can do as you like as far as I'm concerned, but what on earth do you see in our Dan?'

Chapter 15

What did I see in him? My head buried in Chaucer's works but my mind travelling every which way other than the pilgrims' road to Canterbury, I tried to arrive at an answer. He was neither as good-looking as Randy Wesley back home, from whom I was getting weekly letters, nor as full of life as Jimmy Jones. Not as suave as Cliff nor as rugged as our old pal Chuck. He was not as quick-witted as Idris and Trefor. There were boys in the Sixth Form who had ambitions far higher than his. He was just Dan, dark-haired and gentle. He had been part of my childhood and I wanted him to be included in my future.

I was mighty glad when a thaw came and travel became possible up and down the valley. Life returned to more or less normal in factories, schools and shops, and it was good for us all to have a change of company. I took it upon myself to go marketing, bringing home supplies of fresh food, for they were not stocked up for a long spell like Mom would have been back home.

'Not that we don't generally get a few weeks' bad weather,' Auntie Megan explained, 'but it varies from one year to the next.' She was pleased I had been so helpful. We resumed friendly relations and I knew she was near bursting with the effort of not nagging me about Dan.

He had of course had his share of family pressure and of embarrassment, so I would not have been surprised if he had given me a wide berth for a while. I dreaded to think what Idris might have said.

'Nothing,' said Dan when I asked, 'except to tell our Mam he thought she should be ashamed of saying unkind things about you, after all the kindness your Mom had shown us. Yes he did, he stood up in the middle of Sunday dinner and told her straight. Then he said he hoped he could find a girl as good as you, but not until he got a few thousand in the bank. That made them all laugh and we got on with our dinner and no more was said.'

Within a few days, they had something different to talk about, for Trefor arrived with news. I thought at first he had simply come to tell me about his travel article being accepted for publication.

'In this new Travel In Britain magazine it's going to be,' he said, showing us a glossy coloured paper. 'To appear in March and they want me to do another for April, so I'll have to get off to the Wye Valley pretty soon.'

'Congratulations, Tref. You'll have to put in for a pay rise then. Front page in the Press most weeks as well as writing half the stuff inside,' said Auntie Megan. 'Been following your stories on the water supply, I have.'

'For the New Town?' he asked. 'Interesting that, isn't it? I expect they'll build the reservoir after all, but that fellow knew a thing or two about underground sources, didn't he?'

'I wish you would put more in about the Royals,' I said. 'I have to keep buying a daily to get news of their travels - Mom likes to have the cuttings since she saw Buckingham Palace.'

'I'll tell the Editor,' he smiled. 'Now what I really came to announce is that I'm going to be a daddy.'

'Tref! A daddy, you? Wow, will Mom ever be happy?' I threw my arms around his neck and hugged him. 'I sure am glad for you. Hey, guess that makes me Auntie Berta?'

'Sure does,' he mimicked.

'When? How's Doris? Is she giving up her job?' Auntie Megan wanted to know.'

'Middle of June. Very well so far. Not until Easter,' he laughed. I could see Auntie Megan counting.

'She's over the three months then? And to think I never noticed. You are a couple of dark horses. Have you told Jane yet?'

'Not yet, but I shall go up there now. I wrote to Mom last week.'

'I hope it comes on time,' I said, 'then I shall just be here long enough to see it. What do you want, boy or girl?'

'I really do not care, so long as it and Doris are both healthy. She says will you come down Friday night, Berta May, and spend the evening with us?'

He winked at me as he left the house, fastening his motor-cycle gloves. I stood on tiptoe to give him a sisterly kiss and told him to give Doris my love. I had more than a suspicion that he had come with the intention of diverting attention from me and Dan.

Together, we went to the little terraced house on the hill, to find Doris making a meal and Trefor sawing wood in the out-house.

'A crib,' he told us. 'Bit early to be making it, but when the hour comes off I shall want to get around a bit in the evenings, now I've got started freelance writing.'

'I would like to make something for the baby,' I told Doris. 'Would you like me to knit a shawl? Not that I'm a fancy knitter, but I could manage something simple.'

'Lovely,' she said, 'I shall be grateful for anything.'

'Mam and Aunty Jane are busy with the white wool already,' Dan told her. 'This hot-pot's nice and tasty, Doris.'

'My mother's recipe from Lancashire,' she told him. 'Could you get me a nice rabbit for next weekend? I fancy a rabbit but I like to know where it's from.'

'No trouble,' he said, 'I usually shoot a couple when I'm on the mountain. What do you two say to a trip to the theatre on the thirty first?'

'Something good on?' asked Tref.

'Yes, they're doing 'Pirates of Penzance' and I happened to hear Mam say she would be planning something special when it comes to Dad's fiftieth birthday and I thought, why not do the same for hers. A surprise it will be.'

'Count us in then.'

'Me too,' I said.

'I should think you could get enough to fill a bus, with a few friends and neighbours,' said Doris.

That was becoming very popular, to hire a whole coach. Gasoline was cheap and the cost therefore lower than that of rail travel, so parties were going in all directions. I had put my name down for a school trip to Stratford and another to London, for it would be far less trouble for me to go with them than to organise my own visits. I was quite enjoying my contact with the students.

Dan and I walked home; the valley was bathed in moonlight, the frost on tree branches turning them into fantasy creations. Stars shone brightly, the hills stood in stark silhouette before the deep blue of the night sky and our world was at peace. We were in love with life, with the future and with each other.

2

The theatre outing went with a swing, a whole coach load of people going to Newport despite the bitter cold. Dan's mother was radiant in new yellow dress and fashionable tartan coat. Voluble and expectant, the party set out to enjoy itself and was not disappointed.

The musical was splendid. We stood to attention at the end to sing 'God Save The King' and I was nearly caught by surprise when they continued with 'Mae Hen Wlad.' Boy, did they just let rip! I was glad I could sing some of the words and I felt a thrill of intense pleasure to be a part of that crowd. Then we sang our way home to choruses from the Pirates, me sitting at the side of Dan with never a glance of disapproval from the aunts, as far as I could tell.

'Thank you everyone, thank you Dan,' shouted his mother when the coach dropped them at Varteg. Then it did an about turn to find its way down to Cwmavon by way of Abersychan. I was too near asleep to know which route we followed.

Next morning, I went with Auntie Megan to do some shopping in Pontypool, the tunes from the musical still echoing in my head. We had meant to be home in time for lunch, but our errands took longer than we expected and it was about half past twelve when we went into Fowlers to make our last purchase, wool for baby things. Just as we finished counting out our money, someone came in from the street and said:

'The King is dead.'

The whole shop fell silent. All heads turned to look at the speaker, a middle-aged woman dressed in a grey suit. She looked liked Gaynor, well-groomed and confident.

'It is true,' she said. 'I have just heard it on the radio. They read a statement from the Palace.'

Nobody spoke or moved. You could have heard a pin drop. The shock seemed to have struck us dumb. Then a small boy cried, 'Mammy, I want my dinner.'

That broke the spell and I turned towards Auntie Megan.

Her face was white and I thought she was about to weep.

'Poor man,' she said softly. 'Knew he was bad, I did, but not ready to pass over, bless him.'

'And the Princess in Africa, poor dear,' said the shop assistant. 'I wonder, have they told her yet?'

'Sure to have,' it was generally agreed.

'A sorry home coming for her, to be sure.'

The tongues were loosed, King George's illness discussed, recent news items about the royal family recounted, though in streets and buses, trains and offices they spoke quietly, with reverence.

'I was having my dinner when the Supervisor came into the canteen and told us,' said Pat that evening. 'We couldn't believe her. Why, he was there the other day, seeing them off at the airport.'

'Caught his death of cold I shouldn't wonder,' said Uncle Tom from his fireside chair. 'Saw his picture in the paper I did and it made me shiver to see it. The man should have been in bed.'

Now that was an education, to see their concern for their sovereign, though in all the previous six months I had not heard them show the slightest interest, unlike Mom and me.

3

I got my wish and had plenty to read in the Press as well as the dailies after that. My collection of Royal pictures trebled within a week and when I heard there was to be a special book published about George VI, I was hot foot to the book shop to order my copy.

Trefor got to report the local memorial services and took a flying visit to London to the Lying in State so as to write an account of events in the capital.

'You ought to come with me, Berta May,' he said. 'You'll never see anything like this again.'

It was raining, adding torrents of water to the Avon Lwyd, already swollen by melting snow. Grey river, grey rain, grey sorrow. Did I really want to go stand in a grey snake of patriotic mourners, just be able to say I was there? I was feeling my own monthly greyness, tense and strained.

I declined.

'I'll stay here and pray for him in chapel,' I said. Auntie Megan said I was quite right.

'Don't seem reverent to me, just looking at a coffin with thousands of strangers all round. Better bow your head in God's house quiet like.'

Queen Elizabeth II was home from Africa with her husband, the State Funeral was held and I cut out whole pages to mail to Mom. She would want them at once, I knew. A letter came from her, offering sympathy as if the dead monarch had been one of the family. She was a Royalist if ever there was one. She wondered whether Frank had been to the funeral.

'.....I had a visit from Alec and Gaynor last week,' she went on as if this were of minor importance, 'and it was real nice to see them as we've had mighty few visitors this winter. They came to tell us guess what? (Maybe you've heard from them already) She's expecting.

I never thought I'd be having a grand child from that quarter, but there we are and I am so happy I could sing it from the roof tops. In July it will be, so not a lot of difference between her date and Doris's. She looks well, a bit more homely than she did a year ago but better for that. Alec is tickled pink I can tell you and making a nursery in their spare room.

Now as for Bethan, I have to say to her credit that she has got on with her training at the hospital and that boy of hers is a good boy. So Sarah says. But as for the riff raff that come visiting with her at the house, I wouldn't like to vouch for them. Theatrical folk; funny habits and funny manners and dressed like a walking rummage sale. One of them was in court for smoking mariwana (a drug, don't know how you spell it.) Your Pop would die to see his house with that sort in it....'

I wrote back, sending her the clippings and telling her my plans for the next three months. She had not said a word about Dan and me, so perhaps no-one had split on us. Perhaps it would pay me to be bold.

'Dear Mom,' I wrote, 'What a surprise you sprang on us. You'll be Granny twice over within a month and I'll be Auntie Berta. What does Fred say to being Uncle? I am knitting a shawl for Tref's baby and had better think of something for Alec's.

Enclosed are enough cuttings to keep you happy for a week or two. I have ordered a book about the King and when Trefor gets his photos, I can have some prints.

Next week, I am going to see 'A Midsummer Night's Dream' and 'King Lear' at the Shakespeare Memorial Theatre in Stratford on Avon, with a coach load from school. Most of the kids are in the 'Sixth Form' and studying literature and there were seats to spare so Mabel got permission for me to go too. We are staying overnight in one of those hostels I wrote about last year, all perfectly respectable, girls in one room, boys in another. Idris is not going because he's doing Science - going to make a fortune out of that new electrical engineering, he thinks.

Dan and I went to see 'Anna Karenina' last week and when 'Great Expectations' comes soon he will take me to that, so you see we are getting to some good films, not just rubbish and not just wandering on the mountains. Trefor is planning another walking weekend for us. Well, it's for himself in fact, because he wants to write an article about some valley near here, but taking a group helps him. He says it is a good long hike to do in two days, but well worth it for the views. There is a castle or two to see on the way and a big ruined church. I need to read up on it all. It is not in the mountains, so no danger of getting lost in the fog.

Which reminds me, I owe Frank a letter. I have gotten a lot of the family history written out tidily now and am waiting for warmer weather, then I shall go to Somerset and see what I can find about Grandpa Watkins' parents. That should keep me busy through April or May and will just leave time for a tour of the North of England before I come home. A coach tour seems to be the best thing.

With love to all, Yours, Berta May.'

4

When the weather improved, Dan took me to see some ruined castles, way out in the hills towards the north east. He borrowed Uncle Bobbie's truck on the excuse of delivering some lambs to a farmer out that way and then we clubbed together to put some gas in the tank and drove to Skenfrith. It was a good thing the day was fine, for this old fortress had no roof.

'Well and what did you expect?' asked Dan. 'It hasn't been used for hundreds of years. Look, I've got an old guide book here. Let's sit on the grass while you read about it.'

I think he went to sleep there in the shelter of the ancient walls while I found out about the border castles of Wales. Then we went on to Grosmont and White Castle, where we ate our sandwiches overlooking a deep hollow which had been a moat. All around were rolling hills, steep yet tamed into agricultural land. I was glad to be living in the present time and not during a period of feuds and battles.

'Next time you come, we'll put our packs on our backs and walk from castle to castle,' Dan said.

'What makes you think I shall come again?' I asked. 'I'm not likely to have another generous bequest. Oh, I wish we could be together always.' I lay face down on the grass, chin on hands.

'So do I. Sometimes I think I shall die of loneliness when you have gone.'

'I'm not sure I can live without you. But I think of the fuss they'll make if we say.....' I broke off. I could not say I wanted to marry him. He had to ask me first.

'I know. We must wait awhile, at least until you have finished college and got your degree or whatever you have to get.'

'Will you wait for me?' I asked.

'Of course. What about you?'

'Of course. But I shall tell Mom as soon as I get home. They haven't told her yet. I thought they would.'

'I think Emmie and Grancher made them see sense and they think we have come to our senses, too.'

'You don't think they are right?'

'I think they are right to worry about you. They feel responsible and you're only seventeen after all and a long way from home,' he said. 'About the rest, I think we have to be allowed to know our own minds. Give me a kiss and then we must go. Our Dad will have missed the truck by now.'

I think he had a few black looks from his parents, but Auntie Megan was too busy spring cleaning to ask where I had been. Thankfully, I offered to help her for a few days. Then it was time to be thinking of my trip to Somerset. I was none too keen on venturing there alone, but it could not be helped. No-one could spare the time to go with me, so I made up my mind to devote a week to that part of my research and went off to look for Watkins.

I returned with sheafs of notes compiled from parish records and tomb stones, together with memories of days spent either with my head in dusty books or with my feet in long wet grass. I had found some interesting facts, but had not got much further back in time. There had been more movement between counties in eighteenth century Britain than one would have supposed and the Watkins had been more mobile than most.

5

The valley was green, the grass and crops waving new fronds in the spring breeze. Trees were fully clothed, blossom was pink and white in the orchard and the river sang a lively tune to me as I lay in bed with the window open. A lone plane droned high overhead, a milk lorry rattled down the road and cattle awoke to graze the fresh pasture. The world was going about its business, the nation was watching its new Queen, the valley was building its new town, the family was awaiting new arrivals and I was torn apart.

The nearer I came to the end of my visit, the more I wanted to stay with Dan; yet at the same time, I was more and more homesick for Greyroofs. I wanted to be with Mom and Fred, to ride my own horse and get back to my own friends. I had had enough of travelling.

With a smile, I thought of the preparations that were in hand for my eighteenth birthday at the end of May. All the aunts and cousins were determined to make a momentous occasion of it.

'Not that we make as much of eighteen as we do of twenty one,' Emmie has said, 'But you're not likely to be here for that, so we'll make the most of this one.'

They had booked the memorial hall at Varteg, invited all their friends, made out a long list of food to be prepared and warned me to buy a new dress.

All this, in spite of their continuing disapproval of my fondness for Dan. Perhaps, I reflected, they would be glad to give me a resounding send-off in the hope of my disappearing for ever from his life. My eyes watered. I shed a few tears and wished things were not so complicated. I dimly remembered those days, now seeming so long ago, when Mom and Fred were the only truly important people in my life. Turning over, I tried to sleep again.

The preparations went ahead and the big day drew nearer. I bought a nice new cotton dress, green and white striped with a full flared skirt and a wide green belt. The other girls showed me theirs and we all had new hair-dos. Pat and Sheila's boy friends were invited and Doris's parents and sisters too. Back home, Mom had gotten a telephone line brought to the homestead, so Lizzie said I must go to her house before the party and give my folks a call.

'It will be about mid-morning at your place when it's six o'clock here,' she said, 'so you can ring her then and after that I'll drive you up to Varteg.'

'Give us all chance to get everything ready while you're out of the way,' said Auntie Megan. I wondered what surprises were in store.

It was at five in the morning of the day before my birthday when I heard a banging at the farmhouse door. Too soon for even Uncle Tom to be up, the day had hardly dawned and it was several minutes before any of us woke. The hammering continued, urgent and insistent. I was the first to go downstairs.

On the doorstep I found Lizzie, her blue winter coat fastened to the collar and her wild hair uncombed. She pushed her way past me, shut the door and said, 'Is Auntie Megan getting up?'

'I think so,' I said, still bleary-eyed. Below her coat I could see she was wearing an old pair of pants. 'What brings you here at this time of the morning? Is someone ill?'

The stair door opened and Auntie Megan came in, fastening her dressing gown. Uncle Tom followed.

'You'd better all sit down,' said Lizzie, 'I have bad news for you,' She took my hand and pulled me down onto the sofa beside her.

'What is it? Who? What's happened?' asked Auntie Megan.

'I got a telephone call. From Cassie. She had just heard. Freddie went on an educational outing with his school and they went to visit a coal mine. He - there was a rock fall and some of the boys were buried. I'm sorry, there is no way to soften this blow, Berta May. Fred was one of them and when they found him, it was too late. They got them all out but Freddie had been killed. Oh my dear, I am so sorry and I don't know what to say.'

She had put her arm over my shoulders while she was speaking. I sat, rigid and stunned, unable to believe her message.

'You mean he's dead?'

'Yes. Oh my dear, what ever will your mother do now?'

'When did it happen?'

'Does she want Berta May to go home?'

They asked and answered questions and I stared into space. Freddie. Freddie was dead. No, that could not be. He had written to me. I had his letter. But that was a week ago and now there had been an accident.

'I shall have to go home at once,' I said at last. Auntie Megan had made tea and was toasting bread.

'Get this inside you to warm you up,' she said. I was shivering and took the strong tea in gulps, welcoming the warmth.

An hour later, I was dressed and warm but still shaking,

'It's the shock,' they said. 'Do you sit here quiet now close to the fire and we'll see to everything. Lizzie will telephone your Mam and find out what's to do.'

'Will she tell Trefor?' I asked. 'I should like to talk to Tref.'

'Of course she will. He'll be here directly.'

In due course, they all came, the young ones tongue-tied as I would have been if I had been in their shoes. Trefor and I could not speak to each other at first. Then I said, 'Let's go along the lane for a walk, Tref. The air will clear my head,' and we walked beneath the trees, letting nature's beauty sooth our hurt.

'I ought to be travelling with you,' he said. 'Mom would like me to go, but Doris is near her time and has not been well this last month.'

'You have to stay and look after her,' I said, 'I shall be all right. Alec will be helping Mom until I get there.'

'I shall go and get an air ticket,' I said on returning to the house. 'I must be with Mom as soon as I can.'

'But that will cost a fortune and your passage on the ship is paid for.'

'I have enough money and I shall never want to travel again,' I said. 'Please Trefor, help me to get on the first plane I can. If the Queen can fly home, so can I.' I managed to twist my mouth into a weak smile. 'I shall get to see that nice new airport.'

Leaving them to mull things over, I went upstairs to start my packing. Dan had not come to see me and I was puzzled. Something was happening up at Varteg, quite apart from the cancellation of my party. Unknown to me, a loud and long argument was taking place.

I learned afterwards how adamant he had been, how hotly antagonistic his parents and grandparents.

'Pig-headed, they called him,' said Idris two days later as he saw us off at Newport station. 'Never heard him raise his voice before, let alone heard him swear. Had to cover up my ears I did, for the shame of hearing it, but he stuck to his guns, didn't you boyo?' - all this recited in an exaggerated accent designed to make me smile.

Bless them all, the dear aunts and uncles and cousins who had so taken me to their hearts that my sorrow was their sorrow. Through the numbness of those first hours, I was sustained by their love; and to the end of my days I shall remember Uncle Idris.

Dan had come down on the morning of my birthday to fetch me to Penylan, where the old man had taken to his bed after a chest infection.

'Am I going to get a lecture?' I asked, slowly walking up the Snail Creep for the last time.

'No love. Grancher just wants to say Goodbye and to comfort you a little if he can.'

We went into the bedroom, stooping to protect our heads

218

from the low beams and he held out his hand to me.

'Sit you down by here, my lovely and hold my hand.'

I took his bony work-worn hand and perched on the edge of the double bed. Dan quietly left us. For several minutes, we sat in silence. I felt the sympathy and strength that flowed from Uncle Idris without saying a word, while pictures of Freddie flashed before my eyes. I saw him sitting in the hospital, leg in plaster and toy animals in hand. I saw him riding Dusty down the trail and running joyfully across the yard to show how he could manage without his calliper.

'Why?' I asked. 'Why did it have to happen, Uncle Idris?'

'If I could but tell you that, I'd be wiser than God himself,' he answered. 'But let me tell you something, Berta May and you go home and tell your Mammy.' He lay back on the pillows and stared at the ceiling with a far-away look.

'It always seems to be the good ones who go, the ones who have given more to others than they took for themselves. My little brother who drowned, he never did a harm to anyone; nor did our son Edward. As for your dad, I cannot tell you what he meant to me. Saved our lives when our Dad and me was working down the pit. Saved us from the coal and now it have got his own son. A black revengeful beast is the coal. Never did any man do more for others during the whole of his days than your dad, yet he was taken and I was allowed to live on. And the boy gone after him.'

He sighed, drew several deep breaths and then continued.

'They left their love and their example for us, Berta May. You will find Fred all around you and within you, just as your Daddy has been with you since he went. God is love and they are with God and their love is with us. We must not weep at not seeing them, but take their love and make it live.'

Tears were rolling down my cheeks. He turned his head towards me and opened his arms and I let my head fall onto his shoulder so that he could hold me tight. Thus safely enfolded, I gave way to the heartbreak that had been until then under tight control. I cried and cried and could not stop.

'There, there, cariad,' he murmured. 'Take your time and let the tears wash it all away. You'll feel better after a while.' The clock on the tall-boy ticked the minutes away.

When at last my sobbing had subsided, he stroked my forehead, saying, 'Now go home to your Greyroofs and look after your mam. She needs you. And you need our Dan just at present, so he is to go with you. Have no care for the future years, for you will come to decisions in the fullness of time. But please to bear in mind that you are taking with you the heir of Penylan and be kind to him, Berta May. God bless you both.'

Chapter 16

Our bodies flew over mountains and ocean while our minds dwelt alternately in Wales and in Pend Oreille where the hearts of our family lay.

'I suppose this completes my education,' I feebly joked after we had boarded the plane.

'Not completes, just extends,' he said. 'It is never complete until the day....' and stopped. Freddie had been extending his education on the day he died.

There were so many things we could not say, so many sentences begun and not finished. We sat side by side for hour after hour, hands linked, spirits linked but voices unable to be used. It was such a comfort to have him there, yet I could not communicate my thanks.

We were met in Newport by Uncle Henry. It was the afternoon of June 2nd, a day of bright sunshine but chill breezes.

'Mom is waiting in the house,' he said after greeting us.

I was glad of that, not to meet her in a public place. Dan picked up our two cases and followed us to the car. Unable to bring my trunk by air, I had left it and a lot of clothes in Wales. The girls would make use of them.

We found Auntie Sarah and Mom sitting on the back porch overlooking the neat lawn and garden, where long ago we had made our camp and laughed into the darkness of a summer night. I thought I would never laugh again.

She was smaller, thinner and totally without her normal sparkle, was my next thought, but we managed a weak smile before hugging each other in silence.

'It was good of you to bring her home,' she said to Dan rather formally. 'Did you have a comfortable journey?'

'How do you like flying?' asked Uncle Henry. Auntie Sarah was busy making tea and I heard her call from the kitchen, 'Dan, could you come and help me carry this tray?'

'They're going to talk about me,' I thought.

This was not the home-coming I should have had after my year away, my bags full of souvenirs and gifts, my family tree ready to show them, my head stocked with stories to

221

tell. Death had cheated us, beaten and suddued us. It was too much to bear.

Yet as we drove along the valley, the late evening sun lighting the further banks of the river and the forests rising beyond, our tongues were loosed and we began to talk. I told Mom how Auntie Megan's farm had blossomed into Spring, how the valley of the Afon Lwyd had come to life after the winter, so much smaller yet in some ways so similar to the Pend Oreille. Dan told her how we had walked the mountains, how we had seen the morning mist rise from the hollows as the sun gained strength and how good the bread had tasted as we sat on Pen Y Fan.

Then she started to reply, telling us how the stock was doing and what she had planted where. Suddenly we were talking about Fred in the most natural way, all embarrassment and fear gone. We came to the top of the rise and I looked ahead across the meadow to see my dear Greyroofs waiting to welcome me. Unchanged and yet so strange after my long absence, it brought an involuntary smile to my face just to walk through the yard gate. There was no other place quite like this.

2

The funeral was held the next day at our church where we had worshipped all our lives and the whole town packed into the little building. Then we took Fred home to the birch grove above the ravine and he was buried alongside Pop. We put our flowers there and after a few days we set roots of pansies and lupins. I got back into my tee shirt and pants and resumed the life of a rancher.

Mom was wonderful once that was over, but time and again she thanked me and Dan for coming so quickly.

'I thought at first it could be a month before you got here,' she told me as we rode out along the trail towards the mountain's top. 'I couldn't talk to Zeb and so I went to Sarah's and she was so kind but I wanted you.'

'I shall never leave you again,' I said. 'I have been away too long but it took coming home to show me.'

We cantered then, Dan following behind. How I had missed our horses and the familiar saddles, so different from those they used on the Welsh mountain ponies. I had missed the mighty mountains and the tumbling creeks, the tall tamarack and hemlock, pine and silver fir. And now I was home, I missed my little brother; I ached to hear his voice and see him smile. With every day, I cried anew with grief.

Alec came to see us, thanked us for coming so promptly and said Gaynor was expecting the baby within the month. By then, we were all wondering when news would come from Trefor. It was time for his child to be born and we looked daily for a letter. Alas, I had not finished the shawl I had set out to make, leaving it for Auntie Megan to complete the edging.

'I'm sorry, Alec, I have nothing made for your baby, but I will get wool when we go to town.'

'Knit it for a twelve-month-old,' he said. 'We shall no doubt have more than enough of the first size.'

I got out my file and my photographs then, to show them something of what I had done and seen. I believe I talked non-stop for the whole afternoon.

'I ought to go and see Auntie Sarah,' I said soon after that. 'I have so much to tell her about the places she used to know and messages from people who remember her. Will you come with me, Mom?'

'No, you go and spend the day with her alone. It will give her so much pleasure to talk about the old places and to hear you describe what you saw. What about you, Dan? Do you want to go to town or stay and help check out the beeves over Sutton's?'

'If you can do with a hand, I'd like to stay,' he replied. 'I'll go and see Auntie Sarah another time again.'

I was begining to notice that he did not always want to be with me. My old school friends were starting to drop by, to invite me to join them at 4H or to visit with them. It was good to see them again, but I had not yet been out with them a lot, for I knew Dan would not come. Even with Jimmy and Randy he was shy, almost as if afraid of becoming part of their lives. Or was he jealous? Did he fear that my love for him would die now that I was home?

Auntie Sarah was delighted to see me and to sit by my side while I told of my travels. We got out the old box of treasures and I looked at the photographs, telling her which of the places I had seen, which of the chapels I had visited. She had to hear full details of each family, Idris and Jane, Megan and Tom, Bobbie, Emmie, Bessie and Trefor. I told her what Uncle Idris had said to me before I left.

'He is a very wise man,' I said.

'And what about you and Dan?' she asked. I was startled.

'What about us? What have they been saying?'

'You are the only one who has said anything, my lovely,' she said smiling as she took my hand in hers. 'Your voice gives you away, I can hear what you feel every time you mention his name.'

'Oh darn it. Then there's no point in pretending. I love him, Auntie Sarah, so much it sometimes hurts. But they told us we should not love, that we could not or should not marry. I thought they would have told you and Mom, for they were dead set against us.'

'Has your mom noticed?'

'She has not said anything.' I said.

'What is troubling you then?' she asked.

'I do not think we can stay together, Auntie Sarah,' I said. 'Dan fought for them to let him bring me home, but this is not his home. I can feel him slipping away from me day by day. Even while he holds me close and says he loves me, part of him is not with me. I shall have to let him go if he wishes, don't you think?'

'Indeed I do. Life plays some funny tricks, doesn't it? And it hurts us many a time, but we learn to make the best of it. Now read me all you have written of the family tree and then we will have our tea. They will begin to think you are not coming home.'

Bethan arrived before I had finished and I had to tell some of my story again. She was almost a stranger, this half-sister of mine who had left town before I was born.

'How's Mom?' she wanted to know. 'I wish I could do something to console her. Do you think she would mind if I brought Luke up to visit?'

'Of course not,' I said. 'She'd be pleased.'

'She doesn't bear grudges you know.' said Auntie Sarah.

That very evening, our telephone rang and I picked up the receiver to hear an excited voice saying, 'It's a boy. Seven pounds three ounces. Doris and baby both doing well.'

The line went dead.

'Mom!' I leapt down the porch steps and tore across the yard. 'Trefor called. She's had a boy and you're a Granny now and I'm Auntie Berta. Isn't that great?'

'God be thanked,' she said. 'Are they both OK?'

'Yes, but he had no time to tell me more.'

I flung my arms round Mom and kissed her. Then I did the same to Dan, who swung me off my feet as he twirled me round.

I'm going to open a bottle,' said Zeb, wiping his hands on a piece of sacking. 'I been keeping a special one for this.' His whiskered face was beaming from ear to ear beneath his tattered straw hat and he almost skipped up the path despite his seventy four years. Mom and Dan and I were laughing as we followed, happy for the first time in weeks.

Hardly had we got used to that before Alec was ringing us early one morning. I stumbled out of bed, remembering the last time I had been awoken abruptly, but Mom got there first.

'Yes. She has? Oh good. Oh, that's real good news. Tell her we're all thrilled and hope she's feeling well. Be over to visit as soon as we can. Bye son and congratulations!'

'Well? What? Another boy? Oh boy, two little Watkins in a week.' I ran out to the bunkhouse to tell Dan and Zeb, who were out of bed and opening bottles in a trice. Pyjama-clad and tousled, we were merry before breakfast.

'I must call Trefor and tell him,' said Mom.

She could hardly have been surprised to see Dan and me in each other's arms, for each of us would have hugged anybody at that moment, even a silly sheep if one had been to hand. Possibly our kisses were a mite more than brotherly and there was not really any need for me to sit on his knee to eat my grits, but she did no more than to raise an eyebrow and say:

'Now if you've all quite finished, what say we take a day off and go out to celebrate?'

The chores were done in a trice, just as if we were children promised a treat. We packed a hamper into the trunk of the car, put on clean shirts and pants and set off, our spirits higher than I had thought they could ever be again. We did not quite get to singing, but animation had returned.

It seemed appropriate to take the road down-river, through Jared and Ione towards Metaline, for until the impending birth of his son, Alec's chief enthusiasm had been for the Pend Oreille and its power that he was starting to harness. We stopped at Box Canyon to look at the work going on there. It was difficult to see the mighty surge of water through the narrow gap, for men and machinery were excavating and digging and soon the river would flow through a tunnel.

'They're building a coffer dam and diverting the water first,' said Mom.

'What a job,' said Dan, 'Alec must be thankful it has got started at last.'

'Seems a pity to interfere with nature, but we shall be glad enough to have all the benefits the dam will bring,' she said. 'I guess we'll be put on the main power supply then.'

'When will it be finished?' I asked.

'Why, not for three or four years, I guess.'

After a couple of false starts, we found our way up a steep dirt road which led out of the valley north of Metaline. Zeb was acting as our guide, trying to remember how to reach a cave to which he had been years before.

'When I was mining it was, before the Depression. A great bunch of us came on the back of a truck. I didn't recall it being as far as this.'

The road levelled out and we trundled slowly northwards. There were meadows and homesteads to our left, with dark forests rising behind and a few patches of snow still lingering on the shadowed rocks near the summit of Hawk-nose. A few miles ahead lay Canada and the Rockies.

We came to a sign board, Crawford State Park and soon to the end of the road.

'Bring the flash light,' Zeb told Dan, 'and put your jackets on, girls. It will be cooler underground.'

'I could appreciate being a few degrees cooler,' said Mom as we steadily climbed up hill.

It was thirsty work and I wished we had carried a flask with us, but we soon came to the mouth of the cave. It was down at the bottom of a pit and we had to climb a shaky old wooden ladder to reach it.

'I'm none too sure I want to go in there after all,' said Mom.

'Come on,' I told her. 'We can turn back if we don't like it.'

Dan led the way and we followed with difficulty, wishing we each had a torch.

'Take your time,' he kept telling us, shining the light on each change of level.

'Show the light on the roof,' said Zeb. 'There's pretty rocks hanging down somewhere hereabouts.'

We stood still while Dan played the torch light upwards to find thin stalactites above our heads. Then he swung the beam down and there were weird rock formations all around us. One huge grotesque pillar rose from the ground, its surface shining.

Round a bend and we were begining to go slowly downwards when Mom slipped and almost fell.

'Look, these shoes of mine aren't meant for this sort of work,' she said. 'I think I should go back before I have an accident.' To tell the truth, I was feeling about ready to turn round myself.

'I'll come back with you and we'll wait outside,' said Zeb before I could speak. 'Just show us a light past the awkward bit, Dan, then you can go on as far as you like. Not a great distance until you come to the end, as far as I recall.'

'But don't be too long or I shall be calling a search party,' called Mom over her shoulder as she went. 'And mind you behave yourselves.'

We were left in the darkness, where nothing but a slow dripping of water could be heard.

'Do you want to go any further?' asked Dan, holding me close.

'Not really. I'm getting cold and my feet are wet.'

'Then let's just take one peep along the next bit so's we can say we went on, then keep each other warm for a few minutes.' He switched on the torch and we proceeded about twenty feet, then he put it in his pocket.

'Oh Berta,' he said. 'I'm so sorry.' He pressed me closer, seeking my lips with his.

'Sorry for what?' I whispered as soon as I could.

'Sorry I must leave you.' For some minutes he was silent, then he sighed and continued, 'I love you more than I can say, but it is time for me to go home.'

'I know. I have had you for longer than I deserve.'

'Nonsense, you deserve to be happy. When I have gone, you must forget me. There will be someone else, someone whose home is here with you. Give him a chance, Berta May.'

I could not answer. I knew he was right, that neither of us could leave our home to be permanently with the other. We must say goodbye. Passionately, we clung together.

'Time to surface, I think,' he said at last. 'Be careful where you step.' He switched on the torch.

4

'They'll be putting in lighting next year and making a regular way in,' Zeb told us while we were eating our picnic in the woods above ground.

'Then there'll be hordes of tourists. I like it as it is now,' I said.

A chill breeze was riffling through the trees and we were sitting in the shade. We walked briskly down to the car and continued our drive, Zeb giving us a lively account of his life in Metaline as a miner. He took us to a point where we could look down on Z Canyon and see our mighty river's spectacular fall. A flimsy bridge spanned the chasm and he assured us we might cross it with safety, but Mom had had enough excitement for one day.

We retraced our route, dropping down into Metaline and rejoining the highway. The shadows were lengthening on our side of the valley now the sun had passed behind the mountain shoulder.

'What say we stop off in Ione for some food,' said Mom, 'and then we needn't cook supper tonight?'

That agreed, we looked out for a place where we could

That agreed, we looked out for a place where we could get a hot meal and so it was nearly nine when the car crawled up the last mile of our road.

'That was a really nice day,' I said. 'Thanks, Mom, I did enjoy myself.'

'That's good to hear,' she said. 'Fred wouldn't have wanted us to have no fun.'

'Auntie Cass, you're a brick,' said Dan, getting out to open the first gate. He knew as well I did what an effort she must have made to be so cheerful.

When we got into the yard, what should we see but two bicycles leaning on the door of the barn and two figures sitting on the rear deck.

'Just catching the last rays of sunshine,' said Bethan as she jumped down the steps and came to meet us. Luke followed shyly.

'How long have you been here?'

'About three hours I should think. We went in and made ourselves supper, I hope you don't mind.'

'Mind? Of course not. I'm just thankful I didn't lock you out.'

'Are you stopping over?' I asked.

'I hope we can.'

'Sure you can. You wouldn't set off back at this time of night, I should hope. Well, what a day,' laughed Mom. 'Come on in. We'll have to feed the stock, then we can sit down.'

'I'll do the feeding,' said Dan. 'Want to help me, Luke?' and he led the way back to the barn. I decided to leave them to it.

There was a lot of talk about the new babies and who had made what for whom. Their names were to be Gwilym Daniel and Daren Garth Mortimer - no prizes for guessing which was which. After a while I asked Bethan whether she had finished her training and whether she planned to stay at the Newport hospital.

'Oh yes,' she said. 'I have put down roots at last. Luke is happy here and now I have a steady income, I can start to pay my brothers for the house. I have taken so much from them already.'

'I'm glad things are working out OK,' I said.

'Me too, said Mom. 'Well I don't know how you-all feel, but I'm tired out. Will you be alright in the bunkhouse, Bethan? These three boys can have the one room and you can have the other.'

'Fine,' she said. 'Time you were asleep, Luke. If you wake early, you can get out around the farm to do the morning chores.'

'My turn,' I groaned, 'and Sunday too, so every one but me can stay in bed for hours. Goodnight all.'

It was a totally different world that met my eyes the next morning, heavy rain falling from dense grey clouds. June had been the wettest on record and July seemed set to follow suit. Any thought of taking Luke for a ride up the mountain went out of my head as soon as I awoke. I would be surprised if he got up before dinner.

Nevertheless, I found him sitting on the step outside the bunkhouse, ready to help me feed the poultry.

'There's not a lot to do for the stock in summer,' I explained as we scooped oats for the horses. 'They're out finding their own food mostly and just need a boost now and then. But we've got a sickly cow and calf to feed and muck out. You never been on a farm before?'

'No I haven't. I lived in the city before we came to Newport. Will that cow kick me, you reckon?'

I liked him. From what he said, Bethan had rescued him from poverty and neglect down in California. Our brief chat opened my eyes to a side of life about which I knew nothing and to my sister's unsuspectedly tender nature.

'You can come and see us any time you like,' I said, 'but it's a long way on a bike.'

'Nothing to it, there's five gears on mine,' he boasted. 'I went to borrow it from your cousin Danny but Auntie Sarah says I can keep it.'

Mom liked him, too, I could see that, though there was a tender look in her eye that suggested she was remembering Freddie at the same age. Could she picture him in her mind's eye, I wondered, running across the yard with his uneven stride to open the door of the barn? Could she hear his laughter carrying from the end of the meadow?

It was obvious by dinner time that they would get wet on the way home, but Bethan insisted she must go, for she had to work early in the morning.

'Then let Luke stay,' said Mom, but he would not hear of it.

'No way,' he said. 'I'd like to come again, Auntie Cass, but I got to see Mom gets home safe today.'

So we lent them such waterproofs as we could find and saw them cruise across the sodden meadow wearing oversize sou'westers and capes.

'I hope their brakes are good,' murmured Dan.

Soon after this, he went to town himself, to start making bookings for his passage home. I had in the meantime accepted one or two invitations to join my old classmates on outings. Chuck had shown me their class photo; three rows of graduating students wearing suits and ties or white blouses with a scarf at the neck. In the Fall, most of them would be off to the State University or to college and I should rejoin Senior High.

Though my heart at present belonged to Dan, I found it easier than I had expected to pick up the threads of friendship and to rediscover the common ground between myself and the local crowd. A flicker of interest in becoming a part of that crowd awoke in me. I began to make plans for the months ahead.

5

Mom, too, was looking ahead and was making the most of Dan's company before he should leave. The weather warmed up some; our corn was showing by Fourth of July and that in the valley was knee-high, so the old folks were content. On returning home from a visit to Cusick, I found Mom, Dan and Zeb deep in consultation, with catalogues and magazines strewn over the table and many sheets of notepaper covered in scribble. They ignored my arrival.

'Hi. You gonna tell me what's cooking, or what?' I asked.

'Hang about a tick,' said Mom, 'I just got to figure sump'n out before I lose track.'

'You want an iced tea?' I asked Dan.

'Yes please.' I poured four, took a few cookies from the jar and came back to push aside a few papers and make a

231

place for the tray. I waited.

'Now, I been thinking, while you been away' Mom started, 'and I been finding out a few things too. Me and Fred and Zeb, we done a fair bit of talking last winter. Times is changing and we gotta move with them, else sure enough we'll be left behind.'

I nodded. It was good to know she had gotten her mind fixed on the future at a time when many a woman might have broken under the weight of grief.

'Fact is, I maybe should have done this a year or two back, before too many other folk got started.' Would she never get to the point, I wondered.

'Anyways, I got around to telling Dan and asking his advice while he's on the spot and he come up with a few suggestions might help some.'

'Well, some time between now and the end of the century, maybe you'll work your way around to letting me in on the secret,' I was driven to saying.

'Could be,' she laughed, 'you won't want no part of it when you hear. That old Shakespeare and them cathedrals you been studying don't have too much relevance to dude ranching.'

At last, she got on the right track and I listened with growing interest to her plans for Greyroofs. She was aiming to make it a centre for Cowboy Culture.

Chapter 17

Though my first reaction was one of alarm at the thought of my home being invaded by city folk on vacation, I had to recognise that Mom had shown initiative. Many a mountain holding had been deserted since the war, their owners giving up the struggle to make a living and moving into the cities where jobs were to be found and life offered them all modern conveniences on a plate. Increasing mechanisation was transforming our traditional industries or killing them off all together and our sparsely populated county was something of a backwater. Government grants, which had helped revive the economy in the forties, could hardly be expected to continue for ever. Unless we adapted our way of life, Mom and I could find our assets worthless.

Our assets lay, of course, in our property and our own strength.

'I was thinking of your inheritance, yours and Freddie's, when I started,' she told me.. 'I wanted to make sure that when you were both through college, there would be something of value for you to take over. He was with me all the way - said he would major in Earth Science and Business Studies so as to have a useful training and then he would come and help me manage the place.' She sighed. I took her hand.

'Then we shall do it together, you and I. With Zeb's help,' I added hastily, lest he thought I was set to cut him out. They all laughed. All the possibilities were explained to me, including the costing. My eyes opened wide, both at the figures involved and at the scope of Mom's ambitions.

'I still have nearly eight thousand dollars from what Mrs Taylor left me,' she said, 'and our stock is worth quite a lot. We almost have enough horses to begin with and we've managed our timber better than most, so we have a pretty steady income there, but we shall need to take out a loan.'

'But you can grow some of the food to feed them and you're a great cook, Auntie Cass. Fresh farm food and home cooking will be one of the attractions,' said Dan. 'I know that's happening at home already. Tref wrote about that, remember.'

'So the bunk house will become rooms for guests?'

'That's right. Zeb can have Fred's room and leave the bunk house free.'

'In time, we could build another wing, I suppose,' I said. 'Now I see why you mentioned getting mains power - we would sure need that to cope with the extra cooking and washing.'

'And cooling. We'd need fans in summer.'

'Screen doors everywhere,' I added. 'Guests would need protection from the bugs.'

'And some sort of corral for teaching them to ride,' said Zeb. 'I seen one of them some place. Or was it on the movies?'

Dan was busy meanwhile, slowly writing neat lists of all the ideas and all Mom's financial jottings. Then he asked her permission to make a copy to take home for his father to see.

'Like this it is, Auntie Cass. We got the same problems back home only worse, see. Not much land and too many of us to feed. Plenty of jobs around just now, I grant you that, but who wants to work in a factory?' He caught my eye and we exchanged smiles.'Berta May says I am a mountain boy and that is what I want to stay. I reckon I could use a few of these ideas, sooner or later.'

Then we got diverted onto plans for his farm, but the whole of our long discussion was a useful exercise. Four brains were better than one and it was healthier for us to be thus employed than to be remembering our grief. We decided to put every spare minute into getting Greywater Adventures off the ground.

2

Dan's departure was drawing near and some family visits had to be made. We went to Newport for a couple of days and he enjoyed the company of cousins Laurence and Danny for the last time. They all went up to the overlook at Albeni to see that dam which was under construction and friends drove them to Priest Lake where they were building a weekend cabin; I stayed in town, met up with a couple of old class mates and killed time drinking shakes.

On our final evening, Auntie Sarah asked me to bring down her box of treasures. She unlocked it and took out something from the very bottom.

'I think the time has come,' she said, 'for you to take charge of some of the heirlooms. Now Dan, I want you to have your grandfather's watch.'

Dan took it from her, but said nothing. We thought he was weeping, but his head came up and he smiled.

'Oh, Auntie Sarah, there's lovely. It is very kind you are and a beautiful thought. But Laurence and Danny are older than I am. Don't you want to give it to them?'

'No. I think it should be yours, for you are the only Dan Watkins and your name is in the back. Besides, I want it to go home to Wales.'

'Then I shall take it and treasure it and I thank you, Auntie Sarah.' He hugged her close.

'And Berta May is to have Grandma's,' she continued after a few minutes. 'No need for words, Berta May. I know how much you love it.'

For my eyes had filled with tears and I could not speak. Never in my life had I dreamed that this treasure could be mine, though I had fingered its smooth surface and admired its ivory face since babyhood. I threw my arms around her neck and held her close, whispering my thanks.

Then we packed the two in their boxes and the next morning we were off to visit Alec in Spokane, Mom fairly dancing with excitement at the prospect of seeing her grandson. Only twice had we seen him and she would have taken him home with her, had they given her half a chance.

It was easier to talk to Gaynor now, her apartment being no longer as immaculate as it had been before Garth's birth. She was more human and approachable, allowing Mom to hold the baby as long as she wanted and talking to Dan about his home as if she were really interested.

'When we get our house built,' she told us, 'we shall be able to see you more often.'

'In fact, we'll be hoping to spend most of every summer there,' said Alec.

'Where's it to be, exactly?'

'Just north of the Ruby Ferry landing. I've bought two lots and we shall build on one next year.'

'We'll be in business by then,' said Mom, her finger gently stroking the baby's cheek, 'but we'll never be too busy to see you.'

After that, life seemed pretty hectic and Dan's last days sped by. First, the old crowd who'd known him in school came up for a picnic and we went up the trail to our Summer Sea. It was so long since it had been used that the path was quite overgrown and difficult to follow. At the head of a straggling line of twenty or so, I was ducking under branches and scrambling over rocks. Here and there, I had to stop and cut a way through. The pioneer blood in me loved the challenge and the concealment offered by the rough terrain. The six-footers following were unlikely to lose their way but were having trouble with some of the overhanging trees, that much I could hear from their voices. Only Dan was close on my heels. Together, we broke through the final barrier and looked at our little lake.

How small it seemed to us now, how thickly surrounded by reeds and covered with lily pads. We walked all the way round it in ten minutes, before the last of the party arrived. Mom brought up the rear and reported no casualties, though one or two had come close to slipping into the creek. They all put down their loads and dispersed, some to walk, some to sit, some to search amongst the bushes for our old raft. A few paired off. Chuck began to inflate a rubber dinghy which he had brought.

None of us had grown out of having fun, we were all still kids at heart and had a couple of hours watery pleasure with the old raft and the boat. After a while, Jimmy set off with a group who wanted to hike further, saying he would take them clear on up to the top of Boulder and then return down the road. They took lunch packs with them. I set out to collect a good wood pile for Randy and Chuck, who had made a fire on the bank.

'You just better hope no Ranger spots the smoke,' said Mom, but she was as happy as anyone to have them do the cooking and had provided steaks for all. It was not too long before the drifting smell reached the furthest of our wanderers and they homed in on the picnic.

'Guess when Jim smells this, he'll be back at a run,' said Chuck.

'Too late,' I told him. 'We'll have eaten it all before then.' His girl friend laughed and helped herself to another piece of meat and some cold potatoes. She was a big girl all right and could tuck away a man's ration of food, I thought, but she was well suited to old Chuck.

We left the lake to its solitude again when clouds came down over the mountain and rain threatened. Mom and I were the last to set down the trail.

'Don't ever spoil this, Mom. We don't want noisy strangers up here, do we?'

'No fear,' she said. 'Your Summer Sea is too small for motor boats and water skis. When our guests want excitement, there are other places to take them.'

3

There was excitement enough for us during the next two days, when the rodeo was on. We were away to Cusick as soon as we'd done the chores, Dan as keen as I was to see the competitions. As he said, it would be his last chance to watch calf roping and the like and he'd never seen a full-blown rodeo, for the war had cramped our style. To my surprise, he was all kitted out with camera and notebook, just like Trefor would have been.

'Why, you going to take up reporting?' I asked.

'No. Just going to make a note of things. You never know what might be useful and I never had no pictures from the old days. I want some of you riding, though whether this old camera will take you moving, I doubt. Probably get everything blurred, I will.'

'I'll get the crowd together and we'll pose for you,' I told him as Mom and I set off. 'See you.' He and Zeb followed in the car, for we did not have a third horse fit for competitions.

Freddie should have been there. His memory was with us as we rode down the trail and with us trotting along the road and over the flats towards the river. More than once, I looked round to make sure he was following, as I had done

237

all my life. I saw the rise of the green forest to the top of the mountains, but no brother riding ten paces behind me.

Crowds of people thronged the fair grounds, animals were everywhere and children packed closely round the rails of the show ring. Time and again, I was hailed and welcomed home by folks from miles around. The hardest thing to bear was their sympathy, expressed by hand shake, a pat on the shoulders or hesitating words. They were so kind, but I was glad to escape and join in the races.

Mom's horse won a prize as the Best in Show and Dan took a picture of her, then one of me and Mature. After that, I lost him for a while as I was leading Stoney 4H in bareback riding. We came second, but I'd entered Barrel racing too, so had to hang around a good while. It was late afternoon before I was all through and had time to see what was happening in other parts of the ground.

There were displays of crafts and the Homemakers had a good array of preserves and home produce. The Kalispel tribe had a table of Indian woven cloths and bead-work and that was where I found Dan.

'I want to take a few little things for Mam and the others,' he said. 'Do you think she'll like these earrings?'

'They're just fine, but does she have her ears pierced?'

'I dunno. Does she?'

'Sorry,' I laughed, 'I really did not notice but I tell you what, none of the girls does. They thought I was real trendy having mine pierced.'

'Better play safe then and get her a brooch instead.' So he chose a dream-catcher brooch with three tiny feathers hanging from it, some printed cotton scarves and two small wooden carvings.

'That should be enough,' he said. 'How about something to eat?'

We listened to the Cowboy band, sitting in the shade and sipping iced coke with our hot dogs until Mom came along and asked were we ready to go home.

'No need to come until after dinner tommorow,' she said, 'but we'll bring some clean gear and stay for the dance.'

There was a contest for horse-drawn wagons that day and she had lent our old rig to a young family who'd taken the former Stork place over beyond Wesley's. They were sure spruced up and looking good in the parade, she in a long frilled dress with high neck, he wearing an ancient suit and a top hat.

'My, just look at them two kids,' sighed a woman who was standing beside me. 'Ain't they just cute?'

'Could have come right out of a history book,' agreed her friend. 'Why, my old mom had a picture of her and her sisters, all dressed up like that for Sunday.'

Truly, those two little girls sitting with their handsome parents in our buggy had won the hearts of the whole crowd. There might have been bigger and brighter wagons, but none looked so good nor so fitting. First prize went to the Shearers of Greystone Water Road.

'Coming down to the river with me for a while?' asked Dan after a couple of hours. I had done my riding for the day and he had thrown caution to the winds and taken Mature in the obstacle race. There was time to fill before the dancing would begin.

Past the school, past wide-spaced houses set in summer-brown grass, past the silent saw-mill and bulbous water tower, we strolled to the river bank and turned south on the Usk road. The twin rows of black pilings were reflected in the sluggish water, the river now so low that all memory of Spring floods was gone. Hand in hand, we gazed.

'I want to look and look and fix it all in my memory for ever,' he said, taking snaps to finish his film. The wide concrete bridge came in sight. A hantle of geese flew overhead and ducks peacefully paddled upstream without a sound. A drift of smoke rose from houses over on the reservation and the hills above were lit by a bright beam of late sunshine. Distantly, we heard strains of music.

'Time to dance,' I said, but neither of us wished to hurry. We would never be here together again.

At last, we made our way back and joined the twirling couples. Cowboy shirts and hats had magically appeared; clean scarves, full skirts, waistcoats with fringes had transformed our friends. Mom looked real handsome in her brown and white outfit and no-one would have guessed her heart was broken.

'Take your partners and form a square,' said the caller, but Dan and I had no inclination to take but one partner.

I had to beg him have a dance with Mom. All too soon, he was saying his last goodbyes to those he would not see again and we were setting out for Greyroofs. I could not bear to think of the lonely weeks that lay ahead. If I could have gotten out of my bed and into the bunkhouse that night without Mom knowing, I swear I would have done so.

4

Next morning, we all went to church. I mostly went these days to please Mom, for I had not a lot of faith, like most others of my age, and Fred's death had made me question God's existence. Could anything explain the waste of a young life? Even as I sat between Mom and Dan, steeped in the calm of the old wooden place of worship, I had to remind myself of what Uncle Idris had said. God is love.

There were about fifty people in church that day, for we had a new minister and they had turned out in force to welcome him. He seemed a nice guy, come from Montana to work in the mill and living on West Calispel Road. I could not see his family from where I sat, but gathered there were two girls and a boy. His address was inspiring and comforting, so I was agreeable to stopping after for coffee and cakes.

Naturally, he knew as yet little about his human flock, but someone had told him who we were. Working his way round the room, he came to Mom with a gentle, sympathetic hand shake.

'I am truly sorry to hear of your loss,' he said. 'May I visit with you soon?'

Meanwhile, his family had caught up with him and I had a shock to see that his daughters were at least as old as I was and their son was something straight out of Hollywood. Tall, blond, blue-eyed and with a smile that went straight to the middle of me, he greeted me with warmth.

'I'm Ross,' he said.

'Berta May Watkins,' I replied, narrowly avoiding a stammer of nervousness, 'and this is my cousin Dan from Wales.'

'Hi, Dan, pleased to meet you. This your first visit here?'

'No indeed,' said Dan, 'I was here all through the war.'

'No, really? Then I guess you're nearly as American as the rest of us.'

'Not quite,' I laughed. 'Dan is Welsh to the core.'

But Ross seemed less interested in Dan than in me, which was gratifying though slightly embarrassing. We talked for some time. His mother beckoned urgently to him at last, drawing him away to meet other people.

'Well, you've made a conquest there,' whispered Zeb. 'We'll be having him visit along with the minister, you mark my words.' By the end of the day, I was wishing he would stop his teasing.

The final hours dragged by. Dan's packing was done, the car ready for our drive to Spokane and last messages for the folks in Wales were written down. We all wanted to talk but could not think of what we should be saying; afterwoods, we would remember what we should have said.

After supper, the two of us walked up the trail beside the creek and came to a stop some fifty yards below the lake. The Greywater trickled over its stony bed, a slight breeze ruffled the silver birch leaves and far above, light clouds drifted across the reddening sky.

'Time to say Goodbye,'

He pulled me close to him and kissed me gently. Oh, Dan, can I ever forget that kiss? Will ever I know the joy of loving again? Eyes closed, I clung to him and wished the world might end. The thought of parting was too bitter to be borne. Then he drew away and took a small packet from his pocket.

'I got this for you, so you could wear Grandma's watch,' he said, putting a silver chain into my hand. 'Wear it for me and think of me, but be happy.' Then he gently put the chain round my neck and fastened the clasp.

I could not speak, for a flood of silly tears was streaming down my face and I turned away so that he should not see the ugliness of it. Gentle as ever, he wiped my eyes and comforted me. A long time later, I thanked him.

'I will wear it,' I said, 'and I will think of you and you will always be a part of me.' We could say no more. Slowly, we went home.

In addition to the watch, Dan had agreed to take home the old Welsh Bible which his father had sent over for safe keeping in the war. He had it zipped inside a small holdall over his shoulder as he boarded the train.

'Heavy enough to sink the ship it is,' he joked.

Those were the only words I could remember on the way back. The worst of the crying was over, the awful journey after waving farewell nearly done, the three of us making forced conversation as we turned off West Calispel.

'Clean out the barn I will, tomorrow,' said Zeb.

'I'm fixing to make a full inventory of our stock,' said Mom, 'then on Thursday we go to talk to Henry and see the bank manager.'

'You don't need me,' I sighed. My mind was a black void with no thought other than despairing loss; my brain had ceased to function and my body was slumped against the seat. I felt I could never again find the energy to enjoy life.

'Sure I need you. The whole darned venture rests on you. Strong young arms and back and a brain that knows where it's at will be the ace in our pack and you surely have to help me persuade them we know what we're doing.'

I was not at that moment even slightly interested in her plans for Greyroofs, but Mom had courage and a persuasive manner. She was not set to have me knocked down by fate any more than she had allowed herself to be so and it was only days before I was beginning to put my whole strength behind her business project. With less than a month before school opened, there was much for me to do, for she would not hear of my giving up my education without graduating.

'Whether you take a college place next year or come and work for me is not important,' she said, 'but you got to get them grades before you leave and I want a class picture to put on my wall.'

Every morning, I awoke to the realisation that he had gone. I spent the early hours thinking what he would be doing at that moment and the late hours writing what I had myself been doing, so as to mail him daily letters. Zeb told me I was sighing so often the dust on the yard never got to settle. When I went up the trail to the meadows or down-creek on errands, I kicked Mature to gallop like the wind as if sheer speed could blot out my misery.

Sure enough, we got a visit from the Minister and his son, but that great hunk of manhood must have had his vanity dented some by my coolness. He was charming enough to flutter the heart of every girl from here to Seattle, but was wasting his time flaunting his tanned legs and blond hair in the meadow at Greyroofs. I did my duty and showed him round nice and polite like Mom wished, but had no more interest in sharing my leisure with him than in tearing off to swimming parties or regattas with my old buddies. I was selfishly determined to be a recluse.

'So we'll expect you at three,' called his father as they turned their Packard and rolled out through the gate, Ross driving.

'You have a nice evening and come back soon,' said Mom.

'Different,' said Zeb. 'You got to give him that, Cass, he's a different man from the last.'

'Sure is,' she agreed. 'Not that there was any fault in dear old Ben, but a new broom may be just what this town needs.'

'Will someone please tell me what's going on?' I asked, my tone showing my lack of real interest.

'Sunday next after service, Minister's running one of them Treasure Trails. Anybody with a car, they can get a set of clues and go hunting round for the solution.'

'Prize for the winners and a meal fixed over Peter's Place after. Anyone with a car, they can fill up all their seats and that Ross, he got a coupe and wants you to ride with him,' grinned Zeb. 'Told you you'd made a conquest, I did. So me and your mam, we can take Sue and Jack.'

'Oh gee,' I sighed, 'do I really look as if I wish to be a part of that? I'd rather stay at home and mind the house. And will you do me a favour and stop trying to arrange my life for me, Zeb? I do not care to be treated so.'

I tossed my head, glared at him with my angriest frown and swung smartly round on my heel. I set off for the barn.

'Berta May!' Mom's voice came at full volume and I knew before I turned that her face was thundery. I recalled the power of her temper when roused and knew it was about to blast me apart.

But Zeb got into gear before she did and it was his hot air that pretty near pinned me to the barn door.

'Now listen here, you selfish bloody woman and listen real good. Think you're the only one in the world who can't have just what they want out of life, you do. Not a thought for your poor mother you haven't, how hard she have been hit and how many times she could have sat and cried instead of working her fingers to the bone for you. Never saw such an ungrateful girl in all my days, I have not indeed and I can tell you straight, our Dan don't know how lucky he's been to escape. And have you given a thought to......' he went on and on and on.

'Now pull yourself together, girl, and be a Watkins.'

At last, he was finished. I was crying. Mom had disappeared into the house. Shaking like an aspen leaf, I trudged along the garden path, up the steps and into my room. I shut the door and threw myself onto the bed, sobbing.

6

'Here, drink this, honey,' said Mom an hour later, coming quietly in with a glass of cool cordial. I sat up and took it from her, pushing the hair from off my face and keeping my eyes lowered.

'I understand, honey, really I do. The longing and the wishing, I know how they stay with you day after day.' She stood with her back to me, staring out over the flower garden to the birch grove above the ravine and I felt her intense loneliness.

'I'm sorry, Mom.'

We said no more just then. I showered and dressed, we ate supper on the deck and the three of us quietly resumed harmonious living. I did my best to shake off my gloom. There were plans to be put in hand, purchases to be made, crops to be harvested, old friends to be visited and new friendships to be cultivated.

Very slowly, I learned that Uncle Idris had been right. I could keep alive for ever the love of those who had loved me, by living as they would have wished me to do. Both Dan and Freddie had left precious fibres of love with me and it was time I should pick up the threads of my life and make some sort of fabric for the future.

OTHER TITLES FROM OLD BAKEHOUSE PUBLICATIONS

THE LAND OF BRYCHAN
by Nansi Selwood
£6.50
ISBN 1 874538 30 1

Set in seventeenth century Breconshire, this novel chronicles the story of Mary Prichard, the young heiress to an upland estate and related to the powerful gentry families of Brecon and Glamorgan.

As a young girl she enjoys the freedom and privileges of her status while sharing the pleasures and troubles of the common folk around her.

With her marriage to Richard Games, a wealthy landowner who becomes High Sheriff of the County, she is drawn more into the life of the gentry.

The outbreak of Civil War between King and Parliament brings exciting times. But Mary now finds herself caught in the middle as rifts appear among family, friends and the local community.

With her knowledge of the history of her native county and portrayal of her characters, Nansi Selwood gives us a novel full of richness of the life of the gentry class in 'Beloved, lovely Land of Brychan.'

KHAKI SHORTS
by Major Bob Smith
£6.50
ISBN 1 874538 45 X

Hilarious Happenings - Army Style.

Some of the more humorous moments in the 49 year military career of Major Bob Smith are described in this collection of 39 short stories.

The tales range over countries as far afield as Egypt, Cyprus, Sudan, Eritrea, Kenya, Malaya and Germany. The characters to whom you will be introduced include a British Sergeant Major who found that the practice of African 'Askaris' drinking cow's blood was not his 'cup of tea', a pigeon that turned out to be better at carrying messages than radio waves. Then there was a General who broke his leg trying to get out of the author's way on the ski slopes - to say nothing of the 'native goat' that doubled for a real 'taffy' on St. David's day in Cyprus.

This book gives an insight into what the army was like in the 'good old days'. It will be appreciated just as much by those who have never served in the armed forces as those who can identify with some of these hilarious stories.

THE BLACK DOMAIN
by Ralph Thomas
£4.50
ISBN 0 9512181 7 4

Of those who worked in the new collieries being sunk to meet the demand for coal, most found more misery than wealth. Exploited by the mineowners and the infamous Truck Shop system, living in hovels described as 'little better than pigbeds,' and with women and children working below ground in conditions of near slavery, the time was ripe for the threatened Chartist Uprising.

Gwendoline Siston, daughter of Sir Henry, one of the new breed of absentee mineowners, enters this world, first as a carefree girl enjoying a country holiday as the guest of the man from whom her father intends buying his mine. Within two years she becomes the bride of the man her father has chosen to run the mining complex, then his widow, and finally the mine's controller. Her guide and mentor in this venture is the 'educated collier' Robert Morgan, her one time servant.

Can they succeed or will the unrest fuelled by local terror gangs and the difference in their upbringing prove too much? And what of the love which waits to be declared?

Fact and fiction are well mixed in this dramatic and enjoyable story and provides the reader with an insight into the period during which were laid the foundations for events which changed history.

WITHOUT FEAR - THE KEY TO STAYING SAFE
by Diana Lamplugh
£4.99
ISBN 1 874538 25 5

Published by Old Bakehouse Publications for the Suzy Lamplugh Trust, this book is written for you, whoever you are; young or mature; male or female; going out to work or working at home.

This book shows you how to deal with the anxiety that can increase vulnerability and gives ideas on how to prevent problems when out and about or within the home or workplace.

Everyone who wants to stay safe should know what is in this book.

For further details of our range of local history books and novels please send or ring for a copy of our latest catalogue.

Old Bakehouse Publications
Church Street, Abertillery, Gwent NP3 1EA
Tel: 01495 212600   Fax: 01495 216222